Nobody's
Angel

Books by Sarah Hegger

Nobody's Angel

Nobody's Fool

Published by Kensington Publishing Corporation

Nobody's Angel

SARAH HEGGER

ZEBRA BOOKS
KENSINGTON PUBLISHING CORP.
http://www.kensingtonbooks.com

ZEBRA BOOKS are published by

Kensington Publishing Corp.
119 West 40th Street
New York, NY 10018

All Kensington titles, imprints, and distributed lines are available at special quantity discounts for bulk purchases for sales promotion, premiums, fund-raising, educational, or institutional use.

Special book excerpts or customized printings can also be created to fit specific needs. For details, write or phone the office of the Kensington Sales Manager: Attn.: Sales Department. Kensington Publishing Corp., 119 West 40th Street, New York, NY 10018. Phone: 1-800-221-2647.

Zebra and the Z logo Reg. U.S. Pat. & TM Off.

First Printing: April 2015
ISBN-13: 978-1-4201-3739-2
ISBN-10: 1-4201-3739-5

First Electronic Edition: April 2015
eISBN-13: 978-1-4201-3740-8
eISBN-10: 1-4201-3740-9

10 9 8 7 6 5 4 3 2 1

Printed in the United States of America

To Brent,
who loved Lucy first

ACKNOWLEDGMENTS

Thanks to the MoWest Coven (Sue and Chris) for all your support. A continued debt of gratitude to critique partner, Kim Handysides, for all that she does for me. And to my editor, Esi Sogah, for taking a chance on me and Lucy.

I have to give a shout-out to the writers of *Romance Weekly* #lovechatwrite.

Chapter One

Come fly away to a sunnier day
The islands are calling your name
Feel the caress of warm, tropical breezes—

"Sadistic shits." Lucy snapped off the radio and watched the wiper blades sweep the snow apathetically across the windshield, as if they sensed the sheer futility of the task. Her plane from Seattle had body-surfed the crest of the rising storm into O'Hare barely an hour ago. Now the weather settled in enthusiastically. Snowflakes hit her windshield in drunken clumps and gummed up behind the wiper blades.

"Welcome home, Lucy Flint."

From across the street, a light went on in the house—a red-brick Edwardian that had long since drifted past shabby chic and into dilapidated. It was a shame. It was a beautiful, old classic built square and solid out of wood and rufous brick, standing like a citadel against the hostile climate.

A shadow darted past the window as she watched. Lucy pictured her mother moving around in the golden glow from that second-floor light. Mom moved like a squirrel, quick and fearful, darting away from danger as fast as she could and busy, busy, always busy.

Lucy wasn't holding her breath for the fatted calf. In that house, *he* would be waiting too, nursing his spite along with his nightly tipple of cheap drugstore wine—one and no more. Lucy made a snorting sound. She'd obviously not inherited that from her father.

The silhouette was framed briefly against the curtains of her old bedroom and Lucy sighed. Mom would be getting her room ready. Lucy would rather dispense with the frenzy of anxious preparation. It couldn't be helped, however, when you were an only child.

She'd been away long enough to be shocked by the cold that felt as if it would eat your face off before it quit. Ah, yes, Chicago. Other cities had climates, but Chicago had weather—lots of it and all the time.

Suddenly she thought of an old joke. *How cold is it out there? Cold enough for hell to freeze over and the Cubs to win the pennant.* Lucy let out a huge guffaw that was so much more than the tired old workhorse of a joke deserved. Yup, she was so losing it, and she hadn't even gotten out of the car yet. As an augury, it pretty much sucked.

She stared through the snow at the waiting house and took a deep breath and then another. In her head, she chanted the Serenity Prayer. It was all she had against the angry mob of memories clustering around the wooden front porch and jeering at her. The prayer granted her a moment's reprieve, so she said it again. The knot in her stomach unraveled some. She was here for a reason, and that reason was good and just. Lucy reached for her phone and a teeny bit more reinforcement.

"Hey, you." Mads was waiting for her call and answered on the first ring.

"Hey, yourself."

"How was the flight?"

"Fine." Lucy snickered. "Boy, are my arms tired." It was her night for elementary school jokes.

"HA HA HA." A deep, resonant Madeline silence followed, filled, just like when she sang, with the richness of what you'd just experienced and the promise of more to come. "That bad, hmm?"

"Oh, yeah, I'm a big, old mess." Lucy tried to crank some more heat out of the engine. The chill seeped through the metal and surrounded her in her small rental car. "And I haven't even gotten out of the car yet." The heater grudgingly agreed to a degree or two more. "I'm hoping to hide out here for most of the visit."

"Luce." Mads chuckled, hot chocolate over simmering coals. "You can't sit there all night."

"Maybe not *all* night," Lucy muttered.

Across the street, the light in her old bedroom went out. Lucy pictured her mother scuttling across the hallway to the bathroom. Fresh towels—check, full roll of toilet tissue—check, basin and surround—check, and all the time that little refrain playing in Lynne's head. *My Lucy is coming home. My Lucy is coming home.*

Nope. Your Lucy is cowering out in her car and wondering why the hell she ever thought she could pull this off. Mom had been to see her in the intervening years, first in New York and then Seattle, but this was Lucy's first trip home in nine long and undeniably interesting years.

"Are you still there?" Mads called her attention back to the phone pressed against her ear.

"Yup."

"Still hiding out?"

"Pretty much."

"Get out the car, ya big yeller dog."

"Na-ah. You can't make me. You're all the way over there. You can't make me."

Man, Lucy loved that laugh as Mads chuckled again. Years of drinking gin and singing blues in smoky bars honed vocal chords like that. "You have a point. But here's what I can do." An expectant pause and Lucy groaned in anticipation. "I can remind you that you want to be free to move on with your life. It's time to do this, and you're ready. You've done the work, Lucy." Mads stopped crooning and got serious. "Now get out of the damn car."

"But it's cold out there," Lucy whined.

"Get out the friggin' car." Mads didn't want to play today.

"Spoilsport."

"You can do this, babe." A complete change in tone and tears pricked the back of Lucy's eyelids. The faith in her almost crippled her in its sincerity. "And, what's more, you need to do this."

"You're right." Lucy's voice broke slightly and she cleared her throat. "I am about to get out of the car."

"Hallelujah. Speak it, sister, speak it."

The cheering section worked its magic, and Lucy fastened her coat right up to her chin. "I love you, Maddy Mads."

"I love you, too, Lucy Locket. Now, go and do what

you went there to do. Then come home and I can give you a huge hug and tell you how proud I am of you."

"I am opening the door." The grip of the metal felt insubstantial beneath Lucy's fingers.

"Hooray."

"Shit, it's cold." A blast of wind tossed a handful of snow into her face.

"It's Illinois."

"ARGH." Lucy screamed.

A thing lurched out of the swirling snow right beside her.

She jerked her legs back into the car just as the form flew close enough for the air to swirl around her. There was a tremendous thud. The car door was wrenched out of her hand and careened back drunkenly.

"Shit." Lucy grabbed the door and slammed it shut. As if she could quickly take back the last two minutes. No such luck.

A sickening crunch followed, and then an even worse silence. Lucy peered through her window at the spread-eagled shape on the pristine bed of snow.

"Ah shit, shit, shit." Her heart thudded so loudly it drowned out the sound of Mads on the other side of the phone. "This is not good."

Chapter Two

Silence hung heavily over the phone lines. "Lucy? Lucy, are you all right?"

"Um, *I* am." Lucy peered into the gathering gloom nervously.

Her heart sank. Nothing outside the car had changed. The dark thing spread across the snow was definitely human shaped. The object near the human thing, wheels spinning senselessly, was the bicycle it had been riding. Riding, until someone had opened their door on it. And that someone was her. "I've gotta go."

"What was that noise?"

"I doored a cyclist."

"You *what?*" There was nothing dulcet or dreamy about Mads and her smoky vocal chords now.

"It seems I doored a cyclist. I'm going to have to go now."

"Is the cyclist okay?"

"It's moving." Lucy stepped from the car, shut her door, and took a ginger step forward. A soft noise rode the steady sibilance of the wind. "And I think that's it groaning." She held the phone out nervously at the bipedal stain in the snow. "Can you hear it?"

"I can't hear anything but this howling noise. That's not it, is it?"

"Nope." Lucy was reasonably sure on this point. "That's the wind."

"Fuck, Illinois."

"I know, right?" Lucy took a half shuffle closer. "I think it's a him."

"How do you know it's a him? Can you see its face?"

"Nope." Lucy blinked away a sloppy snowflake. "But it's either a man or a very large woman, with a butt that looks like a man." And she certainly noticed the taut, muscular lines of his thighs and ass. She tilted her head to the side to get a better look. Those were male and not too bad, current situation aside. The Thinsulate pants could not be doing much good against the cold, because they left very little to the imagination. The figure on the ground moved again and rolled carefully onto his back. *Yup,* that was very definitely a he and not a she.

"Uh-huh, it's a him," she clarified for Mads without taking her eyes off the cyclist. "Excuse me? Are you all right?"

The cyclist cursed softly.

Lucy inched a little closer, ready to launch a heroic retreat into her childhood home if the injured party got pissed at her, the front steps of which loomed tantalizingly close. Coward. Lucy tried to master her yellow streak. "Should I call nine-one-one?"

"Does he look like he needs an ambulance?" Mads asked.

"I'll ask him." Lucy raised her voice. "Are you hurt? Should I call nine-one-one?"

The man on the ground moaned and struggled into a sitting position.

Her victim didn't look all that injured or dangerous, yet.

He stretched out his legs with a hiss.

"I think he's getting up," Lucy whispered into the
phone.

"Then he can't be too badly hurt, right?" Mads
sounded hopeful. "Any blood? Exposed bones? That
sort of thing?"

"I don't see any blood." Lucy leaned forward and
peered. Now that the cyclist was moving she didn't
want to risk getting any closer. "No bones either. I
think that means he might be all right."

"I can hear you," he spoke.

"He can hear me," Lucy reported to Mads. "Oh."
She stopped talking and stared.

"That's good." Mads kept it positive.

"I think he's going to be okay," Lucy whispered.

The cyclist ignored her and started unbuckling his
helmet.

"It's a good thing he wore a helmet," Lucy reported
into her phone.

"Why?" Mads whispered back.

"Because it's sort of . . . busted up."

"And his head?"

"Seems fine." Lucy stood on her toes for a better
look. "Are you sure you're all right?" Her voice shook
slightly as she risked speaking to the cyclist.

"No thanks to you." The man examined his helmet.
He shook his head angrily.

"I didn't see you." Lucy kept her tone conciliatory.
"You came out of nowhere."

"Then perhaps you should stop talking on the
phone and concentrate on what you're doing."

Lucy froze. She knew that voice. "Ah shit."

The cyclist whipped off his goggles and tucked them into his helmet in short, angry movements.

"This is going to get ugly." She hadn't realized she'd spoken out loud until Mads replied.

"Well," Mads huffed, outraged on her behalf. "Okay, I know you hit the guy with your door. But for the love of God, what kind of dork rides a bike in a snowstorm?"

The wind dropped just then and Mad's voice squawked out of Lucy's phone loud and clear. The cyclist jerked his head up and Lucy swore again. All the way west in Seattle, Mads had no idea. Lucy ignored the steady stream of rationalizations coming through the phone as her stomach sped south, into her boots.

"Bye," she whispered and hung up.

The man in the snow had gone dead still. His gaze locked on her like a heat-seeking missile. And Lucy knew he knew that she knew and he knew that she knew he knew. Or something. Her mind went blank. There must be something to say in situations like this, but she had nothing. She stared at him and he stared right back.

"What the hell are you doing here?" All things considered it was a very reasonable question. His tone and the glare he bent her way shot to hell any vague hope she might have held that Richard had learned to forgive and forget.

"Hello, Richard." Her voice hit the loaded air in a strangled squeak.

His voice was deeper than she remembered, but she would have known it anywhere. Nine years was not long enough to forget any of the small details she could now make out.

Snow powdered one side of his face and stuck to

his eyelashes. His face was leaner and the bones stronger and more decisive, but he was still Richard. Handsome in that Cary Grant, clean-cut, one-of-the-good-guys way. It had played havoc with her teenage heart and hormones. Her grown-up hormones were not dead to the appeal either. His eyes were the same pure, unadulterated cobalt. He blinked to clear snow from the dark veil of his lashes.

Lucy watched him with the helpless certainty that the light at the end of the tunnel was an oncoming train.

His head dropped forward almost onto his chest. He'd propped his elbows onto his knees.

She should say something to ease the tension, but she was clueless. She tucked her chin deeper into her scarf and waited.

"Tell me it's not you," he said, eventually.

She huddled deeper into her coat and tried a friendly smile. "I didn't see you when I opened my door."

"Ah, Christ." A big man, he was surprisingly grace-ful as he rose to his feet, brushing snow off his butt and legs.

She should have recognized those. An hysterical bubble of laughter caught in her throat.

"This cannot be happening to me," he rumbled without looking at her.

She really wanted to ask which part, but was equally sure she didn't want to hear his answer. "Sorry," she said, shrugging again. "I didn't—"

"See me, yeah, I get it." His beautiful blue eyes were colder than the snow seeping through her cheap boots. "What are you doing here, Lucy?"

It was like something out of *Wuthering Heights*. The wind howled, the snow drove against her face, and the large, lurking former love of her life glowered at her in a very Brontë-esque manner. Kate Bush started wailing her lament to Heathcliff in a dark corner of Lucy's mind.

"I came for my mom." She dropped her eyes first. "My dad is sick."

Richard made a strangled sound in the back of his throat. "So, you rushed home to take care of Mom and Dad?" He didn't wait for her reply, but bent to grab his bike and hauled it upright. He leaned over to examine it. Then gave up with a snarl of exasperation. "Perfect, fucking perfect."

"My mom needs me." It sounded lame. Richard shot her a look of clear skepticism. *Okay, he thought so too.* She was tempted to set him right and opened her mouth to do that. She shut it again. There was no easy explanation to this one.

He gave her one last scowl before he turned and stomped away. His feet drove small divots into the snow as he went, dragging his bike behind him. He didn't look back, but strode toward the house next door. He tossed the helmet to one side. It hit the boards of the front porch with a broken splat. Lucy winced. The door slammed behind him with a re-sounding bang that made her jump. This was so not good.

From his kitchen window Richard watched Lucy pick her way carefully along the pathway up to her old home. It was cleared and salted, but would need to be done again when this storm let up. He made sure of that for Lynne, now that Carl was no longer able to shovel. He tried not to look, but his eyes zeroed in like they were on autopilot. *And, oh God, those legs.*

What they did to a man was nothing short of criminal. Richard yanked the fridge open.

He would have described himself as the quintessential leg man. Breasts were good too. He was as partial as the next man to a great pair, but for him it would always be legs. And being a leg man meant he could never let a great ass pass him by without having a look either.

Breast men had it easy. A quick flick of the eyes down and up again and you were good to go. Leg men had more of a challenge. Over the years, and out of necessity, he'd perfected the swift, over the shoulder, window reflection, under armpit, smash and grab eyeful. Of course, that was before he'd had that particular fantasy eviscerated by *her*.

Lucy mounted the three wooden steps to the porch that ran the side of her family home.

And now. Well, now he still loved legs; long, shapely pathways straight to heaven. As long as they didn't belong to blond hell-raisers who blew out of town with his heart in their backpack and never got around to giving it back.

"Ah, fuck it." The orange juice slapped erratically against the side of the carton and Richard took a deep breath. He was a doctor, right. So the shaking hands could be a direct result of the fall. Except it was not the fall. The snow had taken the worst of the impact away. It was her.

He took a long swig from the carton, deriving a sort of savage pleasure from an action that would make his mother stare at him, first in frank and honest amazement, because he never drank from the carton, and next in horror.

"Ah, fuck it." As far as variety went, he was a pitiful

failure, but for impact, his vocabulary was perfect. Just what the doctor ordered.

Lucy Flint, back in town and doing what she always did. Taking his neatly ordered existence between her slender fingers, crumpling it up into a tiny ball, and tossing it over her shoulder. She'd just arrived and she'd doored him, wrecked his helmet and almost his bike, and reduced him to swilling orange juice from the carton. It made him shudder to think what she would do for an encore.

Except he already knew. Richard pulled a glass from the cupboard and poured the remainder of the juice into it. When she got done with turning him ass over end, she would wrench out his innards, starting with his heart, pulverize them, and disappear. Not this time, Lucy Flint. He made a silent promise to himself. *Fool me once . . .*

Her hair was different. It used to be shorter and curled around her beautiful face like a picture frame. This long, silky sweep of blond she had now was like a weapon. Her green eyes played hide and seek with her sexy mane as she peered out at him. This new sex kitten thing was like a knee to the groin.

Who was he kidding? Richard put his glass in the dishwasher and wiped down the granite countertop. Lucy Flint was the quintessential kick in the balls.

"Richie Rich?"
"My only love?"
"Do you think I'm pretty?"
"Beyond pretty."
"Would you love me if I wasn't pretty?"
"Well, I don't know." He looked up from his anatomy text.

"I'm very fond of you, old girl, but . . . love. I don't know about that."

A shriek, as he'd known there would be, and he was attacked by a warm, fragrant armful of pure heaven. Lucy.

Richard hauled his mind back to the present. "Ah, fuck it."

Chapter Three

The front door wasn't locked. It never was. This was Willow Park. Her mother would blink at her in confusion if she suggested otherwise. Nothing ever happened in this forgotten collection of streets just north of Chicago. Stubbornly resisting any attempt to be swallowed into the bustle and jumble of Chicagoland.

The door still jammed. Lucy tugged it slightly toward her, turned the handle, and then shoved. You had to know the magic. She smiled as the door swung inward with a soft groan. The house pounced on her in a waft of wood and old, faded wallpaper. Memories crowded around her, buffeting against her brain for attention. Lucy almost panicked. She couldn't do this. Mads was wrong.

"Lucy?" Too late. Her mother's hopeful voice floated from the interior of the house. "Is that you?" Her mom appeared at the top of the Arts and Crafts staircase standing central to the hallway.

Lucy looked up and forced a smile. "Hey, Mom. Who else were you expecting?"

"Oh, you." Lynne fluttered a hand at her and smiled down mistily. Guilt took a vicious sideswipe at Lucy.

Her mom had gotten older. Lines bracketed her eyes and mouth and her hair was almost entirely gray. She looked faded and tired beyond her sixty-odd years. "I can't believe you're finally here."

The noose tightened a few notches as a couple of joyful tears trickled down Lynne's cheeks. She had stayed away too long.

"Here I am," Lucy said, shrugging.

"Oh, Lu Lu." Lynne moved suddenly, skipping happily down the stairs to sweep Lucy into a hug. It took her a moment to respond; Lynne was not a toucher. The smell of her mother surrounded Lucy; a combination of almond oil and lemon-scented Pledge. The memories in the house pressed closer and Lucy tightened her grip on her mother. She needed to breathe. They were memories and had only as much power as she gave them.

"It's good to see you," Lucy whispered and she meant it. "How are you holding up?"

"Better now that you're here." Lynne gave a watery sniff and held her at arm's length. "Look at you," she said. "Still the prettiest girl in Willow Park. Probably the prettiest girl in the whole of Illinois." Lucy wanted to cringe, but she held still. "And you've grown your hair."

"Yes, I . . ."

"Look at all this beautiful hair?" Lynne caressed the silky ends of Lucy's hair. "I love it." A huge grin lit Lynne's face again. "It's stunning. Wait until they see you now."

Oh, she was waiting for that all right. "I'm glad you like it." Lucy touched a lock self-consciously.

"It makes you look more mature and sophisticated and now we can see those lovely eyes of yours." Lynne sniffled happily.

Lucy resisted the urge to fidget as the examination continued.

"And you've always been careful to keep your shape." Lynne nodded her approval. "It's not everyone who is lucky enough to have a gorgeous figure like yours. Why, Ashley . . ." A stricken expression chased Lynne's smile away.

Lucy swallowed hard. She did not want to hear about Ashley yet.

"Where are your bags?" Lynne's voice rose anxiously. Her mom was already in motion. Her head jerked back and forth as she searched the floor around Lucy. "You are staying, aren't you? You said you were coming for a few weeks. There should be bags if you are staying for a few weeks. I have your room ready. It's your old room and it's just the same. I haven't changed a thing."

"Mom?" Lucy raised her voice and stepped right into her mother's flight path. "I am staying for as long as you need me to. My bags are still in the car. I wanted to come in and say hello first." Lucy stretched the truth a little. She would have brought the bags with her if she hadn't been all shaken up by nearly killing Richard Hunter. Some things, however, didn't need to be shared. So she smiled reassuringly. "I'll go and fetch them, shall I?"

"I'll do it." Lynne bustled toward the coats hanging like dead things on hooks by the door. After nine years, Lynne was clearly not giving Lucy the opportunity to slip away.

"No, Mom." Laughter bubbled in Lucy's throat. It wasn't often that mild-mannered Lynne took a stand, but she took one now. It was like your favorite teddy bear suddenly going a bit feral. "You can't go out there. The weather is hideous and I've still got my coat on. See?" Lucy held out her arms and spun in a circle. "I'll go and get them."

"Now?" Lynne insisted.

"Now."

Outside the storm gave a healthy accounting for itself. Lucy staggered and slipped through the ice and snow back toward the front door. A swift peek at the house next door showed lights blazing. Richard was in that house. She stopped suddenly and the wind slammed into her back to try to get her moving again. Richard was in the house next door? What was Richard doing in the house next door?

"Lucy?" Lynne's querulous wail floated through the gloom and Lucy quickened her pace.

Lynne waited for her, peering through the glass panes of the door as if she were afraid Lucy would not be coming back. The wind shoved Lucy through the door and Lynne shut it behind her. The snick of the lock vibrated through Lucy's gut. The sound reverberated up her spine and she froze for a second.

Her mind clicked back into action and she took a deep breath. She was not trapped. The next breath was easier. She could open the door at any time and leave. The incident with Richard had stirred up all sorts of stuff and she needed a moment or two to put everything back in its proper place.

"Are you hungry?"

"A little," Lucy said, smiling. Any other answer would be blithely ignored in Lynne's ongoing assault against hunger.

"I made tomato soup." Her mom led the way into the kitchen. "Just the way you like it." The last time Lucy had eaten tomato soup was in this kitchen. "Would you like a grilled cheese with that?"

Lynne didn't wait for a reply, but started her bustling.

The kitchen was a distinctly unlovely room. The counters were scarred and misaligned and the cabinetry way past tired and well into burnt out. Yet, in this ugly, L-shaped cave, Lynne had rustled up magic day after day.

Carl didn't see any point in fixing a room in which he spent almost no time. He had never eaten in the kitchen. Lynne had always taken her husband his meals. Lucy felt the familiar bite of resentment. Not five minutes in this house and she was doing it. It was as if it was hardwired into her.

She pulled a stool up to the counter and Lynne put a steaming bowl of homemade tomato soup in front of her. The earthy tang came straight out of her childhood. Cold, cold days spent outside in the snow and ice. Braving the weather until your fingers and face went numb and then staggering home for grilled cheese and soup, followed by a bath and hot chocolate. Then, crawling all full and sleepy between fresh, chilly sheets.

"So you're back? To what do we owe the honor?"

The nostalgia was too sweet to last. Lucy blew on the soup gently as she turned to look at him.

"Hello, Dad." She was shocked. Her mom had aged, but Carl had become an old man. In her mind he was such a powerful figure. Now, he stooped in the kitchen doorway, his shoulders slanting forward over his sunken chest. He still wore his pajamas and a tatty bathrobe, which had been old when she still lived here.

"How are you, Dad?" Gingerly she slipped the hot spoon between her teeth. She tasted nothing, as if Carl had robbed the entire place of any flavor or texture.

"Would you like some soup?" Her mother bustled into the mounting tension. "Lucy was having some soup with me. Doesn't she look wonderful? Did you see she's grown her hair? I think she looks lovely. Of course, you always loved her short hair, but you have to admit she looks a treat."

Lucy wanted to reach out and put a gag over her mother's mouth. She rested her spoon against the side of the bowl carefully. The hostility came off her father in waves as he stood and glared at her.

"I don't want any goddamned soup," Carl snarled in the direction of his wife, effectively ending the chatter.

Irritation tightened in Lucy's gut as her mother subsided into a wary silence. For over thirty years, he'd been doing the same thing.

A short man, built like a pit bull with broad shoulders and almost no neck, Carl had looked every inch the thug in his youth and had reveled in it. If it weren't for identical green eyes, Lucy would have questioned her paternity. Also, not forgetting a less-than-charming shared propensity for being bloody-minded and stubborn.

She wanted to yell at him not to speak to her mother like that. When she was younger, that's what she'd have done. He knew it too. The taunt glinted in his eyes. He may look like hell and his mind might be slipping, but his eyes were still daring her to do her worst. Goading her to join the chaos.

She forced her hand to pick up the spoon, dip it into the bowl, and bring it to her mouth. "It's good," she said to nobody in particular.

"You here for money?" Carl demanded from the doorway.

Lucy looked up from her soup as he stepped farther into the kitchen. She could see more signs of age on him as he moved into the light. The march of years had diminished him like the faded fabrics on the furniture. He had no power to wound her. It was hers to give, that power.

"No, Dad." She took another sip of her soup. "I have money and I have a good job now. I'm not here for money."

"Good," he jeered, breathing heavily through his nose. "Because you'll have to wait until I die before you get another cent out of me."

Good old Dad, what a charmer.

"Now, Carl." Faithful Mom rushed into the fray like a frantic squirrel guarding her kit from the rabid neighborhood stray. "The things you say."

She turned her back and carried on chattering.

Lucy pushed her soup bowl away. Carl looked ready to fight back and she cut it off quickly.

"I won't be here for long," Lucy said, keeping her tone level. "I need to tie up some loose ends and then I am going back to Seattle."

That successfully deflected him. Carl went silent before he grunted and turned away. "What time is dinner?"

Lucy could have answered the question for him. What time was dinner always?

"Six-thirty?" Lynne glanced at her husband for approval as if she hadn't been putting a meal in front of him, at that time, for over thirty years.

"Good."

Of course it's good, Lucy thought savagely as her mom slid the grilled cheese onto the counter beside her. It was always good in Carl's world. The universe Carl controlled with an iron fist was always good for Carl. *Stop it.* Lucy pulled her thoughts up short. Her father was who he was and now he was a sick, old man. Lucy tore into the bread to keep her mouth busy.

Carl reached the doorway and stopped suddenly. "I suppose you know who lives right next door?"

Lucy looked up from her sandwich.

Her mom sucked in a loud, shocked breath. "Carl."

"You're talking about Richard." The penny dropped in time to cheat Carl out of his surprise attack. Though, to be honest, she wished she'd had that little nugget of information about twenty minutes ago.

Carl looked momentarily deflated, but recovered quickly. "He bought up the old Crowley house. Spent a goddamned fortune, doing God knows what to it." Carl sniffed and shoved his hands deep into his pockets. "Waste of money, if you ask me. There was nothing wrong with that house."

"I was worried your flight might not be able to land in this weather." Her mom picked up a sponge and attacked the counters.

"Richard and Ashley renovated the Crowley house?" She turned to her mother for confirmation, but Lynne was not looking at her.

"Sometimes they shut the airport if they can't clear the runways in time. Isn't that right, Carl?"

He ignored her and kept his sneer locked on Lucy.

"I am sure they did a wonderful job." Lucy was proud her voice sounded so even. "Ashley always did have excellent taste."

"Listen to you." Carl chuckled. "I bet you want to rip her eyes out."

Lucy took a controlled breath. She was not jealous of Ashley. Richard and Ashley had found their way back to each other, despite her best efforts to the contrary. She was not here to stir up the old trouble. She was here to put it to rest.

Carl watched her carefully for any sort of reaction. Lucy gave him nothing. "Do you see much of them?"

"We see him all the time." Carl's jeer widened into pure malice.

"Mom?" Lucy put a little starch in her voice and her mother stopped and blinked at her.

"Well, he is our family doctor now," she confessed in a rush and sidled over to the old oven and started cleaning around it.

Lucy blinked at her mother's back. This was going to make Richard super happy. She had the insane desire to laugh hysterically. "What happened to Dr. Barnes?"

"He retired four years ago and went to Florida." Her mother scrubbed around the spotless burners, her entire body vibrating with the effort. "He and his wife left town. They said they couldn't stand the cold anymore and who can blame them. I hear they have a nice condo in Florida now, right on the beach, as well. I am sure—"

"They're splitting up." Carl leaned his shoulder up against the doorjamb. "She left him."

"Mrs. Barnes left Dr. Barnes?" Lucy frowned at her mother.

"I'm talking about lover boy from next door." Carl grinned at her maliciously. "She left him high and dry, just like you did."

Lucy stared at her father. He couldn't have that right. "What?" *No, Carl is making this up.* She frowned down at her sandwich. *He must have this wrong. It must be his illness making him say things.*

"They are getting a divorce," he replied with relish.

"Carl, I don't think . . ." Her mother twisted the cloth in her hands.

"Is this true?" Lucy looked from Lynne to Carl.

"What does it matter?" Lynne banged the dishes. "That unpleasantness is all over and done with. It doesn't matter what happens to them. He is our neighbor and our doctor. Finished."

"I can't believe this." Lucy rescued her sandwich from her mother who swept away all in the path before her. Ashley and Richard were like the perfect couple. No, they *were* the perfect couple.

Lynne sprayed the fridge door with disinfectant. "We should mind our own business."

Carl scoffed loudly. "Here's your chance to take him away from her again."

He didn't quit, but Lucy kept her eyes focused on her mother. "Ashley would never leave Richard."

"I think it's a temporary thing," Mom told the inside of the kitchen sink. "At least that's what Richard says."

"What happened?" *Perhaps it's salvageable.*

"She left him." Carl chewed the words out with relish. "He seems to have difficulty holding on to his woman, for all his fancy education and money. Makes you wonder why. What's wrong with the man? You know though, don't you, Lucy?"

"Carl." Her mother tossed her sponge into the sink. "Richard Hunter is a wonderful young man and a good doctor. Don't you start saying terrible things about him."

True. Lucy grimaced ruefully. *All-round, marvelous Richard.*

"Ashley is crazy about Richard," she said aloud. So crazy about him, it had ended years and years of friendship between her and Ashley.

"Shows how much you know," Carl scoffed. "She walked out and is living above that shop of hers on Main Street."

"What shop on Main?" And the surprises kept coming. Mom had been holding out on her.

"Ashley owns a shop now." Her mother threw Carl a look loaded with meaning. Typically, he ignored her.

"Oh, yes," he told Lucy. "Ashley is quite the career girl. Opening more and more shops and becoming some sort of fashion person." He waved his hand in the air when the right phrase wouldn't come.

"Shops?" Lucy's eyes opened appreciatively. "Shops? As in more than one?"

"Three." Mom gave it up with another glare at her husband. "Ashley has this shop on Main and two others. One at Lakeview Mall and another downtown." She crossed her arms over her chest and thrust out her chin. "And she is about to open another one in San Francisco. Although why anyone would want to open a shop there, I cannot fathom."

"What sort of shops?" While she had been screwing up her life and scrambling to get it back on track, Ashley had been busy shaping her world.

"Clothes," her mom responded shortly.

"Rich women clothes," Carl drawled. "Fancy stuff for women with nothing to do and too much money burning a hole in their pockets. You would love it. Why don't you get that fancy man in Seattle to come here and buy you something?" Carl warmed to his theme enthusiastically. "In fact, you would enjoy that. Lording your rich boyfriend over your old enemy."

Lucy grit her teeth. *Ashley had left Richard?* It didn't make any sense. "She always loved fashion," Lucy said out loud. Ashley loved fashion and Richard, those two things made Ashley's world turn. She shook her head. Her mom was right. This really was none of her business.

"Now she's busy and out of your hair." Carl scented blood. "You can have another crack at her man."

"You know," Lucy let the impulse rip and smiled beatifically. "You're absolutely right. I thought I might get started after my grilled cheese."

Chapter Four

There were times when Carl's rigid habits were a blessing. He insisted on his dinner at six-thirty, but it also meant he was in bed by nine-thirty. Nothing shifted her father from his stance. Not school recitals, Christmas, or New Year's Eve. It didn't even matter if the Cubs were finally in the play-offs and looked a sure thing to win. Carl went to bed at nine-thirty.

And he assumed the rest of humanity did the same. The rest of Willow Park could have told him different. Lucy had run wild from the time her father went to bed until somebody dragged her home. Most of the time it had been Ashley and then, later, Richard.

Now, it meant after the dinner dishes were put away and the kitchen cleaned, Lucy had her mother to herself. It was the opportunity she'd been waiting for most of the day.

"How is he?" Lucy asked, as she made her mother a cup of coffee.

"He has good days and bad days." Her mother's expression grew pensive. "Lately, the bad days are outnumbering the good."

It was pretty much as the phone calls had suggested.

Carl had never been an easy man to live with, but he was getting worse. Mood swings and vicious bouts of paranoia were taking over.

"Have you given any more thought to selling the house?" Lucy kept the tone light.

"He feels safe here." Her mom got up and wiped down the spotless surfaces.

"I was thinking more of you." Lucy caught her mother's hands and held them still. "This house is a lot for you to manage."

"He hasn't left the house since he heard about that swine flu." She gently removed her hands from Lucy's and went back to her wiping.

"Never?" Lucy watched her mother. She wished her mom would put the stupid sponge down and talk to her.

"Oh, no," her mom said, shaking her head vehemently. "When it's sunny out, he will sit on that balcony upstairs."

Lucy did a quick mental calculation. So, Carl had not been outside the house in about two years.

"Besides," she rattled on. "This is our home. You grew up in this house."

"But if you sell you could get something smaller." Lucy waved an expansive hand through the air. "Something more manageable. It's called downsizing and all the best people are doing it."

"But where would we go?" Her mother didn't smile at her silly attempt at a joke, but looked around the old kitchen nervously.

"Anywhere you like. Florida, like Dr. Barnes." Lucy reached over the counter and touched her mother's hands. Gently, she cradled one between her palms. Her mother's hands were wrinkled and dried from years of hard work. Nowhere on Lynne did her age show as much as on those hands that had spent a lifetime being busy with the needs of others. "Or Glen Ellyn. Didn't you always want one of those smart new condos they're building? Somewhere close to the lake?"

Her mother thought about it for a second and then gave her a small, shy smile and her eyes danced. If Lucy showed very little resemblance to her father, there was absolutely no resemblance to her mother. Lynne's eyes were a pale, pale blue that seemed to have faded with the years. She had been a medium blonde, but that color had all disappeared and Lynne would never justify the time or the money to have her hair colored. Lucy watched her mother process the information.

"Close to Lake Ellyn would be nice." Lynne squinted at her as if the idea had never occurred to her. "Do you think we could find one like that?"

"Or you could have something similar close to downtown," Lucy pressed as she took a sip from her coffee.

"I don't like being downtown." Her mom's eyes widened. "There are far too many people. And, oh my, the crime. I was reading the other day—"

"The where is not important, Mom." Lucy cut her off before the objection could gather steam. "You can go anywhere you like. The idea is to find something with virtually no upkeep."

"Oh," her mom said, nodding. "It would be nice to have a bit more time to do . . . things." She sighed wistfully, as if Lucy were suggesting a trip to the moon.

You couldn't rush Lynne and getting her mother to see there was life outside of the old house was probably going to be Lucy's hardest task. Lynne was born in this house, grew up in it, brought her husband to her family home and had her own child here. It was as if her mother were grafted into the sagging, maple floors. And in this old house, Lynne had slowly had the life sucked out of her, first by her domineering father and then by her husband.

While Lynne had gone quietly, Lucy had put up a fight. The house and her father became twisted into each other in her psyche. She spent her teens rebelling. Her final act of rebellion had taken her not only out of the house and away from the suffocation, but all the way to New York. Not so smart, as it turns out. But twentysomethings are not, as a rule, known for their foresight—twentysomething alcoholics, not at all.

"I am sure you would get a good price for this place." Lucy took another inch forward. "I spoke to a Realtor and they told me a lot of young families are buying up these old houses and fixing them up."

"Like Richard?"

"Well, yes, like Richard." It still seemed strange to say his name out loud. He'd existed in her mind almost constantly since she'd been away. One big regret she would do anything to change. No time like the present, nagged her conscience. Her conscience always sounded like Mads.

"I don't think I could ever sell this house." Lynne shook her head, her eyes troubled.

"Why can't you?" It was hard to keep the impatience out of her tone. "When we spoke on the phone, you seemed keen."

"Did I?" Lynne got up and bustled around the kitchen again.

"Do you think it's the best place for Dad?" Lucy fired her best shot.

Lynne stopped her busywork and frowned. "I'm

not sure." She sat down again and clasped her hands around her mug. "He does struggle with the stairs. I thought of getting one of those stair lifts installed for him."

"You could do that," Lucy agreed. "Or you could leave the stairs to a young family with younger legs and find a condo all on one level."

"I don't know." Lynne's brow furrowed. "I can see your point, but it all seems so drastic."

"It's a big step." Lucy packed her voice with reassurance. "But you don't have to do this alone. That's why I'm here, remember?"

Lynne made a noncommittal noise and took a sip of her coffee.

"I mean it, Mom." Lucy touched Lynne's wrist and her mother looked at her again. "I know I haven't given you much reason to believe me, but I am here now and I will stay for as long as you need me." She gave Lynne's wrist a small shake. "And if you need to, we can talk about the past. It's not something I'm proud of, but it happened and we can talk about it."

"I don't think I want to," Lynne said, surprising Lucy. "I want to appreciate that you are here now. I was never one for jawing over my problems."

"Then why don't we do something about this house?"

"Like what?" Lynne narrowed her eyes suspiciously.

"Well." Lucy took a bracing breath. *Into the fray.* "If you are even going to think about selling, the house is going to need a thorough going-over."

"Are you calling my house dirty?" Lynne stuck her chin out.

"No." Lucy chuckled. "All I meant was that any house, all houses, in fact need to be cleared of all the stuff that gathers over the years." She added some enthusiasm to her voice. "It will be a sort of special project we tackle together."

"Hmph." Lynne looked as if she might balk. "It may be stuff to you, but it's my stuff."

Lucy did a lightning fast mental catalogue of the house. "What about my room?" Inspiration struck. "We could get rid of all those old posters and stuff."

"But you loved those posters," Lynne objected immediately.

Lucy felt an insane urge to start laughing hysterically. "I loved them when I was sixteen, Mom. I think I'm a bit beyond Hootie & the Blowfish."

"Oh, you really liked them." Lynne gave her a misty, nostalgic smile. "I still have all their records."

"CDs." Lucy fought down the incipient panic. It was a bit like fighting her way through cotton candy. "I've moved on since then."

"Well, of course you have." Lynne rolled her eyes and got to her feet. "You're thirty years old now and I would think you're way beyond that sort of thing." Then, she stopped in the center of the kitchen and gave a soft, sad sigh. "Oh, but you did love to dance, didn't you, Lu Lu?"

The cotton candy crawled up her chin and into her nostrils and gummed up the roof of her mouth. "Anyway, I think it's time to clear out my room."

"If you're ready, Lu Lu."

Lucy stopped the wince from showing. She hated that pet name. Lu Lu was a wild, drunken little girl full of rage and sadness so deep there wasn't enough booze in the world to wash it away. Lucy pushed ruthlessly past the rising dark of memories.

"I think it's time, Mom."

"Okay, then." Lynne smiled at her. "Like you said, it can be our special project."

"Right. I think I'll head up." Lucy returned the smile, not able to meet Lynne's eyes or her mother would see the smile for the lie that it was. "I'm tired."

"Of course you are, darling," Lynne said, going immediately contrite. "All that traveling is exhausting." She gave Lucy a coy smile. "Would you like me to make you some hot chocolate? I got the kind that you liked and I still remember how to do it."

"Sure, Mom, that would be great." Lucy took the stairs two at a time. Across from her window, a light blinked on in Richard's house. The curtains were thick and all she could see was a shadow against the fabric. She snapped her own drapes shut. It would not do to be caught peering into his windows.

Around her the house was nearly silent, other than the familiar settling sounds: the soft protest of wood and the metallic pop of the radiators as they pumped heat into the rooms. Lucy forced down another mouthful of hot chocolate. It was sweet enough to make the most exacting five-year-old happy. Her mother had left it with her before going to bed.

Her bedroom was a bizarre shrine to her youth. Posters stuck to the wall with Scotch tape curling up at the ends. A corkboard pinned above the simple pine desk, painted white and chipped where she'd scratched it. Lucy approached the board cautiously.

There she was, all long legs and attitude hair: Lucy Flint, teenage goddess, in all her various incarnations. Other girls got gawky or thickset as their bodies changed, but not Lucy Flint. Lucy Flint flowered like an exotic bloom. A beautiful child seamlessly transformed into a lovely young woman. Right beside her in most of the pictures was Ashley. Adolescence had not been as kind to Ashley. Puppy fat and braces conspired against her.

God. They were almost a caricature of themselves; the blond beauty and her plain, studious friend. Except it was Ashley who had first captured the prince.

And there he was, the prince in question. A couple of years older and carrying those two years across his broad shoulders with the tautly held dignity of a boy becoming a man. Richard. Lucy's heart gave a little thump. He had certainly been beautiful. The years had been kind to him. She'd caught that much as her mind got busy trying to process the fact she'd nearly killed him.

Lucy chuckled. It was kind of funny. Actually it was very funny. And the joke was on her. She touched a strip-leather bracelet carefully pinned in place with heart-shaped thumbtacks. The first thing Richard had ever given her. Made, inexpertly, by his own hands and given to her with an offhand gesture and his heart in his eyes. Lucy's heart gave another thump, even bigger this time. She may have stolen him from Ashley, but for a while there, it had been magic.

Beside the bracelet hung a photo and Lucy's laughter died. Damn, she had loved him. It streamed out of the captured image. Him with his arm casually looped around her neck, his nose and mouth buried by her ear and her laughing. She'd been happy in that moment. True, wondrous, and unfettered happiness she'd thought would be enough to fix the aching cavern inside her. Reflexively she reached up and rubbed the place on her chest that still ached a little.

Chapter Five

"Ring the doorbell, Lucy." She took another deep breath and dropped her hand. Richard was home. Lucy knew this because she had been watching his house for the last two hours. He had driven up, gotten out of his car, and entered the house without even glancing in the direction of her house.

So, here was her dilemma. She would reach up and press the button. Inside the house the doorbell would ring. She would wait and hear footsteps, perhaps a light would go on and then the door would open. And then? This was where things headed south for her. Her finger dropped away. With both hands wrapped protectively around her peace offering, she stood on Richard's doorstep, getting colder by the minute and procrastinating.

"This is stupid." She had to do this. If he was her father's doctor, and he was, then she was going to be seeing rather a lot of him. They needed to establish neutral ground.

"For Christ's sake." Lucy leapt back a step as the

door was suddenly yanked open. "Are you going to stand there all night?"

And she got her first good look at Richard. Her tongue got glued to the top of her mouth as she stood on his doorstep and stared. *Holy Mary, Mother of God*, but he looked good. He'd been a handsome boy, but he was so much more now. Her gaze roamed over features that had hardened around the edges, having lost the softer fullness of youth and been replaced by sharply hewn angles. His mouth was still the same, only the lines bracketing it were deeper. It was a stern mouth, but it always seemed to look as if there were a smile waiting to appear.

Except for now.

Now, it was drawn into a single, harsh line. Lucy realized he stood there and glared at her, his eyes colder than the February weather.

"My mother sent over some of her soup." Lucy lifted the container to show him. Soup sloshed convincingly against the sides.

"Tell her thank you, from me." His voice sounded a bit deeper and more gravelly. Or perhaps that was because he was thoroughly pissed off. It was still a great voice. She used to call him up just to hear him say her name. His father had been from Willow Park and his mother French Canadian. The accents mixed in Richard's single-malt baritone like old friends. She wondered if his voice would still caress the two syllables of her name like a lover. Not likely, if the look arcing her way was any indication.

He reached out.

Lucy almost leapt back again before she realized he was going for the soup. *Damn.*

He raised an eyebrow at her and she gave him the

soup. She felt stupider by the second. He stepped into the house again and the door started to shut.

"Um."

"Yes?" Richard glared at her.

"May I come in?"

She could see him mentally battling that one. Richard had the manners his father ground into him and the natural chivalry of a born gentleman. He wanted to slam the door in her face. She could read it in his white-knuckled grip on the wood, but his good twin wouldn't let him do it. With a grudging nod, he stepped back and made a brusque motion with his hand for her to enter.

He turned and strode down the corridor and Lucy trailed him obediently.

His jeans were old and worn, but they clung to his thighs and butt in a way she would have to be three weeks dead not to notice. Lucy stepped into the bright light of a kitchen and gulped.

A white, long-sleeved T-shirt molded his body in all the right places. This might have been easier if he'd had the decency to grow the smallest paunch or perhaps be losing his hair. But no, Richard looked better than ever and angrier than hell. Lucy realized she was stretching even his legendary gallantry to the breaking point.

"I offered to bring the soup round because I wanted the chance to speak to you."

He crossed his arms over his chest.

"I wanted to apologize for . . . um . . . the thing with my car door. Out there in the storm. I didn't see you until it was too late." Silence descended between them. Lucy could hear the soft tick of the kitchen clock behind her.

"Is that it?" His eyes were like a shark's, all relentless focus and no leeway.

"No," she responded carefully. "But I might be here for a while." He started looking murderous. "I'm here to help my mother and I thought it best to break the ice, so to speak."

Not a flicker, not a twitch, just the same hostile silence.

"Break the ice." She motioned to the snow and ice outside the window and attempted a light laugh. "Anyway . . ." She cleared her throat when she got nothing. "We got off to a bad start and I wanted to apologize."

There, that wasn't so bad. She could do the adult thing, even with her heart going like a jackhammer inside her chest.

"You came over here to apologize for us getting off to a bad start?"

"Yes," Lucy said, nodding. "I thought we could be civil, maybe, for the time that I'm here."

The silence in the kitchen hung heavy.

"You did, did you?" he spoke at last. "Like we could put it all behind us."

"No." That's not what she meant. He was due an apology and he would get one, but not like this.

"Would that be after dooring me the other night or the way you ran out of my life nine years ago?"

Lucy's heart stopped and then lurched to a start again. There would be no easing into this if Richard had his way.

He carried on in a frigid voice, "I want to be clear about what it is that we are sweeping under the rug."

"Yes, I—"

"If I don't get my questions in fast, you might skip

town again and I might spend another nine years wondering why."

"You've been wondering why all this time?" That took her by surprise. She realized it was the wrong thing to say as his eyes went glacial.

"Don't flatter yourself," he snarled. "But now that you're here I thought I might ask, for shits and giggles." He didn't look much like he was laughing. "Why did you do it?"

Oh, man, she didn't want to get into this. There would be a time and a place for that, but now wasn't it. "Does it matter?"

"Humor me." He jerked his chin in her direction. It was a gesture she recognized. Richard was more than mad. He was boiling on the inside. "I'm still hazy on the why. Because you"—he took a step closer to her—"you didn't even have the balls to break up with me to my face, but left a message on my phone."

She had been stupid to come here. She thought they could agree to disagree or something. *Yeah, right.* She stepped away from him, brushing against a stool that screeched loudly in protest. The noise scrambled her already jangling nerves. "I'll leave the soup and go. This is not a good time, clearly."

"I must have left over a hundred messages for you." He kept coming.

"Yes, I know." Lucy backed up. "I . . . um . . . threw the phone away."

She needed to get out of here.

"Ah." He stepped around her so that he stood between Lucy and the door. His eyes were piercing. "Thus, eliminating any possibility I might contact you."

"I can . . ."

"Tell me?" he murmured and put his head on

one side. "Was that your idea or Jason's?" The name ricocheted around the kitchen as they stood in silence. Richard spoke first. "That was the name of the guy you ran off with, right? Brooke Taylor's boyfriend. Have I got all of this right?"

"Perfectly." Lucy let out a shaky breath. "And you are long overdue both an explanation and an apology, but perhaps now isn't the time."

"You're probably right," he said, his tone now downright nasty. "Perhaps you could text me something touching?" There it was, the truth in all its glory. "Or, I am sure you can find an e-card to express the right sort of sentiment."

"You look fine," she yelped, desperate to shut the flow of eloquence. He was being a prick, but no more than she deserved.

"What?" He blinked at her in confusion.

"I mean, you don't look injured."

"Really? That's probably because some scars are hidden."

"I was talking about yesterday." *Anger is hurt,* she reminded herself fiercely. *Stay out of defensive and in the moment. Get out of your goddamned head. This is not about you, it's about him and he has every right to be pissed at you.* She ran out of AA poster material. "I wasn't expecting someone to be out on their bicycle."

"Really?"

"It was snowing."

"I'm in training."

"For what?" She eyed him skeptically.

He clammed up and went back to glaring.

Lucy couldn't take too much of the ensuing silence. It was time for a good exit line. "Anyway. I am sorry for what happened and I hope you weren't hurt."

"Nine years, Lucy." His eyes bored into the back of

her brain. "You come back here after nine years and you want to brush everything under the carpet and talk about yesterday?"

"I don't want to brush things under the carpet," Lucy insisted gently. "I think . . ."

"Fine." He made a decisive motion with his hand. "Let's play this stupid little tragedy out your way. That's how we did it in the past, anyway." He crossed his arms over his chest, biceps bulged against the white of the shirt, and Lucy fixed her gaze there. It was easier than facing the fury of his eyes. "Tell me again what the hell you're doing here."

"I'm here to help my mother." Her voice was barely louder than a whisper.

"You're kidding, right?" Richard gave a harsh bark of laughter. "You?" He sneered at her. "You've never helped your mother in your life."

"Nevertheless." Lucy clutched her tattered dignity and held his hostile gaze. "She is struggling with my father and she needs my help." Lucy sucked a ragged breath into her lungs. "You're right, I wasn't there for her in the past, but I can be there for her now. And I intend to."

"Bravo," he jeered in a soft voice. "Look at you getting all noble. You know I'm your father's doctor, right?"

"I just found out." Lucy forced herself to meet his gaze.

"Change of plans?"

"No." She kept her eyes steady. "I said I would help and I meant it."

A muscle clenched in his jaw and he unfolded his arms to jab a finger in her direction. "Just so you know, Lucy. I will be watching you. I take care of your mother as well as your father and the last thing that poor woman needs is your crap. Are we clear?"

"Crystal." Lucy snapped her spine straight and glared right back. She had nothing to fear.

"Lynne is as fragile as hell right now." His eyebrows closed over his eyes like thunderheads. "You pull any of your shit, any of your tantrums or bring your fucking drama into that house and I will tear you to pieces." He meant every word of his threat and Lucy felt a slither of fear snake down her spine. That, more than anything, pissed her off.

"There will be no tantrums, no drama, and no need for puerile threats," she said, putting a bit more force in her voice.

"I mean it, Lucy." Another step brought them so close she could feel the heat of his body.

"I understand," she said, nodding and crossing her arms over her breasts. Her mouth felt dry and she swallowed carefully. "But you have nothing to worry about. I'm not going to do anything to hurt my mother. Or my father, for that matter."

He didn't speak for the longest time. He stood there, staring down at her. His hand shot out.

She jumped, but not quickly enough to evade the hard grip on her chin.

He tilted her head up to the light and stared at her, his eyes raking her features as if he could see some truth beyond the exterior. "Still so fucking beautiful."

His face was perilously close to hers and Lucy's breath caught. He traced her features with a long, slow look. Something flickered into life in the tense silence, a shiver of awareness that hovered in the air between them.

Richard felt it too. His eyes darkened; a small frown

creased the skin above them. It unnerved her and she jerked her chin away.

She stepped to the side and put some physical distance between them. Everything inside her felt shaken up and out of place. "Well"—her voice sounded loud and jarring in the torpid atmosphere—"if you are sure there is no lasting damage from the other night, I will let you get back to whatever it was you were doing." Probably constructing little voodoo dolls of girlfriends past. "Please let me know if there are any repairs needed to the bike and I will take care of them."

"The bike is fine."

"Good." Lucy turned tail and headed for the door. "My mother is waiting for me to get back."

"I don't remember that ever having any impact on your plans before," he said, going for another body shot.

"People change, Richard." Lucy wrenched the front door open. Freezing air rushed through the door and made her eyes tear up.

"Not you," he said from somewhere behind her.

Lucy took a moment to stop and stare. "I think you'll find that you're wrong." She shut the door behind her before he could reply.

Outside the weather did its best to add drama. Hard pellets of snow were being hurled against her by a frigid wind.

"So," she said to nobody in particular. "That went well."

Chapter Six

Lucy did not expect to sleep well and she was right. It was with a sort of grim satisfaction she stomped downstairs the next morning. The staircase protested her weight all the way down. When she'd been a child, she'd played a game with the staircase. It was her mission to make it all the way up or down without a creak. Information she'd put to much use as a teenager.

This morning, she didn't give a shit. The stupid old thing needed a good carpenter and she needed caffeine and she needed it now. No booze and, as of six months ago, no cigarettes either, and caffeine took on a whole new meaning in your life. That and cheese-cake.

Lynne had beaten her downstairs. Lucy was ashamed to say that she took one look at her mother and nearly snuck away.

Lynne looked like hell. Her shoulders were slumped like a kicked dog's as she sobbed quietly into a cup of tea. Lynne always cried like this, silent and unseen tears, anything to keep Carl from hearing and relishing his handiwork. Impotent fury for her mother turned to acid in Lucy's stomach. A lifetime of being bullied and belittled and now the old man was losing his mind.

"Mom?" She kept her question gentle.

"Good morning, Lu Lu. Did you sleep well?" Lynne scrubbed tears from her cheeks with the heels of her hands. Her face was blotchy and her eyes puffy from weeping. Bits of salt-and-pepper hair had escaped and clung to the sodden mess of tears on her cheeks. Lynne looked pitiful.

"I slept great, Mom." Lucy slid into a stool opposite her. "What's going on?"

"It's nothing." Lynne managed a watery smile.

Lucy watched her, and Lynne's smile started to slip away. Lucy grabbed a box of Kleenex and slid them toward her. "Tell me."

Lynne plucked a sheet out of the box and blew her nose. She took a long pause and then a soft sob escaped her, then another and another.

"I haven't got any milk," she hiccupped.

"What did you say?" Lynne never liked being held when she cried, so Lucy stayed on her side of the scarred work counter. "You don't have any milk?"

Lynne gave a snuffle and shook her head. She rattled the empty carton at Lucy for emphasis. "I ran out of milk."

Lucy took it in: the cup with the tea bag in it, the kettle starting to boil, and the penny dropped. Carl's morning cup of tea and there was no milk. Lucy peered closer at Lynne's face.

"He will want his tea," her mother wailed.

"I am sure he'll wait, Mom," she suggested gently. "Is he even awake?"

"No . . . o . . . o." Lynne looked at her wide-eyed. "But he will be and then he is going to want his tea."

Lucy sat nonplussed. This was uncharted territory.

Carl must have gotten a whole lot worse. *I should have come sooner,* whispered guiltily in her head.

"I tell you what," Lucy said, inching forward carefully. "You keep getting his breakfast ready." Lucy kept a close eye on her mother. Last night, Richard had told her how fragile Lynne was. Looks like he was right. "I will pop up to the store and get the milk. You put the coffee on for us and by the time the rest of his breakfast is ready, I'll be back. Dad will get his tea and be none the wiser."

"He will notice." Fresh tears welled in Lynne's faded blue eyes. "He notices everything, everything I don't want him to see."

"Oh, Mom." Lucy sat down again. "What's this all about?"

Lynne seemed to hesitate, as if wondering how much to say. She took a handful of tissues and blew her nose enthusiastically. "I had a terrible night," she said quietly. "Sometimes, he doesn't sleep well and then he gets angry."

"He gets angry?" Unease tightened in Lucy's belly as more tears seeped down her mother's cheeks. "He doesn't hurt you, does he?"

"What?" Lynne stopped crying all of a sudden and stared at her, aghast. "Why would you think such a thing about your father?"

Lucy's mind juddered to a jarring stop and her jaw dropped open. Part of her wanted to snap back that it was maybe because she'd never heard him say a civil word to his wife? Or perhaps it had something to do with the way he had bullied and blustered his way through both of their lives? Or could it even have a little something to do with the fact that Lynne was down here, weeping into the tea and looking like running out of milk was a fate worse than death?

In the end she said none of that, but murmured something about having done some research on Carl's condition.

"Well." Lynne huffed and snatched up a couple more Kleenexes. "This is not some stranger on that Interweb. This is your father we are talking about and he gets so angry and then he cannot rest and he needs to get it all out." She blew her nose and tucked the Kleenex under the cuff of her sweater. "Carl rants and raves, but he would never lay a finger on me. I am shocked you would think such a thing, Lucy."

"Why don't I go and get that milk?" Lucy knew when she was beat.

"You have to be shitting me." Lucy planted her hands on her hips and glared. She took a step toward the mound of snow that was her rental car. The brush in her hand looked a bit like a whistle squaring up to a thunderstorm.

She started back toward the house, stamping snow off her boots as she went. This was strictly a shovel job and there was sure to be one in the basement. She opened the front door and was hit by a blast of warm, humid air.

"You let her go for milk? Did you give her money?" Carl's peevish tone drifted down the staircase.

Lucy shut the front door decisively. A walk it was then.

The store was less than a ten-minute amble away. The day was cold, but clear and crisp and she really, really didn't like shoveling. She lived on the damned West Coast with all the worthy and worthless of the U.S. to avoid shoveling, for the love of God. Lucy pulled her cap tighter around the top of her ears and took a deep, bracing breath. The cold air scraped through her sinuses and froze the hairs to the side of her nostrils. *Not a good day for licking a lamppost.* Lucy grinned like a kid and started tromping.

Hate the cold as she did, there was something magical about those clear mornings after a fresh fall of snow. Around her the gleaming, white world snapped and crackled in the sunlight, diamonds danced underneath the treacherous surface and invited her to step knee-deep into its pristine beauty. Lucy resisted for half a block before the urge to leave her mark overcame her and she planted two perfect footprints into a glistening, flawless snow bank. The snow gave with a crack beneath her feet and she sank up to her thighs with a happy shriek. It was a good day for a walk, after all.

As she walked, the huge snowplows worked beside her, grinding and scraping against Main Street ahead of an impatient morning buildup. The cold made her eyes water and she ducked her head, tucking her chin into the neck of her coat to avoid the wind. Across the railroad tracks she went. The tracks that led straight into the heart of the city, humming all day with the busy people on their way to and from downtown Chicago.

These tracks separating the north from the south side of Willow Park were a sort of rite of passage. You were a big girl when you got to cross these on your own, first on foot and then—joy of all joys—on your bicycle. Lucy smiled to herself. A flood of memories raced at her. She and Ashley riding up to the pool in summer, dashing up to the skating rink in the winter, or ambling along after school trying to attract the attention of the boys who went to school at St. John's, up the road. *Well, that was a thing of the past.*

The video shop was gone. A Realtor had moved into the space instead. But the bakery was still there, doing a roaring trade in breads and pastries. Memories of chocolate croissants that melted in your mouth and baguettes still warm from the oven made Lucy's mouth water. The smell of fresh roasted beans got her moving faster. As soon as she got that milk home, she could have her java fix.

The store was exactly the same. It even smelled the same. Of wet wool, candy, and stale beer. Wire bins almost blocked the entranceway, selling dollar-store gloves and hats. The beverage fridges hummed loudly in the quiet of the shop. There was nobody else around and Lucy peered down the first aisle.

She saw him before he noticed her. Old Man Martin. Nine years ago, she'd thought he was old along with any other adult in her radius. Now, he looked only a little past middle-aged. He worked toward the back of the shop, hauling slabs of beer off a pallet and into the fridges. Lucy watched him in silence before she spoke.

"Hello, Mr. Martin." Her voice sounded breathless and girly.

Mr. Martin paused and looked up. He frowned as if struggling to place her.

Lucy pulled her cap from her head and stood still as the realization crossed his face. His craggy face went from surprised to wary as he straightened and looked at her.

"Lucy Flint?" He pushed his glasses up his nose with grubby, dusty hands. Those hands were as she remembered, lined with years of dirt and grime that seemed ingrained into the cracks and crevices. "You are back?"

The fact he knew her name was a statement in

itself. The old man never bothered to get to know any of the names of the kids who grew up in and around his store. But he remembered Lucy Flint all right.

"Only for a short time," she told him. His look of relief was not encouraging. "My dad is not well."

He nodded as if he already knew that. Of course he did, this was Willow Park.

"And also," Lucy added when he bent back to his beer, "I need to say that I'm sorry."

He crossed his arms over his chest and stared at her impassively. It looked like he still wore the same woolen jersey he'd had nine years ago. It was a shapeless, dusty thing of an indiscriminate shade somewhere between gray and brown. It matched his trousers perfectly.

"About the thing with the window." The compressor on the beer fridge switched up a gear and reminded her to get on with it. "And I know my parents paid for the damages, but I have never told you how much I regret my actions that day."

Mr. Martin looked at her for a long moment, in which her heart pounded loud enough to drown out the sound of the compressor. She was not sure he would respond at all, when he suddenly turned the corners of his mouth down and grunted.

"Good," he said with another nod.

Lucy waited for more.

He looked mildly confused.

And that was it, Lucy realized with a hysterical bubble of laughter rising up in her throat. Her first amends done and accepted. The older man gave her a small smile and bent back to his beer. She was already forgotten.

Lucy found the two-percent milk Carl liked, still grinning, and approached the cash register.

A woman stood with her back to Lucy. Her hair was

an impossible shade of red and her plump figure was compressed into a pair of bedazzled skinny jeans. Something about the woman's posture rang a large bell with Lucy. The woman turned to the side and Lucy's stomach hit an air pocket.

In slow motion, Lucy watched the other woman turn and catch sight of her. Both of them stared. The hair was different and she'd put on a bit of weight, but her face retained the soft prettiness of a doll. It was almost the same face Lucy had seen since her first day in first grade. It had been hate at first sight. She guessed by the way the other woman looked at her not much had changed. Someone had to say something. Lucy took a deep breath.

"Hello, Brooke."

Brooke's blue eyes went even wider.

"Lucy Flint?" Brooke wheezed in disbelief, her pretty Cupid's-bow mouth almost disappearing into her face. "Lucy Flint?" A huge breath rattled through Brooke as she struggled for composure.

Lucy took a cautious step back.

Brooke's eyes narrowed viciously as shock gave way to recall. There was rather a lot to remember. Jason, the weasel, sat top of the list. Aside from that, however, the incident of the sixteenth birthday party had also been rather noteworthy. Brooke had been known to carry a grudge. As far as Lucy knew, Brooke had yet to forgive Ashley for dipping the end of her braid in purple paint in fourth grade. The absconding boyfriend, the ruined sweet sixteen, not to mention some rather creative name-calling could, quite possibly, rate much, much higher on Brooke's shit parade.

"How are you?" Lucy made it to the cash register and put her milk down. "You certainly look well."

"You're back." Brooke moved between Lucy and the exit.

"Only for a little while." Lucy kept a sharp eye on the talons at the end of Brooke's fingers. "I am here to see my mother, help her out a bit, and then it's back to Seattle for me."

She paid Mr. Martin, intensely aware of Brooke's eyes making smoking holes in the back of her coat. "Well," she burst out. "It was lovely to see you. I hope to see you again before I go."

"I'm married now," Brooke announced, and Lucy stopped in midflight.

"I beg your pardon?"

"I'm married." Brooke tossed her fiery hair back. "I wanted you to know."

"Congratulations," Lucy managed past the constriction in her throat.

"And I have two children." Brooke stuck her chin out. "You aren't married, are you? And you don't have any children."

"No." Lucy edged a foot closer to the door, cursing herself for the coward she was as she went.

"You have nobody." A smug smile spread across Brooke's face.

It was a look Lucy remembered well.

"Well, I have friends." Lucy stamped on the desire to go into a long, face-saving explanation and swallowed. "Nope. Nobody," she agreed with a nod.

"Just like you did to me," Brooke sneered. "But now I have my Christopher and our children and what do you have, Lucy Flint?"

Lucy got her hand on the door and pushed it open. The small bell overhead gave a cheery jingle that did absolutely nothing to lighten the atmosphere.

Even Mr. Martin looked over the top of one of his perpetual word searches to watch the action.

Outside, escape beckoned and Lucy hurried away quickly. Brooke was right up there on her list, number four behind her mother, Richard, and Ashley. She was a yellow-bellied dog, as Mads would say, to be almost running down the street in the opposite direction.

Chapter Seven

"Hi."

"Hey there"

"Are you sleeping?"

"I was." Mads chuckled in her Colombia roast voice. A mighty yawn crackled down the phone wires. "So, what's going on?"

"Nothing much." Lucy squirmed a little. It was only a slight evasion of the truth.

"Nothing much at seven-thirty in the morning, hmm?"

"Well, it's nine-thirty here."

"Quit stalling."

"Okay." Lucy took a deep breath and shifted the phone to her other ear. Outside her window, the little blond girl over the road was busy walking a scraggly looking mongrel on the end of one of those expanding leashes. The dog had the leash at full extend and went for broke. "I delivered my first amends."

"You're a superstar." It always sounded so much better in that voice and Lucy preened. "Which one?"

Some of the gilt came off her cookie. "Mr. Martin."

"The man whose shop you egged?"

"That's the one. Only, I broke the window as well."

"How did he take it?"

"He was nice." Lucy watched the raddled fur ball drag his owner around the corner. "He barely remembered, but he was nice."

"Good."

A deep silence followed. Lucy wanted to fill it with inane chatter. Instead she watched the little girl's vanilla braid disappear out of sight.

"And?" Mads sounded more alert, as if she'd shaken off the last vestiges of sleep and Lucy knew her moment of reprieve was over. "Have you seen him?"

"Uh-huh." Lucy pulled a face she knew her sponsor would not be able to see, but it made her feel a bit better. "Ah, jeez, Mads, I screwed up so badly."

"Tell me."

"I doored him."

"You what?" Madeline's voice came fully awake.

"Remember last time we spoke?"

"Vaguely, I haven't mainlined my caffeine yet."

"You and me talking, me cowering in the car, you kicking my butt to get out of the car."

"Would we call it butt-kicking?"

"We most certainly would. Anyway, butt-kicking worked and I stepped out of the car."

"Ah." The fog cleared for Mads. "Horrible screaming coming from person lying in the snow." Mads went silent for a long moment and Lucy waited for her to do the math. Mads did not disappoint. "Tell me you're shitting me?"

"I wish I could."

"What was he doing out there?"

"He was riding his bike."

"What kind of idiot rides a bike in a snowstorm?"

"That's what I said."

"To Richard?"

Lucy debated whether lying to one's sponsor was really that counterproductive. "Not in so many words," she managed in a small voice.

From downstairs drifted the faint sounds of her mother rattling around in the kitchen. A quick glance at her watch confirmed it was getting close to second teatime. Carl Flint liked his second tea at ten, which meant his wife would make it so. The familiar tightening of rebellion grabbed onto Lucy's gut and she took a deep breath.

On the other side of the phone, Mads grew serious again. "Make the amends, Lucy. You have to do this now."

"I know," she replied into the building silence. "I will get to it, but this is . . . harder than I thought it would be."

"I know, babe." And the instant understanding wrapped around her like a comfort blanket. "But you can do this." A warm, loving silence stretched between them. "You have to do this, to move on with your life."

"I know." The fight bled out of Lucy and she reached for the small, hovering peace fairy dancing just outside of her grasp. The fairy allowed herself to be caught and Lucy took another, healing breath. "And I will speak to Richard. I was kind of working my way up to him."

That earned her another one of those dark roast chuckles that made Lucy smile automatically.

"I saw Brooke Taylor as well," Lucy added.

"Remind me?"

"Sixteenth birthday party, me getting naked and jumping into the pool and everyone following. Brooke in a pretty pink dress crying as her party dissolves into a wet T-shirt competition."

"Hmm."

"And I stole her boyfriend."

"Of course you did."

"Hey!"

"Hey yourself. Was he worth it?"

"Hell, no."

And Lucy got another chuckle and this time she joined in. "The only one who was ever really worth it was Richard."

"I don't like that tone, girlfriend."

"What tone?"

Mads ignored her token protest. "You are not there to make things worse or repeat old mistakes."

"I know that."

"Good. Now get it done and come home."

"I will."

"Soon."

"Soon," Lucy lied, crossing her fingers.

"You're lying," came that voice. Shit, Mads could be scarier than God sometimes.

"Okay, I'm lying, but only a little bit." Lucy squirmed again. "And I will get to it."

"And then come home."

"Yup."

Home, Lucy thought as she hung up. Now that was an interesting concept.

He knew it was from her before he even bent to retrieve the parcel on his doorstep. It had been a truly miserable day. The Willow Park jungle drums had worked with their usual, ruthless efficiency.

With few exceptions, almost every one of his patients had been happy to share the glad tidings. Lucy Flint was back in town.

It was a relief to pack up for the day and come home. Until he saw the parcel sitting on his doorstep, right in front of the door and tied up with a big, red bow.

He ignored the uneven thud of his heart as he bent to pick it up. It was a brand new helmet, complete with reflector stripes. With it was a small horn siren. And despite his shitty day and the even shittier fact that Lucy Flint was back, Richard smiled. She always could make him smile. The wave of nostalgia totally broadsided him.

This was how she operated and this was what she did. She ripped his world upside down and inside out and then made him laugh, despite it all. It was those eyes, lurking beneath his awareness all the time, all green and sparkly and peering at him through the veil of her hair. Laughing up at him, drawing him closer, sucking him into her world. Richard shook his head in irritation.

He was a thirty-two-year-old man and not some testosterone-driven boy seized by his first major crush. She was not going to do this to him again, because he wouldn't allow it. He dropped the gift into the snow by the side of the door. If it was still there in the morning, he would return it with a polite note.

Knowing Lucy, she would be watching, wrapped up in the delight of her little plan. Her eyes crinkling in the corners and her wide mouth split in a goofy grin. He shut his door and removed his coat. Been there, done that and bought the entire shipment of T-shirts.

With a soft curse, he ripped open the door and snatched up the helmet. She'd even gotten the size right. That was Lucy for you. She could drive you absolutely fucking crazy and then turn around and do something so sweet and thoughtful it almost swept the pain away—until the next time.

And of course, his pisser of a day would not be complete without a visit from his mother. And Richard knew from the moment he saw her marching toward the front porch, Donna had heard the news.

"Hello, darling." She gave him that special smile he'd been getting since she fetched him after his first day of kindergarten. Donna was not a beautiful woman, but it was easy to forget that in the charming symmetry of her neat, delicate features. Her eyes were the same as those he saw in the mirror, the sort of clear, impenetrable blue that was not merely a shade of green in disguise.

Her skin was flawless and her bone structure good, if a little too definite for feminine beauty. But it was her smile that drew people to Donna. It appeared as suddenly as the sun through the clouds and was as welcome. She turned that celestial grin on him now, but Richard wasn't fooled.

"You've heard." He folded his arms over his chest and planted himself in the middle of the Oriental rug Ashley had insisted would give the entrance hall a "pop" of color. Whatever that meant. Beige was good enough for him; it went with the wood and the walls.

"What, darling?"

"Are we really going to do this tonight?" Richard wasn't buying the vague thing for a second. Donna was her most penetrating and deadly like this. His mother looked up at him, her smile at half wattage, but just as charming. "I've had a living shit of a day, I'm tired and I'm hungry and I don't feel like playing games."

"You never did feel like playing games, Richard." She used the mother voice that took all the starch out of his shorts and made him want to squirm. "Even as a little boy. You were always so serious." She amped up on the friendly and waved a shopping bag at him. "And I brought dinner with me."

"What is it?" Richard eyed the bag warily; man enough to know the way to his heart and not too proud to go with it.

"Spaghetti and meatballs." She had him and her eyes told him so.

"Your spaghetti and meatballs?" He would at least go down swinging.

"Richard Hunter," she said, taking a menacing step forward. "Have I ever, ever fed you store-bought spaghetti and meatballs?"

"Non, maman, je m'excuse."

The French got her every time and she melted like a snowball in front of him. Richard could reach out and touch the glory now.

"Verse-moi un verre de vin, espèce d'enfant ingrat."

Yes, indeed, her ungrateful child would pour her a glass of wine. The prospect of a good feed always made Donna's boys more malleable.

"So, tell me?" Donna settled on the opposite side of his kitchen table.

More of those "pops" of color in the bright, green flower things on the seats. He didn't get it. He really hated those cushions, he realized, as he watched Donna get comfortable. He didn't like flowers and he especially didn't like flowers that looked like they should be painted on the side of a sixties passion wagon.

Stripes. He dug into his dinner with relish. What he needed in this room was something manly, like stripes. And not in that girly green color either. Blue. Blue stripes. When Ashley came back, he would speak to her about it. Make her see that stripes were a much better option. That settled, he risked looking over the edge of his wineglass at his mother.

Donna looked at him, her eyes unfathomable but full of love, and Richard sighed. Her love wound around him like a spider's web and he knew she would outpossum him.

He tried for nonchalant. "She's back."

Donna, however, had the advantage of having handled him since the day his ass was cracked and she sat perfectly still and waited.

"Aw, jeez, Ma. What do you want me to tell you? Lucy Flint is back."

"I want you to tell me how you feel, Richard." Donna took a hefty sip of her wine.

"I am a guy," he barked at her. "We don't have feelings. We have urges."

"*Richard, tu me tapes sur les nerf, fais pas le niaiseux et dis-moi ce que tu penses de tous ça.*" It all came out in a torrent and he knew he was beat. She was not going to back down and Donna could turn this into the War of 1812 if she chose to.

"All right." He threw up his hands in disgust. His fork clattered noisily against the side of the bowl. "She's back and she's as beautiful as ever. No." He slashed his hand decisively through the air. "She's even more beautiful. Leave it to Lucy not to get fat or dumpy looking. She's smoking hot and just as deadly."

"And you feel?"

"FREAKED OUT."

Donna looked at him for a long moment, her face inscrutable. And then she just smiled. His mother did a dumb little Mona Lisa thing with her mouth and went back to eating her dinner.

"What?" he demanded as he retrieved his own cutlery.

"Nothing," Donna said, shrugging innocently. Richard glared back at her until she started spilling again. "I thought that's how you would be feeling and I asked. No big deal."

"You're weird, Ma." Richard gave her the benefit of his professional, medical opinion.

"You may be right," his mother said, grinning back at him.

There was a lot he wanted to say, but none of it would sort itself into coherent utterances. So, he fulminated in silence for a while. Eating didn't interrupt his fuming and he carried on with his dinner.

Donna had always been the perfect mother for three healthy, active boys. When you fell down, she picked you up without all that fussing and fluttering. If you were bleeding, you got a Band-Aid; if it was worse you got a trip to the emergency room. All of it handled in the same calm, no-nonsense manner that left a boy feeling like he was in capable hands.

She was still that woman, but his mother had changed in so many other ways. Insisting on grubbing around in his feelings and demanding that he talk about them. Jeez! She had his brother Josh for that with his designer duds and monthly manicures.

There had been no "feeling" talk when his dad was alive. This had all started after Des's death, when Donna had gone into bereavement counseling over the loss of her husband. Bereavement counseling. And out of it she'd come, not even wearing the same clothes.

Case in point. Richard examined the ankle-length red skirt and greenish sweater his mother wore. They should have looked ridiculous. Donna should have looked like Santa's oldest little helper. But she looked . . . Richard shrugged, she looked nice, attractive even, but she didn't look like the mother he knew.

The jeans were gone along with the Gap sweatshirts, de rigueur for all good soccer moms. They'd been replaced by chunky bits of ethnic jewelry that jangled and crashed when she moved. Donna herself was different, more assertive and more definite in her opinions. It made him feel like he'd lost his mom and she'd been replaced by her upgrade. Richard had liked the prototype fine.

"So, Richard . . ." She always caressed the *ch* in his name to the sibilant French *sh*. "I am not only here to get all up in your grill."

Richard frowned. Had she been watching YouTube videos again? He must be the only son in the world who thought about restricting his mother's Internet access. The thing with the nude tennis players loomed large and ugly in his recent memory and he shrugged it off hastily. If that was research for art class then he was . . . well, he didn't believe it.

"Okay?" he responded carefully and refilled both their glasses. It was a very decent Australian and Richard made a note of the label.

"I have come to a decision and I wanted to share it with you. Actually, I have come to a number of decisions lately, but I think it best if we dealt with them one at a time."

This did not sound good and Richard braced for impact. "Why don't we start with the one that's going to make me yell the loudest."

"Oh, Richard." She giggled and waved an arm at him, sending silver and green bracelets smashing together. "You are still so like your father."

"That's a good thing, Ma," he reminded her.

Donna made a little moue with her mouth and

Richard glared at her. His father had been a good man, a great dad, and his parents had always been happy.

"*Maman?*" he growled. Donna didn't so much as flinch.

"Richard, I loved your father. I was happily married to the man for over thirty years," she snapped at him impatiently. "But that did not blind me to the fact he was domineering and repressive sometimes. I was eighteen when I married Des. If I'd been older . . ." She trailed off in thought.

"*What?*" Richard demanded, outrage surging through him. She could change everything else, but the past was sacrosanct and he didn't want her messing with his memories of a basically happy family.

"It doesn't matter," Donna said, shaking her head. "But it does get me to my decision. Like I said, I was eighteen when I got married and I had to run away to do it. Richard . . ." Here she paused and seemed to take the time to pick her words carefully. "My father wants to see me and I have decided to go."

"WHAT?" Donna didn't flinch as he exploded from his chair. "You cannot be serious?" Richard wanted to punch something. He pressed his fists firmly onto the table in front of him and leaned toward Donna. "The man threw you out," he reminded her through clenched teeth. "He tossed you out like garbage because you married an American. Remember?"

"Of course I remember," Donna flashed back at him, color high on her cheekbones and sparkling through her eyes. "I was there, Richard. It was me who did the running away."

"Then why?" He stared at her uncomprehendingly. His mother had been thrown out for daring to marry an English speaker and an American, at that. She had been ruthlessly cut off from all forms of support and the company of her large, boisterous family. She'd even changed her name from Adeline to Donna and moved to Illinois. She hadn't been back to Montreal since. Richard thought she'd turned her back on all of that. Donna was better than the lot of them. She didn't need them. She had him and Josh and Thomas, when his youngest brother got around to remembering he was not the center of the universe—ETA on that currently unknown.

"Sit down, darling." She tapped the table with her hand in a way that was supposed to placate him. Richard clenched his teeth. "And I will try to explain."

Richard sank into his chair and reached for his wineglass.

"He's old, Richard, and not very well." Richard stared at her, unimpressed. "And me"—she did the French, one-shouldered shrug—"I want to have peace around me and that starts here." She tapped the center of her chest.

"I don't get it." And he really didn't. Donna was young still, younger than most other mothers. Only after Des's death had the realization hit Richard that she was in her early fifties and a long, long way from being done.

"I feel like there is this part of me out there that is unfinished business and I want it over and done with." Donna placed her hands carefully on the table in front of them and splayed her fingers. She kept her face bent over her hands as if she were examining them. Richard had inherited those long, elegant fingers. "I have no idea what it will accomplish after all this time, but I do know I will regret it if he dies and I had this chance to go and make peace and I never took it."

"Would he be wanting to see you if Dad was still alive?" Richard couldn't quite keep the bitter resentment out of his tone.

"I don't know." Donna glanced up at him. "I can't work in the realm of what ifs and maybes. I can only deal with what I know to be true today. And for today"—Donna took a deep breath—"my father would like to see me before he dies. He regrets what has happened and is reaching out to me."

"I think you're being naïve."

"And I think you are very sweet." Donna smiled at him suddenly and Richard blinked in the afterglow. "You are so protective and outraged on my behalf, but this is not your battle, darling. You have your own battle looming." She jerked her head in the direction of the house next door.

Richard felt his features stiffen into rigor mortis. "There is no battle," he said, trying for casual and ending up sounding electronically generated. "She's home, but it's nothing to do with me. She'll leave again and I will get on with persuading my wife to come home."

"Richard?" Donna sighed and rolled her eyes.

"Don't." Richard held up one hand as inside his stomach pretzeled around itself. "Don't say it, because you don't know. Ashley will be back and we will fix this. I did not get married to give up and get divorced."

Donna growled and started clearing plates, loudly. "You are the same stubborn bastard your father was. You know that, right?"

"It's a good thing, Ma." He refilled their glasses. "And it's not being stubborn; it's called being focused." *See that?* He could psychobabble too.

Donna made a rude noise and stacked the plates next to the sink. She started energetically rinsing them and putting them in the dishwasher. "I blame your grandmother." Richard tried not to wince as she tossed his flatware into the machine.

"Always telling you that you were a little, miniature version of your daddy. And you know what?" The cutlery got flung into the tray. "You became like him. But Richard," she said, drawing the long, French syllables through her mouth tauntingly. "You are thirty-three."

"Thirty-two."

"In two months you will be thirty-three," she hissed like a rattler. "I give you permission to be your own man. I also give you permission to take the stick out of your ass and live a little."

She mumbled something Richard caught the edge of. Along with her eyes and her hands, his mother had bequeathed a little continental flash fire. Up came his hackles. "What did you say?"

"Nothing." She pursed her lips and crossed her arms over her chest.

"What did you say?" Richard took a menacing step forward.

It was too much for his mother, who would be hung, drawn, and quartered before she allowed one of her boys to ride roughshod over her. "I said that at least Lucy was good for that. She ripped that stick right out of you."

He reeled as her words slammed into him and took his breath away. They stared at each other for a long moment, stunned and silent.

As suddenly as the fire had surged, it died down and Richard saw the heat in Donna's eyes dampened immediately by regret. She reached out and cupped her palm over his cheek. "Unfortunately, the silly girl nearly ended up beating you to death with it."

"And now she's back." He let his mother embrace him for a moment before gently disentangling himself. "I wonder if Ashley has heard."

Donna shrugged again. "This is Willow Park, Richard, of course Ashley has heard."

Chapter Eight

Lynne was so sure this was not a good idea, but Lucy had been adamant and here she was. She had pledged her support and, by God, her mother was going to get it. It also meant seeing Richard again, but she couldn't let that stop her.

It had taken most of the night to get it straight in her head, but she had it now. The shock of seeing him again had combined with the guilt and nostalgia and had messed with her thinking. She was back on course. She was here to help her mother and it was long overdue. And she was home to put the past to bed, for his sake as much as for hers.

"Are you sure about coming with me?" Lynne sat in the car beside her as Lucy parked outside the doctor's office on Main Street.

"Absolutely." Lucy threw her a confident smile that didn't even vaguely match the condition of her nerves. "You said you didn't feel you could go in there alone and here I am."

"Hmm." Lynne peered through the windshield at the front window of the doctor's office. "He is an excellent doctor, you know." She fluttered her hands anxiously.

"I'm sure he is." Richard was good at many, many things. Your classic, pain-in-the-ass overachiever and she'd loved how driven he could be. She'd never gotten around to telling him how much that impressed her about him. Chances were she wouldn't get another opportunity to do so now. "And I am sure he will know exactly the best thing to do about Dad."

"I'm sure you're right." A small, worried frown puckered up Lynne's forehead.

"I promise not to do anything to upset him." Lucy had no idea what Lynne thought she could possibly do in a crowded doctor's office with her mother beside her. Then again, Lynne had been there since the birth of the legend of Lucy Flint and seen quite a bit of what her daughter was capable of. "There really is no reason to be nervous. He is your doctor and a professional." Lucy mustered up a confident tone. "He will be perfectly civil. We've known him since I went to day care."

"You bit his arm." Lynne looked pained.

"What?"

"Your first day at Mrs. Clark's Day Care, you bit Richard's arm."

"No." Lucy blinked at her mother. She did a rapid memory scan, but came up blank. Of course, she had been a holy terror and the biting thing went on for a while. Actually, until the day another kid had bitten her back. A plump princess called Ashley and Lucy remembered the day well. Over wails and tears, they had looked at each other and seen an even match. They could fight to the death or join forces.

"You were three." Lynne nodded her head sadly.

"Richard came with his mother to pick up his brothers and you bit him. You almost broke the skin."

"Are you sure?"

"Positive. I wouldn't forget something like that," Lynne stated decisively. "Donna was very understanding about it." Lynne shook her head in amazement. "She didn't make the slightest bit of fuss."

"Donna had three boys," Lucy said, laughing softly. "I'm sure she'd seen worse by that stage."

"Still," Lynne said, shaking her head and frowning. "If it had been the other way around, if he had bitten you, I don't think I would have been so casual about it."

That was true enough. To this day, her mother was blissfully unaware of the Ashley equalizer. Otherwise, Lucy felt sure, her friendship with Ashley would never have been allowed to prosper. Lynne always kept her "from children who were rough." *Also, if he'd bitten me,* Lucy thought as she climbed out of the car, *I would now have one less thing to make amends for.*

The office was busy with a steady stream of people moving in and out. On the other side of the central desk, a receptionist ruled the office with phlegmatic disinterest. A bit like a large, sedentary toad directing the flow of insects from her lily pad. She eyed Lucy speculatively over the rims of her round glasses and Lucy resisted the urge to fidget as she and her mother found a seat.

"Lynne Flint." Lucy jumped a bit. Her mother threw her a concerned look. "Exam room two, Dr. Hunter will be right along."

Lucy viciously suppressed the insane urge to giggle hysterically as Richard walked into exam room two.

He was conservatively dressed in a pair of khaki chinos and a pale blue shirt. He carried his white coat in one large hand and hung it neatly on the back of the door. He turned back, folding his arms over his chest, and her stomach bungeed.

"Lynne." He smiled at her mother. "Lucy." He cut a glance in her direction. His smile vanished and she found herself on the receiving end of an arctic blast.

He turned to talk to her mother, having the sort of inconsequential chat friends and neighbors always shared. Wasn't the weather awful? Everybody was hearty and hale? Were the Cubs ever going to get it together?

Lucy caught that telltale little muscle jumping in his jaw. Richard was not as composed as he looked. It helped to steady her nerves.

"Lucy?" Her mother motioned for her to have a seat on the exam table.

Lynne took the only chair and Richard perched on the edge of a high stool.

"What can I do for you?" There was that voice she'd loved.

"Richie Rich?"

"My flower?"

"Would you love me if I was fat?"

"Nope, I would dump your chubby butt and find myself a skinny chick, but we could still be friends."

"Richard!"

"Don't ask stupid questions, Luce. I'm always going to love you."

* * *

A strangled twitter got away from her. Her face burned as the other two turned and stared at her. "Sorry," she whispered. "I was thinking of something else."

Richard turned back to look at Lynne expectantly, the muscle in his jaw going into overtime.

Lucy cleared her throat and looked at her mother. Lynne looked from Richard to Lucy and back again.

Lucy kept her eyes away from Richard.

"Lynne?" Richard prompted gently and her mother jumped. "Is there something you came to see me about?"

"Well." Lynne mashed her hands together, twisting her fingers painfully within each other. "I'm not so sure."

Silence. Richard waited patiently. Lynne threw Lucy a look of desperation.

"Actually, Richard." His name came out of Lucy in a breathy whisper. She cleared her throat. "We are here about my father."

"I see." His body tensed as he turned to look at her.

Lucy stuttered to a halt. She remembered those eyes so clearly. Laughing, serious, lovely Richard eyes looking at her, always watching her and so packed full of love and adoration that she could barely believe it was real. She'd killed that. The eyes looking at her now were cold, unreachable facsimiles of the other pair. It helped get her thoughts back on track.

"We wanted to discuss his condition and what to do about it."

"What to do about it?" His eyes narrowed on her.

"Our options." Lucy battled on, feeling the sharp horns of a trap close around her.

Richard made a small sound of disgust, more a sigh than an actual noise, but Lucy felt the impact.

"Is this what you want to talk about, Lynne?" Efficiently he shut her off and turned back to her mother.

"Well—" Lynne looked between her and Richard, her eyes huge, as helpless as a child, and Lucy felt her gut tighten in frustration.

Richard's eyes bored into her.

"Mom"—Lucy took a deep breath and gently picked up Lynne's hand—"you wanted to come here, right? You wanted to talk to Richard about Dad."

"Yes," Lynne said, but sounded like she meant something entirely different. "Lucy thought it would be for the best."

And Lucy wanted to scream as she saw Richard snap to the inevitable conclusion.

"He's getting worse and you're struggling to manage." Lucy prompted her mother. Her heart sank as Lynne fiddled with the straps of her purse.

"Right." Richard stood. He gave her mother a tight smile. "Lynne, would you mind if I had a word with Lucy?"

Now her mother looked truly torn, her eyes darting from one to the other frantically. "I'm not really sure—"

"It will only take a minute." Richard took Lynne gently by the elbow.

Lucy almost panicked. She wanted to beg her mother to stay, but she stood her ground.

Lynne slunk reluctantly out the door and Richard shut it gently. He turned back toward her, the tension palpable through his body. "I warned you, Lucy." He looked suddenly much too large, eating up all the space in the room.

"I didn't force her to come here," Lucy protested quickly. "She wanted to come and talk to you."

"Cut the crap." He took a step toward her. "Lynne and Carl have been my patients since I started practicing. Give me a little credit here. You may not have forced her to come, but this has you stamped all over it."

She wanted to keep protesting her innocence, but his expression was set. He had accused and condemned her all in one huge leap of presumption. God, he could be such a sanctimonious ass sometimes. She'd almost forgotten that little treasure. "What, exactly, are you accusing me of, Richard?" She folded her arms over her chest defensively and then rethought the reaction and dropped them to the side.

"Don't play dumb," he snapped. "I have a waiting room full of people and I don't have time to play games with you."

"No games," Lucy replied quietly; she didn't fully trust her own voice. "I told you the other night, I am here to help my mother."

"By having your father committed?" he flung at her. "By waltzing in here after all this time, having no idea what is going on with your Dad or what has happened since you've been gone. Lucy arrives and suddenly Lynne gets the idea to lock her husband away."

Lucy stared at him, aghast. It took a while to get her tongue moving. "That is so unfair." She got to her feet. "She doesn't sleep at night because he keeps her up, ranting and raving. She's a mess, a bundle of nerves. Yesterday morning, I found her sobbing at the kitchen table because she'd run out of milk for his tea." She was somehow standing toe to toe with him. "He has always been a bully and you know that, but he's worse now. I am worried for her. I am worried about what he is capable of. Don't let your anger at me cloud your judgment, Richard."

She hit home with that one and he opened his mouth and shut it again.

"I wanted you to hear what she has to say," Lucy continued in a softer tone. "She always keeps everything bottled up inside and I wanted her to tell you what is really going on, because I think, as his doctor, this is stuff you need to know."

"She knows she can come to me." He had his temper under control, but he still glared at her resentfully. "I have been watching the situation for a while now."

"But she won't." Lucy pressed forward. "It's not her way."

He grunted as he absorbed her words. Then he gave a curt nod and strode to his desk. He picked up his phone.

"Carmen," he spoke into the phone, but his eyes were still locked on Lucy. "Would you send Lynne Flint back in?"

He didn't speak or even look at her. They heard Lynne's step approach. Lucy carefully let her breath out as Richard opened the door. Lynne stuck her head around the jamb cautiously, looking ready to bolt at the first sign of trouble.

"Come in, Lynne." Richard ushered her mother back into the room. "Lucy says Carl is getting worse?"

Lucy felt weak with relief. He wasn't happy about it, but he was going to listen.

"What should I say?" Lynne opened her eyes huge and turned to Lucy.

"Tell Richard about Dad." Lucy gave her mother an encouraging smile. "Tell him what you have been telling me over the phone." Lynne seemed to draw courage from her and Lucy caught her mother's hand and gave it a squeeze. "Tell the doctor how Dad has been getting confused about who is who and how he gets so frustrated and angry."

"I'll tell Richard that, should I?"

"Yes." Lucy nodded and gave Lynne a smile of encouragement. "You tell . . . him . . . all the stuff you told me. I am sure he can help you."

It took Lynne a while, but she got it out in the end. Agonizing syllable by agonizing syllable she let the entire story unfold.

Richard's full attention focused on Lynne as he listened. He locked onto the person he listened to and seemed to absorb every last scrap of information. Her mother unfurled underneath the magic glow of his attention.

Lynne kept nothing back. Lucy felt guilt turn the knife even deeper into her flesh. Her mother had been dealing with all of this on her own: the increasingly wild swings of emotion, the paranoia, the vicious bouts of temper. Lynne had been virtually locked in that house like her own private hell. When she fell silent at last, Lucy was more than ready to let Richard take over.

"Lynne, I am going to need to examine him," Richard insisted gently. "I hear what you're saying and I don't doubt it for a minute, but I have to see him and form a professional opinion."

Lynne folded like a deck of cards.

"That could be a problem," Lucy spoke up. Richard jerked in her direction. "My father won't come and see you. He's terrified of leaving the house."

His eyes narrowed in thought, but he didn't look away.

Lucy swallowed, her throat feeling as dry as after a three-day bender.

"He won't come," Lynne confirmed. "He says I am going to lock him up somewhere." Richard flicked his eyes briefly in her direction and Lucy stiffened. "I would never do that," Lynne stated vehemently.

"It might not need to come to that." Richard got to his feet. "The situation needs to be assessed and considered and once we have all the information, then we can look at options."

"That sounds reasonable," Lucy choked out and earned herself a hard stare.

"You don't get committed for being a bit difficult." The accusation went straight for the jugular and Lucy gasped.

"That is not what I am doing."

"No?"

"No."

"How is Donna?" Lynne chirruped desperately from her place in the chair.

"Fine," Richard ground out with his eyes still locked on Lucy. He must have realized he was growling, because he lightened up slightly and managed a tight smile in Lynne's direction. "My mother is well, thank you for asking."

"I am trying to do what is best for both of my parents," Lucy insisted.

"How novel," he drawled.

"And Joshua?" Lynne piped up again. "I hear he is doing very well for himself. Something to do with the banks?"

The corner of Richard's mouth twitched. Reluctantly, as if he had no intention of smiling, but the ridiculousness of the situation was not going to let him out of it. "Everyone is fine," he told Lynne mildly. "And everything will be fine," he said, turning the full potency of Richard on to Lynne and her mother opened up like a flower to the sun. "You leave this with me. Okay?"

Lynne nodded happily and simpered. Lucy realized he was now looking at her.

"Okay," she said, stumbling into agreement. He had this and she took a step back and perched awkwardly on the end of the examination table behind her. The disposable paper covering crackled loudly beneath her butt and she cringed and tried to ease away.

"It's been a while since I've seen Carl," Richard said.

"He doesn't like doctors." Lynne looked agonized by the confession.

Richard took it in stride and nodded. "I could always come around on some or other pretext and do a house call."

"You would do that?" Lynne beamed at him in delight. "You already do so much for us."

"Leave it with me." He gave her mother another reassuring smile. "I will call you and set up a time you think would be good."

"Oh, thank you," gushed her mother.

Over Lynne's head, Richard looked up suddenly, his expression unreadable.

Lucy looked away first. She trailed her mother out of the office.

Richard had already turned toward his next patient.

They were in the car and on their way home before her mother spoke to her.

"Richard is still rather angry with you, Lucy." Lynne's forehead crinkled up in concern.

Lucy heaved a sigh. "You think?"

"Oh, yes," Lynne said, and nodded her head seriously.

Chapter Nine

"Lucy Locket?"

"Maddy Mads?"

"How's it going, girl?" Mads sounded unbearably chipper.

"Not so good." Lucy tightened her grip on her phone. It was so cold outside the house and her hand ached where she'd taken her mitten off to make the call. "Richard is my father's doctor."

A long silence. "You are *shitting* me."

"I wish I was." Lucy grimaced and pushed aside a small mound of ice outside the door. "And guess what?" Her breath hit the air in a white plume. "He doesn't trust me."

"And this is a surprise, how, exactly?"

"You're all heart." Lucy shook her head as a throaty chuckle hummed down the line toward her. She wouldn't be Mads if she were any different.

"Oh, stop whining." Mads had a smile in her voice. "You knew this was going to be tough."

"I know." And it was getting tougher. "I also know what I've got to do now." Lucy peered up at the house next door. A light was on in the downstairs window.

She now knew that was the kitchen and Richard was in it.

"Oh?"

"Stop being a ballbuster because I need a little cheering here." She took a deep breath. "I'm going in."

There was silence on the other end of the phone as Mads put the pieces together and then she gasped. "No?"

"Yes."

"Are you ready?"

"Absolutely not." Then again, she didn't think she would ever be ready. "But he's the one taking care of my dad and unless I get this part out of the way, we are going to continue circling each other like a pair of stiff-legged dogs."

She had her phone in a death grip and Lucy tried to flex her frozen fingers. "Sweet Mother of God, but it's cold."

"Duh. That's why you have to get your skinny ass back to Seattle as soon as all this is over. How's your mother?"

"You want to talk about my mother? Now?"

"We both know you need a couple of minutes to stall. So, yes, let's talk about your mother. Or even better yet, your father."

"Damn, you're good."

"Uh-huh." Lucy could hear Mads shift the phone into a more comfortable position against her ear.

"My mom's not so good, actually." The wind whipped around the corner of the house and stung her eyes. Overhead the clouds were looming ominously. Lucy decided to ignore the rather obvious portent. She was not much of a symbolism girl, anyway.

"Your father giving her a hard time?"

"He's a lot worse than I thought." Lucy took the stairs down to the sidewalk carefully. Salt crunched under her boot heels. She suspected Richard had been up doing his thing again. He really was one of the world's last good guys. And she'd let him go. Nope. She'd not just let him go, she'd tossed him, like a caber, as far as she could. And he still shoveled and salted for her parents.

"So, she's depressed, unhappy, scared . . . ?"

"It's not that, Mads," Lucy said, struggling to articulate a circling suspicion she hadn't quite worked out for herself. "She's hesitant, as if she is not sure she wants to do anything."

"Ahh." All that wisdom was a tad annoying sometimes.

"What does that mean?"

"Nothing." Mads compounded her sins by laughing. "You'll work this one out."

"Thank you, Obi-Wan."

This was it. She stood on the walk in front of Richard's house. "I'm standing right in front of his house."

"Is that a song lyric?"

"No." She'd been watching and seen him come home from work. A few minutes later, he'd come out again, dressed for a run. Oblivious to her bemused gaze, he'd trotted off and not returned for a good three hours. Who did that?

She'd given him an hour to have a shower and something to eat. It was now closer to eleven than ten thirty and very late for a social call, but she knew he was there. The element of surprise was on her side.

"Elliot called me," Mads said into her left ear.

"What?" Lucy was momentarily distracted enough to stop her sharp focus on the cheery red door that marked the entrance to the dragon's lair. "Elliot called you? Why?"

"He wants to know when you'll be back."

"I told him, not for a few weeks."

"You know Elliot," Mads murmured. "He likes specifics and anyway, it's fair for him to ask. He deserves some answers from you."

"And he'll get them," Lucy said through gritted teeth, aware she was irritated with Elliot and trying not to take it out on Mads, but, really? They so didn't have to do this right now. Not when she was so nervous cookie-tossing started to feel imminent. "As soon as I have them," she finished grimly and took a deep breath.

"That's what I told him."

"And he said?"

Mads laughed again, like Lucy wasn't on the brink of one of the most defining moments of her life, but was sitting with Mads in her small apartment and eating something decadent and wicked. "Again, you know Elliot. He had plenty to say about it. I didn't listen to most of it. It's all about the same stuff anyway. He loves you, he wants to be with you, and he wants you to be on the same page."

The small, paned window in the red door gaped like a troll mouth. Lucy stepped forward. She was now officially on Richard's property. It was not quite the point of no return, but she was approaching it fast. Her breathing accelerated with her pulse rate. "I can't deal with Elliot now. I'm almost there."

"Is that why this is sounding more and more like an obscene phone call?" Mads teased and then said, "You are there to settle this thing with Richard, so you can move on. You can't separate that from Elliot. I think you should bear this in mind when you go in there.

You are doing this for a number of reasons. Your father is one, but getting on with your life and being able to commit to a relationship is another big part of why."

"You think Richard is the reason I can't commit."

"Duh!"

"I suppose you're right." Lucy chewed her lip. No other man in her life had compared to Richard. She was almost at the front step. Unlike her parents' house, Richard's was fronted with a small covered portico. Beneath her feet, matting scrunched. "But do you think that's because of guilt or residual feelings?"

"Lucy." Mads suddenly lost patience with her. "That is what you are there to find out."

Lucy didn't rise to the bait. She had arrived. The door, with its grimacing glass, was right in front of her. It hadn't seemed nearly as unfriendly the other night when she was here. Or maybe it had. Who knew? She got a firm grip on the mental jabbering.

"You can do this, Lucy Locket." Mads grew serious. "You got yourself sober and this, you can do."

"Bye, Mads."

Lucy reached out and rang the doorbell. Half afraid he wasn't there anymore and more terrified that he was.

He opened the door on an impatient yank. A *who the hell is ringing my doorbell at this time of night* type of gesture and Lucy jumped back a step. All the air left his body in a great whoosh and they stared at each other.

"Um . . . hi."

Silence.

He stared at her.

Lucy stared back.

"It's late."

"Yes, I know. I'm sorry about that, but you went out earlier."

"I was out for a run."

"Oh, that's what I figured. Since you were wearing all the . . . um . . . running stuff."

Lucy's eyes roamed a bit. He wore a ratty old T-shirt and a pair of track pants, both of which should have been consigned to dishrags a couple of years ago. They clung to the muscular lines of his body.

"I wondered if I could come in? Again?" That didn't sound one bit like her voice. She sounded like a frightened teenager. Come to think of it, she felt like a frightened teenager. "You are Dad's doctor and I am here to help out and I . . ." She stuttered impotently as he continued to turn her to a statue with his eyes. "I would like about half an hour of your time. It's important." Now she almost sounded adult.

"Yeah," he finally spoke. His voice sounded a bit rusty as if it came from some place deep inside him. Still, he didn't move, but stood in the doorway looking down at her. He hunched his shoulders against the cold.

"Should I come back at another time?"

"Um . . . no." He stood a moment more, and then must have realized what he was doing and stepped back to allow her in. "Now is as good a time as any. I was . . . er . . . " He gestured toward the inside of the house vaguely. "I was . . . er. Jesus, Lucy." He exploded all of a sudden. Lucy's heart skipped a beat. "What is this all about? Is your mother ill? Your dad?"

"No, it's nothing like that." Lucy froze in the middle of shrugging out of her coat. "I wanted to speak to you. About something personal." He still looked mulish. "Something to do with you and me and the past."

"Ah, shit." At least that's what she thought he muttered. It was difficult to tell with him spinning on his heel and stalking away into the shadowed depth of the house.

She hesitated a moment before finally wrestling out of her coat and hanging it up. He disappeared through a doorway as she bent over and unlaced her boots, slipping them off her feet. She took a step into the house, preparing to follow. Lucy stopped, dashed back, and carefully placed her boots side by side on the rubber matting. She took a soothing breath.

The inside of the house was immaculately clean. There was nothing out of place and the floors gleamed like a ballroom. It made her feel like even more of an interloper. The faint smell of what he'd eaten for dinner hung about and it smelled good. He must have learned to cook. He would have had to. Ashley had barely been able to boil an egg without causing a major incident.

She peered around the door frame cautiously. The kitchen was a cheerful space that could have easily absorbed a family of ten, but it appeared lonely and abandoned and, once again, spotlessly clean.

Richard waited for her. His hips propped up against the far counter with the window behind him. A large, central island stood between them. His arms were crossed over his chest and his face cast in stone.

"May I?" She indicated a spindle-backed chair pulled up to a table. She didn't trust her knees right now. The table was tucked into a neat little alcove and cheerfully curtained in lime green and white.

He nodded and shrugged, uncrossed his arms, and then crossed them again. "Do you . . . er . . . want anything to drink? I have beer, wine?"

"A soda would be fine, if you have it."

He handed her a can.

Lucy took it and popped the tab. She had no idea what she was drinking, but she drank it anyway. It gave her hands something to do instead of fidget. She noticed he took a Landshark and popped the cap without taking a sip. He used to drink Heineken.

Actually, he never used to drink much at all. She'd covered that part of their relationship and done a rather thorough job of it, which brought her to what she was doing here. Lucy put the can onto the table with a dull thunk. She was not sure, but Richard might have jumped slightly.

"I wanted to talk to you because of my dad," she said, wincing. She could do better than that. "Actually, that's only part of it. The other part is about what you asked me the other night."

The only sign he was still alive was the occasional rise and fall of his chest.

"You asked me why." She cleared her throat and took another breath. "You wanted to know why I . . . you wanted to know why I left like I did."

He shifted slightly, his jaw muscle clenching and unclenching rapidly.

"I think you deserve some sort of explanation." She wished he would say something, but the silence clawed between them. She spoke again. "Um . . . it probably isn't going to be huge news to you, but it turns out I am an alcoholic. I have been in recovery for the last three years." It seemed the most logical place to start.

He didn't look exactly blown away.

She'd certainly never hidden her drinking from him. Only then, when they were all doing it, it was easier to convince herself there was no problem. She was just a girl who liked to party. "And as such I am tasked with making amends."

"So you're in AA?" His deep, smooth voice cut her off.

"Yes."

"I know about the Twelve Steps. I researched it for a patient or two."

"Oh, right." Lucy mentally cut out the middle bit. He clearly didn't need a summary of the Twelve Steps.

"Why now?" He broke into her thoughts.

Lucy swallowed and weighed her answer. "I think it's time." Her mouth twisted into a rueful grimace. "Actually, it's way overdue, but I—couldn't before."

He stood totally still with his arms crossed over his chest, his beer hanging forgotten in one hand.

"I owe you this." She stopped talking and looked at him. Silently asking permission to continue.

Finally, he made a soft noise in the back of his throat and nodded.

"Um . . . you and I." Lucy took a juddering breath and another sip from her soda. Something sweet hit the back of her throat and made her cough. Forget about hard, this was like ripping her soul out. "I should never have, what I mean is, that you and . . . ah. Damn, this is not coming out the right way."

"You haven't said anything yet," he replied in a flat voice.

"Right." Lucy blew out a breath. *Start at the beginning, Lucy.* "I suppose, it all really starts with Ashley and me. Even before you and me or you and Ashley, there was Ashley and me." His face grew harder and she rushed through her words. "You see the thing with Ashley and me; I was always jealous of Ashley and if she had something, then I wanted it. And Ashley had you."

"How flattering," he drawled, and took a long sip of his beer. His hands were not quite steady. It gave her a small shot of courage.

"It was more than that." Her voice grew stronger. "I took one look at you and knew that I wanted you for myself. Taking you from Ashley was icing on the cake. I deliberately set out to break you two up and I managed that." He flinched slightly as if she had struck him. "I wanted you and like a spoiled and ungrateful child, I took you."

"Again, how flattering." His eyes flashed blue ire at her. "You girls passing me from one to another like a pair of . . . what . . . high-heel shoes. You borrowed them from Ashley for a while and then gave them back?"

"Ah, damn." Lucy dropped her head into her hands. She knew he would be hostile. She had no right to expect any less.

"Is that it?" he asked in a tone that made her flinch. "Are we done with the important thing because I have to give myself a root canal once you're done."

"Were you always such a hard-ass?" It slipped out of Lucy.

"No," he snarled back. "I save it up for people who treat me like shit and then want to walk back into my life and have me play nice again. What the hell were you expecting, Lucy? That we would sit around, have tea, and laugh about the good old days?" He exploded from the counter, slamming his beer bottle down. Foam fizzed up over the lip and onto the counter. "Jesus. I don't need this shit. Go back to Seattle, Lucy. Do us all a favor and go back to Seattle and don't come back."

* * *

"Richie Rich?"

"My Angel."

"What would make you stop loving me?"

"We could start with you not giving me my fries back."

"I will." Her breathing sounded loud in the sudden silence. His face was set and furious and she almost took the gap and ran. She dragged in a ragged breath, her heart thundering so loudly in her ears, it made her voice seem muted. "I will go back to Seattle and leave you in peace. But first, I need to tell you how sorry I am."

His eyes grew hotter and angrier and she had to close hers to regain her composure.

Her legs shook and she gripped the edge of the table for support. "I wanted to tell you how sorry I am. How I know I screwed up and I hurt you and I wish to God I could take it all back, but I can't. I can only say that I'm sorry. I'm sorry. I am so, so sorry."

Neither of them spoke. Lucy could sense him still standing there, watching her, but she didn't have the courage to look up. She pushed her chair back from the table. This was pointless if he didn't want to hear it. "There's more, but if you don't want to do this, you have every right not to. Just, for now, if you could know that I am sorry. It doesn't fix anything, but it's true."

"Wow." He blew out a long, tortured breath. "This sucks."

"Should I go?" Lucy heard the telltale quiver in her voice. "I can go, if that's what you want."

He gave a sharp exhale that was almost, but not quite, a laugh. "I have no goddamned idea," he admitted reluctantly. "Until I figure it out, why don't you keep talking?"

"Thank you." Lucy reached into the pocket of her jeans and pulled out a piece of paper. With shaking hands she spread it out onto the table in front of her.

"Is that a list?" Lucy nodded and he gave a short, hard bark of laughter. "You made a list?"

"I wanted to get it all down. If I ever got the chance, I wanted to be sure I said all that needed saying." She steadied herself and sent a quick Serenity Prayer out to whoever and whatever was listening. Serenity, courage, and wisdom, it was all there and she took it.

And Lucy started the recitation of her sins. One by one she went down the items on her list. The screaming matches over nothing, the hysterical phone calls in the middle of the night, the bar fights she used to incite. The times she made him jealous, the times she let him down, and the times she stood him up. The odd occasion that the police got involved. The many, many encounters with pissed off barmen, bouncers, and other patrons. All the men, always man trouble and throwing him front and center. The list seemed endless, but she was here and Lucy spared herself no detail, however grisly. She did it by the book: what she resented, why, and then her part in it. No excuses and no justifications, just the facts, ma'am, and the pure, unvarnished truth.

Lucy noticed out of the corner of her eye that Richard did not move. She was too much of a coward to look up, so she kept her eyes down and fixed on the table under her palms. All the way to the end she went. Last item on the list: Jason, and she stuttered to a premature halt.

"Don't stop there." His voice whipped across the

kitchen toward her, and she flinched. "Now we're getting to the good part."

"I . . . ah." The blood drained from Lucy's face as she tried to pick up the train of her thoughts again. She didn't want to say this stuff, to hurt him anymore than she already had.

"What's the matter, Lucy?" He moved, stalking toward her on nearly silent feet. Lucy kept her eyes locked on the table, but she felt him move closer. She felt the air stir against her neck as he leaned down toward her. "You're at a loss for words?"

She raised her chin. Her throat felt clogged and she coughed to clear it. "You were getting serious," she managed past the lump. "We were in love and you were . . ."

"I wanted to marry you," he drawled beside her ear. "Not immediately, we were too young, but I wanted to marry you. You knew that, didn't you?"

"Yes," she whispered, every pore attuned to the silent menace of Richard, hovering angry and dangerous beside her. "It scared me," she admitted. "I didn't think I deserved it and it scared me. I thought you would realize I wasn't any good and you would leave me."

"So you left first?" His voice became a low, menacing whisper. "You snuck away because you were frightened. I could almost understand that." He gave a humorless laugh. "The real fucking kicker here is the other man. That's the part I want to get to. Say it." His voice lashed at her and Lucy winced. "I want to hear you say it."

"I left you and ran away with another man." Lucy trembled so badly she could barely speak. "I humiliated you and hurt you and I can never fix that but I am . . ."

"You're sorry?" He moved away from her and Lucy

drew a ragged breath into her starving lungs. "Forget the humiliation, Lucy," he said, his voice shaking as badly as hers. "You almost fucking broke me." Out of her peripheral vision she saw him grab his beer again and tip the bottle back.

"I know that," Lucy whispered. "I know that and I broke me, too. I know you don't care, but I broke me, too."

"Jesus." Richard stood frozen in the center of the room. "It was bad enough living it the first time."

Across the space she dared to look at him. His eyes were tortured and stormy and it was like watching an emotional kaleidoscope chase its way through their depths. There was anger and hurt, confusion, disillusionment, and fear all crammed within one man. He looked away.

A trickle of wetness snaked down her cheeks. She was crying. She scrubbed away the moisture with her sleeve.

He moved toward the fridge and yanked it open, considering if he wanted another beer.

She should go, but she wanted to stay and she wavered indecisively.

"What happens now?" he asked, breaking the silence.

"That's up to you." The hand around her soda can shook so violently she had to put it back on the table. "Richard, you are under no obligation to forgive me. I am here to tell you I know I hurt you and if I could take it back, I would. I can only own up to what I did and ask for your forgiveness, over time."

He shook his head, his expression colder than the weather outside when he turned to look at her. "Just like that?" He placed his palms on the top of the counter and bent his head forward. He looked defeated and angry. "It's taken you all this time to come here and say this. There were times when I would have given anything—anything—to have you come here and do this, but now, after all this time? Nine years, Lucy."

"I was drunk for six of them." Lucy swallowed past her dry throat. "I spent those years blaming everyone else for what I did. It was Ashley's fault for being jealous of me. It was your fault for trying to trap me." She stopped, wondering if she'd said too much.

"Can I ask you something?" He didn't wait for her nod. "Did you love me?" He kept his head lowered. "Because I was crazy about you. After you left with that prick, that is the one thing that kept going around and around in my head."

Shit. That was an easy one. Loving Richard had never been a problem. "I loved you," she said quietly. "I loved you to distraction."

"But still you left." His head came up and his eyes blazed at her across the width of the kitchen. "You left for another man. Did you love me when you did that?"

"Yes, Richard, I did." Lucy eyed his beer bottle enviously. It would be so much easier to drown her pain in the oblivion of a good drunk. But that option was closed to her now and each day she made it more and more so.

"I don't get it." He threw his hands up. "You're going to have to explain that one to me because I am just a poor, dumb asshole."

"I don't think I have an explanation." Lucy clasped her shaking hands together. "At least, not one that will make any sense to you."

"Try."

"There was this brokenness inside me." The words clawed up her throat. Her honesty was really all she had to give him, when it came right down to it. "I tried to drink it away, party it away, but nothing worked. I even thought if I loved you enough, you could fill the void for me and make it all better."

"I tried hard enough." He glared at her as if daring her to contradict him.

"Yes, you did," Lucy agreed. "But it was not something you could ever do. It was something I needed to do. It's like I was broken and I wanted to strike out against anything that held any meaning for me. I wanted to hurt myself, ultimately. And I did."

"Yeah, Luce." His shoulders drooped as the fight went out of him like a deflating balloon. "But you took the rest of us down with you."

"I know that." It came out as a whisper. "And I have to live with that, too. The only thing I can do is ask your forgiveness and give you my promise I have changed."

"How long have you been sober?" His abrupt change of subject shook her.

"Three years."

"Well done."

"Thank you. It was very rocky in the beginning. It took me a long time to admit defeat but I hit bottom, eventually. And thank God I did."

Lucy was killing him, as surely as if she had taken a scalpel to his guts. Christ. He should be harder than this. Especially when it came to this woman and after all this time. Apparently, they were both slow learners, because she could still get to him.

He'd seen her in all sorts of moods, from blackest depressions to giddy highs that terrified him she would never come down again. He'd seen her weep, wail, scream, and rant, but he had never seen her like this.

She sat there, so still and so quiet. Her dignity lay around her slim shoulders like a force field and pulsed with life. Despite the difficulty of what she did and despite her position as supplicant, she had never been stronger.

She awed him a little and frightened him a lot. Tears slipped, mostly unheeded, down her face and he tracked them, fascinated. It was as if they came from a place so deep it was beyond the petty performances of her youth. It reached out to him and fastened grim fingers around his heart.

Richard had never ached to hold her more. His hands shook with the need to pull her against his body and hold her until he could absorb all her hurt into himself. It was what he had tried to do all those years ago. Tried and failed, his memory put in quickly. In the end, her brokenness had been too much for him. For a while, it looked like it might be too much for her. And yet, here she sat. A survivor, a victim, and a perpetrator all rolled into one.

It scared him shitless. This need he felt to make a connection with her again. She still had it. All the Svengali-like appeal for him she'd always had. He stood here and listened to her rehash crap he didn't like to even think about, and all the time part of him watched the way the light played on her silky hair. How her skin still looked like a peach and how those huge eyes could still strip him down to his essence. He was one sick son of a bitch.

"I don't know, Luce." He had to say something. The silence in the kitchen was beginning to make all sorts of dumb shit seem possible. "I'm glad for you, I really am." That much was the God's honest truth.

"But I don't know if I can do this about-face and everything is all right again."

"I can understand that. I'm not asking for anything like that." Man, did she have to look so completely crushed? Not that it showed, but he knew Lucy. She hadn't changed completely. She was trying not to cry again. He'd seen her do it so many times around her dad that he could see right through her mask.

"I'm not saying I can't, ever, forgive you," he put in quickly. Despite it all, he was on the back foot now and feeling like the biggest shit and a bully. She had come here with her heart in her hand and her pride on a platter. And what did he do? "I just . . ." He searched for the right words. "I don't know what I'm saying."

Lucy took a breath and straightened her shoulders in a graceful unfolding that held him spellbound. She had always had a kick-ass body. You didn't have to like Lucy Flint to admit she was the stuff sweaty fantasies were made of. She was slim, but not skinny, and all her curves were deliciously positioned in the right places. He'd heard she'd done some underwear modeling in New York. No big surprise there.

And there were the legs. Richard let his eyes stray down. Those legs that used to drive him animal, crazy, wild. Given the chance, they might still do so. Richard dragged his gaze away.

"So what are we now?" He risked a few steps around the counter.

She choked out a funny little laugh and it stroked luscious fingers down his spine and drew a smile from him. "Battle weary?"

They stood looking at each other awkwardly.

"I should go," she said, her voice dipping a little lower.

"I'll walk you out."

They moved in silence through the house until they came to the front door. They stopped just inside the vestibule by tacit agreement. So much emotion gathered up in his chest he felt squirrelly with it. He couldn't let her walk out like this. There was more to be said.

"I almost feel like I should thank you, Luce." It came out gruff and raspy, which was what the place inside him felt like.

She turned to him in surprise, those green eyes opened wide and luminous. It was all there for him to see, the best of Lucy Flint in glorious detail. With no subterfuge or manipulations, pure and unadulterated Lucy. It hit him like a two-by-four to the back of the head and before he'd even consciously recognized the impulse he reached for her.

She seemed to move toward him at the same time. And she was in his arms. Lucy Flint was in his arms, again. It felt like fucking heaven. Every curve of her pressed against him. She held him like she used to. One arm wrapped around his waist and one around his neck. As if she couldn't get close enough to him. It was like she tried to melt into him.

His body remembered. It woke up with a great, big roar of interest that rushed straight to his crotch. He should move away and put some inches between them. His track pants would do nothing to hide his visceral reaction. Not yet. For a few seconds the need to indulge in her was too strong and Richard dropped his head and inhaled the scent of her. L'Eau d'Issey, still the same subtle scent after all these years and mixed with the cinnamon undernotes of Lucy.

The small hitch in her breathing rocked him to his core. And then he kissed her. Without his mind having formed the thought, his mouth found hers and feasted on the forgotten sweetness. The taste and feel of her exploded through his sense memory like a tsunami. His tongue thrust between her lips to find the honey his body still remembered was right there for him. A rough sound grated in his throat. Hot and needy, he wanted more of her. Shock slammed into him and he wrenched away. Dragging his mouth away, he scrambled back a few steps to put distance and sanity between them.

Her eyes were huge in her face, mirroring the shock he felt. "I . . . ?" She pressed her shaking hand to her mouth.

"GO," he growled, furious with her, furious with himself, and shaking with the effort it took not to reach for her again.

Chapter Ten

Lucy woke up to a familiar sound and her stomach clenched. Carl's voice became more insistent from the room next door. In direct proportion to his increased agitation, Lynne's tone grew more conciliatory. The call to action of her youth: Carl harangued and Lynne capitulated. Even now the lash-out-irrationally button blinked at her. *Push Me.*

For a moment she was a little girl again, lying in her too-big bed and listening to her parents in the room next to her own. She took a deep breath and re-minded herself she was not that little girl anymore. Last night and Richard hovered outside her aware-ness, but she was too cowardly to go there yet. She pushed the memory of the scene away, especially the last part, the part where he had kissed her. Richard kissed from his soul. It was pointless to think anyone else would ever kiss her like that. And wasn't that a cheery little thought to start the day on.

Lucy focused on Carl as he progressed to the name-calling. Her mother never retaliated. Where the hell had Lucy learned to stand up for herself? Actually, she grimaced, she had not always stood up for herself and certainly not against Peter. A brief interlude between Elliot and more Elliot landed her with Peter. Even now it was hard to fathom she had allowed some man to make a punching bag out of her. She got out of bed, more to escape the dark thoughts than anything else.

Elliot. It seemed the safest place to put her thoughts this morning. He'd been calling Mads and that couldn't be good. Elliot had been her knight in shining armor, the quintessential prince, waiting patiently in the wings to rush in and rescue his tattered princess. Only, the princess was not so sure she didn't want to have a crack at the dragon herself right now.

Elliot always urged her to take responsibility and stand on her own feet. He just never meant where he was concerned. She had left Seattle with things very much up in the air. Last night and Richard had, unfortunately, made a few things glaringly obvious. Lucy pushed the memory away ruthlessly. It was over, done, and best forgotten, a product of too many raw emotions spilling out of control. The thing to focus on was the amends and she'd delivered it. She took a deep breath. It was done.

The voices next door snatched away her moment of peace. A new note crept into Carl's voice and Lucy slipped out of bed and closer to the door.

"You're a stupid woman." Lucy sucked in a hard breath.

"Now, Carl, it's just a chair." Her mother always placated him.

Lucy pulled on a pair of sweats.

"I know what you're doing," Carl said, his voice growing louder.

"I'm not doing anything, dear," Lynne wheedled.

Why didn't her mother leave him? Lucy frowned at

her own thought. It seemed strangely disloyal, but it stuck like peanut butter to the roof of her mouth.

Well, why hadn't she left Peter? Her thoughts came full circle. You didn't have to be at the business end of someone's fist to feel isolated and unworthy. It had taken a stranger, appearing as if by magic at the side of her hospital bed. A stranger with café au lait skin, obsidian eyes, and a voice like gin and cigarettes, to tell her there was another way to lead her life. Lucy smiled despite the grim direction her head went.

Peter had landed her in the hospital the last time. After a drunken brawl between them, Lucy remembered nothing except waking up and seeing Mads standing by her bedside. And Mads had offered her a way out of the increasing insanity of her life. Surely her guardian angel must have been on duty that day because, despite everything, Lucy had listened. She had still been hearing those words three days later when Mads had picked her up from the hospital. She'd been sober ever since.

Lucy opened her door and snuck into the bathroom. She really didn't want to get dragged into the argument. Her teeth felt as if she had a layer of fur growing on them. She made it to the bathroom with a small sigh of relief. Now, it was time for coffee. Getting to the kitchen would be more of a challenge.

"Lucy?" Her mother's voice and Lucy groaned. The coffee might have to wait. Lynne had always dragged her into these fights. As if her presence ever did anything to soothe her father. One look at Lucy would send Carl straight over the edge. "Lucy, would you come here, please?"

But, no, this was how they did things in the Flint household and not much, if anything, had changed in her thirty years of being part of it.

"I'll be right there, Mom." Lucy splashed water on her face and braced for Carl. Thus far, his success in drawing blood had been limited. But Carl was like HAL 9000: He watched, he waited, he listened, and he learned. Lucy pulled a face at her reflection in the mirror. Was there some kind of special place in hell for people who had these thoughts about their parents?

She remembered something that made her grin. In the French version of *2001: A Space Odyssey*, HAL had been called CARL. That was better than a shot of caffeine. Lucy trotted across the hallway.

"What's up?" She leaned her shoulder against the door frame.

"You still here?" her father snarled at her. Nope, Lucy decided, no place in hell for her. More like a haven of eternal reward for tolerating the old fart.

"Still here," she confirmed with a pleasant nod. "What is it, Mom?"

"Oh, Lucy." Lynne turned huge, pleading eyes in her direction. "It's that chair."

Lucy almost burst out laughing, but Lynne's face persuaded her this was not a laughing matter. The chair in question was only a little younger than God. In fact, it may even have appeared in the painting of the Last Supper.

"What about the chair?" Other than the fact that it was cat-sick yellow and unmentionable brown, ripped and sagging. It no longer Lazed at all, the handle long broken and the footrest sort of hung half-mast between the floor and the swaybacked seat.

"It must go," Lynne wailed.

"Over my dead body," Carl growled. It was too easy. Lucy kept the pleasant expression on her face.

"I am trying to clear out some of the debris." Lynne turned to her in mute appeal.

"And you will try and get rid of me next," thundered Carl as he sat in the chair defiantly. Springs groaned in protest, but Carl stayed put. "The chair stays for as long as I do."

Again, Lucy bit her tongue.

"Now, Carl." Lynne went into her soothing routine. "You know that's not the way it is. I want to give the place a bit of a spruce-up. Maybe we can get that Realtor in, like we talked about. And maybe you and I can move to something smaller. You always said you wanted us to have a house of our own."

"The chair stinks." Lucy added her two cents worth from the doorway.

"It does not." Carl rounded on her belligerently.

"Just saying." Lucy shrugged and the full force of her father's wrath turned in her direction.

"You put these ideas into her head, didn't you?" His eyes narrowed venomously in his face. "You want to get rid of me."

"It's not my decision," Lucy told him frankly. "But I do think Mom is looking tired and somewhere smaller would be easier for her to manage. One level would also be better for both of you."

"We do fine without you and your suggestions." Carl's face went alarmingly red.

"You're upsetting him, dear," Lynne whispered urgently and Lucy stared at her. That's what you got for waking up in the Flint house.

"Okay." She straightened away from the doorjamb. Last night she'd delivered an amends to Richard. This morning she was exhausted, wrung out like a dishcloth, but strangely liberated. She was not going to get dragged into her parents' battle. "Does anyone want a cup of coffee?"

It was comical the way both Carl and Lynne stopped and turned to stare at her. Lucy kept a pleasant expression on her face. "Coffee?" she prompted.

Lynne frowned a little and then turned back to Carl. "There is not enough room in here for two chairs. So, I guess we'll have to cancel the new one and leave that one there." And the battle was on again.

"What new chair?" Carl narrowed his eyes suspiciously at Lynne. "Have you been spending money again?" Lucy looked at her mother. This was news to her too. When had Lynne been ordering new chairs?

"Well," Lynne said, screwing up her face. "It will cost twice as much to have that one repaired. I thought it would be better to get a new one. They have such lovely fabrics now and leather in all sorts of colors. But there is not enough space in here for two chairs."

"Mom." Lucy turned to leave. "He doesn't want a new chair. If he wants his smelly old chair, let him have his chair."

"I never said that." Predictable as clockwork, Carl thundered at her.

"Whatever." Lucy shrugged over her shoulder.

"We don't have money to spend on nonsense," Carl decreed from his tatty throne. "You would know that if you ever bothered to come home."

Now that was an out and out lie. The money part, at least, because Lucy knew Carl had squirreled away a small fortune over the years. God knows, he hadn't spent a cent on anything in her lifetime. Somehow, she couldn't drum up the enthusiasm to engage the battle. Coffee, on the other hand, now that she could get excited about.

"Well, that's that then." Lynne said it so calmly Lucy snapped back to attention. Her mother was up to something.

Lynne started to gather up the debris from Carl's breakfast. "It doesn't really make any difference to me."

"What are you blathering about?" Carl snapped, intrigued despite himself.

"Oh, nothing," Lynne breathed airily. "We were talking about putting the house to order. One thing led to another and we got to thinking it might be time for some new things."

"What new things? We don't need any new things."

Yup, good old Dad. Tight as a bear's ass in fly season. Carl was business as usual but Lynne, now there was the revelation. Lucy decided to stay a while and watch her mother at work. Which triggered another thought. For all her unobtrusive and submissive behavior, Lynne managed to make her will count when it was important to her.

"You're quite right, of course." Lynne picked up the tray. "It was nothing important really, or even useful. A new chair, definitely. That one is in a terrible state. And then Lucy suggested one of those new televisions."

Say what? Lucy blinked at her mother.

Lynne headed for the door. "The ones that go on the wall and get high definition and all that stuff. I know nothing about it but the nice young man at the store explained how much clearer the picture was and, I must say, they had some hockey playing and it was almost like being at the game."

Way to go, Mom. Lucy almost cheered out loud. Clearly, Lynne had skills that were vastly underestimated. Lucy knew she had a new appreciation for Lynne's methods, and she was fairly sure Carl hadn't a bloody clue he was being calmly and quietly arranged into a useful position.

Carl looked marginally less bellicose now. A crafty grin played around the corners of his mouth.

Man, had she ever underestimated Lynne. Not only did he play right into his wife's hands, he thought he had the win. It was all something of a revelation.

"I don't need a new TV," Carl grumbled.

"No, you don't," Lucy agreed quickly. "It would be wasted on you, you never watch anything." She thought she'd give her mother a hand.

"I watch TV all the time." *Yup, you could bet the farm on it.*

"Sure, you do." She snorted. *That should just about do it.*

"Perhaps a microwave instead?" Lynne mused as she left the room. "Or you know what, Lucy. That old dishwasher of mine has clearly seen better days."

"You just got a microwave." The enraged bellow followed them down the stairs.

Lucy watched her mother with newfound respect as she followed her into the kitchen. Already more questions were starting to crowd her brain. Lucy pushed them away. She had more than enough to deal with for the moment.

Lucy wrestled the grim-smelling old relic out onto the driveway. Lynne offered to help, but Lucy left her doing what she did best, appeasing Carl.

The weather had improved slightly today and the temperature was bearable. A light snow drifted like tiny cobwebs through the air. That should really put the chair past saving.

She shoved it down the porch, her legs slipping and sliding as her feet failed to gain purchase on the new snow. It may not be a thing of beauty, but the chair was certainly built to last and weighed it. Determined not to be daunted she gave another mighty push and the chair moved a gratifying two feet. This was her badge of honor, her medal of courage, her triumph over Carl. It was not much, but it was the thin end of the wedge.

Good. Lucy stepped back and surveyed her handiwork. "Only another twenty or so feet to go."

"Are you talking to yourself?"

Lucy's heartbeat accelerated all by itself and it had nothing to do with her difficulties with the chair.

His dark head covered in a navy cap, Richard appeared at the end of the driveway. He was all wrapped up in his winter coat and boots, carrying a snow shovel. The moment hung awkwardly between them as Lucy searched for something to say.

"You seem to spend your life doing that," Lucy said, nodding toward the shovel.

"I don't mind it," he said, shrugging. "It gives me a chance to clear my mind."

"Is that why all the running and cycling?"

He smiled at her. It was the first honest, real Richard smile and it lit Lucy up from the inside out like a storm lantern. She stood there and basked in its glory.

"Richie Rich?"

"My pet?"

"Pet?"

"Give me a break here, I am running out of names."

"I love your smile, you know."

"*Of course you do, it's part of my awesome package.*"
"*Package?*"
"*Uh-huh.*"

"So what's with the chair?"

Lucy jerked her attention to the malodorous mess she was heaving around. "This," she said, patting it gingerly, terrified of what might be hiding in there. "This is more than a chair. This is a moral victory."

"Uh-huh?" He folded his arms over his chest.

He was different today, a bit more relaxed and almost—approachable? The air between them felt clearer, freer, as if they had both managed a bit of breathing space. If she'd done nothing else with her amends, she'd done that.

"I managed to liberate this from the house. Over the voluble protests of my father, mind you. This chair is a portent of change."

"And here I thought it was a really old La-Z-Boy."

"That's because you lack vision," Lucy said, grinning at him. For once he didn't stare at her as if he were cast in granite. He cracked another smile and Lucy's cup ranneth over.

Then, he did one of those Richard things she hadn't remembered, but it all came back to her in a rush. He strolled over and hefted the chair onto his shoulder. He carried the chair effortlessly to the sidewalk. It would stay there until somebody decided they must have it or the city came to get it. Lucy's money was on the latter. She was reasonably sure it should be condemned as a biohazard.

She followed Richard down to the sidewalk and smiled. It was always like this with Richard. He opened doors, carried heavy things, stood when a lady left the table, a hundred small, old-fashioned, and nearly forgotten courtesies he performed as easily as if he were breathing. All the brothers were the same.

"What are you smiling at?"

"You." Lucy's smile widened when he looked surprised. "You always had the most beautiful manners. Other boys were not like you. If they did do something polite, they made a big deal. You got on with it as if it were the most natural thing in the world."

"Aw, Lucy, stop already."

"Are you actually blushing?"

"No."

"You are too."

"It's the cold."

"Pshaw!"

The moment drew out long enough to feel ungainly. Lucy looked at her feet.

He shifted on his.

The hostility was missing and in its place was a wide abyss that throbbed with possibility. Lucy was not entirely sure what to do with that, yet.

"Um . . . Luce?"

"Yup." It was a relief one of them spoke.

"I think it's incredible." He pushed his hands into the pockets of his coat. "You getting sober. I've seen people come through the practice who are struggling with addiction. I don't absolutely understand what it is you guys go through, but I am in awe of what you manage to achieve."

"Thanks." She wanted to squirm like a happy puppy.

"I was in shock when you came around. It was hard to listen to you dredge up the past." His breath hit the air in white plumes of vapor. "For the most part I try not to think about it and then, you appear out of nowhere and want to hash it all out. I haven't thought about some of that stuff for years. Truthfully, I didn't want to think about it ever again."

"I didn't do it to upset you, Richard."

"And I get that, Lucy." He cleared his throat. "I guess what I am trying to say is, I am finding this harder than I would have thought. And because of that, I didn't tell you last night how much I admire your courage in getting sober."

Lucy looked up at the clean, classical lines of his face. The snow had thickened into fat, sleepy flakes that clung lovingly to his head and shoulders.

Inside her chest, her heart gave a queer tug.

"It's not as if I don't want to let the past go, Luce, but being angry with you has become a sort of habit." He scrunched his shoulders next to his ears and dropped them down. "I never foresaw a time when it would stop."

"Would it help if you gave me some sort of task?"

"Hmm?"

His look of confusion made her chuckle. "Some of the old-timers say when you make an amend you should ask the person if there is anything they need you to do to prove yourself to them. Would that help?"

"Like what sort of thing?" He frowned in concentration and it took her right back to the days she had lain on his bed and watched him study. So serious and so focused on what he was doing. It had been a sort of challenge to see if she could get him to look up. In the end, she'd always managed it. And a whole lot more.

"Oh, I don't know," Lucy said, and shrugged, keeping it light. "You seem to have the shoveling pretty much under control." He was still studying her carefully.

"Anything you can think of that will reassure you I am sincere and you can trust me again."

He raised one of his dark, dark eyebrows in disbelief. "That's a pretty big blank check you've handed me."

"Well," Lucy said, grinning up at him. "You can ask. It doesn't mean I have to do it or anything. You ask and I will make a judgment call at that point."

He nodded abruptly. "I'll think about it." The snow was starting to settle all around them as they stood, not looking at each other, but intensely aware of the other person.

Richard shuffled his feet suddenly and Lucy looked up. She watched with fascination as his cheeks went a little pinker. "As for the . . . um . . . other thing."

Lucy felt her own face heat. "Don't . . ."

"A reaction to the situation . . ."

"Absolutely, I totally understand . . ."

"Shouldn't . . ."

"Right, clearly."

"Okay." He blew out a long breath. "I'm glad we got that out in the open and cleared up."

The small space between them seemed alive with all the wasted possibilities. The sadness nearly sent Lucy to her knees. If it hadn't happened the way it did, where would they be now? Would that be her house? Would this be her beautiful, kind, strong man?

She couldn't tell what he was thinking. Only that his eyes were trying to probe the layers of her and see beyond.

"It's cold." Lucy looked away first.

"Very." He gave a jerky motion toward the house. "Is your mom inside?"

"Yes," Lucy answered, snatching at the conversational gambit.

"Um—good." He straightened his shoulders and his

expression firmed into purposeful lines. "I thought I might try and visit with Carl."

"Oh?" Lucy realized what he meant and smiled. "Oh." She motioned toward the chair. "He was in fine voice this morning about that."

"And Lynne?" A small frown creased the skin between his eyes. "Is she all right?"

"Actually," Lucy said, "she handled him very well. It was quite an eye opener."

He frowned as if weighing his words. "You know, Lucy, it might not be the best thing for Carl or Lynne to have him placed in a home."

"I know that," Lucy responded quickly, but there was none of the former accusation in his eyes and she settled down again. "I know that. And I want to do the best thing here. Whatever that is."

"Okay." He nodded slowly and motioned for her to proceed.

Lucy made a face and stepped out of his way. "All things considered, it's probably best if I make myself scarce while you visit. I only bring out the worst in him."

"Oh, right." He opened his mouth to speak and then stopped as if his mental censorship board had reached for the red pen.

She waited a moment more for him to finish what he was going to say. It didn't look like he would, so she turned.

"Let me know if you think of anything," she called over her shoulder. "About the amends."

He raised one hand and waved it in acknowledgement.

Chapter Eleven

"There you are. I thought I'd hear from you first thing this morning." Mads didn't keep her waiting.

"Yeah." Lucy wrapped her scarf around her neck as Richard disappeared into her house. "I had a thing this morning, with my dad, but it's done now."

"So, how did it go?" Mads wanted to know about the amends.

"It went . . . okay." And she really didn't have any other words to describe the scene with Richard.

Mads listened in silence as Lucy went through the details, omitting the last part.

"You did well, Lucy Locket," Mads said after a pause and Lucy's conscience twanged. "We all have a few that feel like an open nerve ending."

"Uh-huh."

"I don't like the sound of that." Mads was like a bloodhound on the trail.

"Let me ask you a hypothetical question." Lucy tramped up the street as Mads went silent to listen. "Say, a person was trying to get her life in order and needed to make peace with her past to do that?"

"Hmm?" Mads rumbled softly. "Hypothetically speaking, right?"

"Um, right." Lucy tucked the phone securely against her ear as she checked for traffic before crossing. "And that person discovered, or thought maybe it was possible, that her feelings might not be what she thought they would be."

"In what way?" Mads pricked her ears.

"Like, say, there were still residual feelings for a past flame." She really shouldn't be asking this. She knew the answer, but that stubborn part of her couldn't let it lie.

"What sort of residual feelings?"

"Complicated ones."

"I see." Mads took a deep breath. "Then I would have to, hypothetically, remind that person that they were not there to screw anyone over any more than they already had."

"Right." Lucy swallowed past the dry lump in her throat. Stupid to have expected anything else. "Right."

"Ah, babe." Mad's instant empathy made Lucy's eyes sting. "This program can help you free yourself, but it can't always give you a happy ending."

"I know." And she did know. Time to man up a bit. "It could be because it's all so fresh and I haven't seen him in so long. I look at him and suddenly my head is full of what-ifs."

"Lucy, girl," Mads said gently, "are you good for him though?"

There it was. The uppercut straight to the chin. "Maybe I could be now."

"What about Elliot?"

Lucy groaned and looked up. Snowflakes drifted down and fell like a cold kiss on her cheeks and lips. "I think I have an answer for him."

"Okay, then," Mads said. "Then that is one good thing going there accomplished. For the rest, I really don't know. I think you should do what you need to do and get out of there."

"I know." Lucy's heart twisted and withered. It was the right thing to do. Nine years ago, she'd gone after a man for all the wrong reasons. She couldn't spend her life making the same mistakes.

"Finish up and come home," Mads said.

All along the street, the snow had stopped and the sunlight played tag with the icicles, turning the residential neighborhood into a picture postcard. Already the clouds that would banish the sun were starting to create wisps on the horizon. But for now, the day had turned clear and crisp and beautiful. It was the right sort of day for blowing the cobwebs out of your brain and she started to walk.

The new snow crackled and squeaked beneath her feet. She rapidly searched the pockets of her coat for her cap and pulled it down over the top of her ears. They gave a grateful throb as warm blood started to flow to her extremities again. She was sober. She tasted the clean air on her tongue. She was alive and she was living each day as it came.

She made it to the end of the street and turned right toward the town hall. A great, square, brick edifice, the city hall stood in pride of place at the corner of Main and Clarke. The Christmas lights were still strung around the windows and doors, but the tree had already been hauled away. Lucy went past the town hall and toward the cenotaph. Every Veterans' Day, Lynne had brought her here to watch them lay the wreaths of poppies at the feet of the stone soldier.

Behind the soldier, the children's fountain lay closed and boarded up against the cold.

That was the place for the hot summer days of July and August. She and Ashley had stripped down to their underwear and danced in and out of the water sprays. The roads were quiet as Lucy crossed over to the community park. On the corner, the old billboard still stood. Every happening in the small neighborhood was religiously recorded and advertised here.

Life went on and sometimes it hurt to stand up and feel it flow through and over you. It was why she drank, to escape this. There was no escape, however; sooner or later you had to start facing each moment and living it.

And in the center of the park was the outside skating rink that went up every year. There were only a handful of hearty souls braving the cold today. A group of four boys matched up in a game of hockey. At the edge of the rink, a small girl skated in tentative circles around her father.

Lucy felt as if she had gone miles into the darkest parts of her soul, yet life in this place plodded on much as it always did. Lucy was not sure if she hated that thought or drew a strange sort of comfort from it.

The little ice fairy wobbled, regained her balance, only to wobble again and go over on her butt with a thump. Her father was there immediately, dusting off the ice and wiping her tears. That had never been her. She had never been that little princess.

Instead, Lucy had been one of those boys. Trying so hard to impress and look like they didn't give a shit at the same time. From the time she had strapped on skates or soccer cleats or whatever, she had been one of those boys. She always had to be better, faster, tougher, and stronger. Most of the time she had been.

Lucy was blessed with a healthy athletic ability, but it
wasn't enough. She hadn't been a boy. Sometimes
that meant a severe disappointment to Carl and, at
best, an almost-good-enough. But she wasn't that anymore and that was the bit that mattered.

"You used to skate rings around all the boys," said
a voice Lucy knew well. She nearly didn't turn around.
The urge to run and hide was like jungle drums in
her chest.

"Hey, Donna." Lucy braced herself and turned to
greet the coolest mom in Willow Park.

Only Donna was nothing like Lucy remembered
her. Gone was the shoulder-length hair; it was cropped
and tousled like a boy's. It suited her. Donna had
never been a pretty woman, but this new haircut
showed up the clean lines of her face and drew attention to those amazing blue eyes. Richard's eyes, Lucy
thought, with a little slither of regret.

"Lucy." Donna wasn't smiling, but there was no hostility in the measured stare she turned on her. "And
back in Willow Park."

"Um . . . yes." Lucy hunkered into her scarf. Another regret and another person whom she'd hurt.
Donna had been like a second mother to Lucy.

The boys on the ice shouted and cheered as Donna
studied her. Donna frowned slightly and sighed. The
soft exhalation hurt more than all Carl's bluster. "I
didn't think it was possible, but you are even more
beautiful than you were when you were a girl." She
gave a short, wry laugh. "No wonder Richard is in
such a confusion." Donna was taking every inch of
Lucy in. Looking beyond the surface, as if she could
see more.

"Richard's in a confusion?" Lucy found her voice.

"What did you think, *chérie?*" She clasped Lucy's

face tenderly between two mittened palms. Lucy gasped as much for the unexpectedness, as the sweetness of the gesture. "Did you think he could not be affected by you, ever? You underestimate the size of the footprint you leave."

"I don't think I do," Lucy said.

Donna looked at her deeply and then took her hands away from Lucy's face. Her expression grew sad all of a sudden. "Perhaps you don't, at that."

"No, I don't." Lucy cleared her throat. Donna had welcomed Lucy into her home and her heart while Lucy had done what she always did, hurt people. "But I didn't want . . . I never meant . . . I want to try and make it right."

"So I've heard," Donna said, nodding slowly. Her blue eyes were still avidly eating up Lucy's features, as if she could find some great truth there. Lucy wanted to tell her not to bother. "Des always hoped you would come back," she said. "He passed two years ago, did you know?"

"Yes." Regret tightened her chest into a hard ache. "I am sorry for your loss."

Des had been the blueprint for his son and, like Richard, Lucy was candy to him and he had spoiled her rotten. Lucy, desperate for any fatherly approval, had lapped it up. One of her true regrets was that Des's funeral had been and gone and she had lacked the courage at the time to come back. Des had deserved more from her. Hell, she had deserved more from her.

"Des always did have a big, soft spot for his Lucy." Donna echoed her thoughts. "He was devastated when you left."

More pain, more regret, and more guilt and Lucy's shoulders sagged beneath the weight. So many good people had been hurt, people who didn't deserve her treatment of them. She had no words, so she looked at Donna mutely and shook her head.

Donna took a bracing breath and gave her shoulders a small shake as if she could free them from some invisible pressure. "Enough," she announced suddenly and Lucy jumped slightly. "Des would have been thrilled to see you and he would have been proud of the way you are facing your troubles now."

Lucy couldn't keep the skepticism from her face.

Donna smiled, as if she accurately read her expression. "He was not angry with you," she insisted. "Des always saw so much more than we gave him credit for. He was angry for you. Me"—she shrugged—"I wanted to take a piece out of your hide for what you did to my baby boy, but Des, he saw things differently. He said if you had been his, you would never have felt the need to run so far or so fast. It made me look at the whole thing differently. It took a while, but I saw what my Des was trying to say . . . eventually."

Lucy's mouth dropped open and Donna reached up and shut it gently with one finger. "And I am glad, because now I can say, with some fairly large reservations, that I am glad to see you again, Lucy."

Lucy blinked rapidly. "I . . ." The rest came out as a garbled strangle and Donna, thank God, took pity on her and changed the subject.

"And this is Rasputin." She gestured to a rather ratty looking mongrel, unhappily trying to pick snow out of his paws. "He does not like to walk, this dog of mine." Donna threw Rasputin a disparaging glance. "But he likes to eat and he likes to sleep, so we get along fine."

"I see you changed your hair as well." Lucy marched them into safer territory. Hair was the ultimate equalizer amongst two or more women. Forget fashion, weight was too fraught with pitfalls. Hair was the tried and true game changer.

"Yes." Donna patted her hair into place before pulling a cherry-red cap on over her curls. "Des, he liked it longer and you know how he could be." Donna pulled an expressive face. "I wore my hair that way for over thirty years, to please the man. But after he died, there was nobody to tell me how to wear my hair anymore." She winked at Lucy and then said, "I am walking my ungrateful dog, but what are you doing out here on a day like this? You must be soft after living in Seattle all this time."

Lucy laughed. "I needed some fresh air," she said. "But I think it's fresh enough for me and, you're right, it's time to get out of the cold."

"I will walk with you." Donna tucked her arm through Lucy's. "I am going your way."

"How are the other boys?" Lucy ventured tentatively as they tramped along together. "Joshua and Thomas, are they well?"

"Ah, oui," Donna responded, smiling. "Thomas, he is an engineer now and working over in South Africa on some project."

"Really?" Lucy tried to imagine the awkward boy she'd left behind doing anything but chewing gum and skateboarding. She gave up the attempt.

"Oh, yes." Donna nodded and gave a tug to the recalcitrant Rasputin. The dog got to his feet with a small doggy moan. "Thomas is over there now and he e-mails me all the time and we talk on Skype. Do you have Skype?"

"No."

"You should." Donna patted her arm. "It is the most marvelous thing. I can see my Thomas, clear as anything." She leaned into Lucy. "I can see when he is trying to lie to his mother."

"Does he do that a lot?" Lucy couldn't resist.

"Pftt!" Donna threw up her arms. Rasputin almost left terra firma. "That one."

They walked to the end of the street.

"And Joshua?" Lucy asked about the second oldest brother. A year younger than Richard, Joshua had been the best-looking brother. The other two brothers were no slouches, but Joshua held the undisputed title of heartbreaker. In his time, his reputation had spread beyond the sleepy streets of Willow Park into the neighboring areas. Joshua Hunter was hot. H. O. T. Strangely, he had held no appeal for Lucy, nor she for him.

"Joshua." Donna rolled her eyes. "He is still around, but he has this big, fancy apartment in downtown Chicago. It's one of these modern ones with all the exposed piping and lots of light. I would love to live there. My son doesn't have any idea how lucky he is. He's never there. He uses it as a place to put as a mailing address and bring women home to." Despite her words, Donna's voice radiated warmth. Joshua had been the sort of charmer it was hard to get angry with and impossible to stay angry at. "He is doing something with computers, but he was always good with money, that one." Donna gave a short laugh. "Two things Joshua could always find without even trying: girls and money."

"I'll bet." Lucy smiled, remembering that twinkle in the middle Hunter brother's eye.

"So, tell me, Lucy *belle fille,* where you have been and what you have been doing? I asked Lynne once about you, but she got terribly embarrassed and upset and I didn't want to do it again."

That was news to Lucy and her old friend, guilt, gave the knife another hefty turn. "I went to New York, at first, with Jason. He said we were going to be famous." Lucy smiled at her own naïveté. "With my looks and his skill with a camera, how could we fail?"

Donna surprised her by not joining in her short, self-deprecatory chuckle, but gave her an intent look instead. "And?"

"And?" Lucy puffed up her cheeks and blew the air out slowly. It created a little cloud of vapor that turned to crystals against her scarf. It was the first time anyone from home had ever assumed the result might be anything other than an abject lesson in humility.

"And we found out we were one more set of dreamers amongst thousands of others. There were lots of photographers as good as if not better than Jason and New York was drowning in lovely girls. Jason, or 'JP' as he styled himself, found every single one of them."

Donna made one of her continental noises that could mean anything from *I told you so* to *Aren't all men such bastards?* "He was always such a one."

"Yup." Lucy planted her boot into a patch of virgin snow, lifted it, and studied her pristine footprint with satisfaction.

"And then you went to Seattle?" Donna chuckled at Lucy's look of surprise. "It's not as if I have heard nothing, *belle fille*. This is Willow Park, after all."

"I like Seattle," Lucy said as the unfortunate Rasputin's short legs disappeared into the buildup of snow beside the sidewalk. "And I wouldn't say I took the town by storm, but I made a living. I'm happy there, now."

"Hmm." Donna peered up at her with those piercing blue eyes. Richard had that way of looking at her. It was as if he were taking what she said under advisement and would give her his conclusions later. "Now we are here."

They were standing outside Richard's house.

"You are not coming in." It was a statement. "Not yet, but soon. Isn't that so, *belle fille*?"

"The Willow Park grapevine must be having a field day with all of this." Lucy writhed a bit inside.

"Oh, yes," Donna said, rolling her eyes. "You being back was enough to get the tongues wagging. Your revelations and Brooke's spite have done the rest."

"She worked fast."

"She is not one to forgive a slight and you did a little more than that." The truth in that stung, but there was no point in denying anything. "Speaking of people you have harmed, I will ask only one thing from you, Lucy." Donna's face was dead serious. Even Rasputin stopped fidgeting and sat with a sigh. "Do not hurt my son again. I am not angry with you. I think, now more than ever, I understand what drove you to do what you did. But I ask you to treat him with care. He doesn't look it, but he is fragile right now and where you are concerned . . ." Donna shrugged eloquently.

"I don't want to hurt him any more than I already have." Lucy held Donna's look.

"*Bien.*" Donna reached up and patted Lucy's cheek. "You are a good girl, Lucy. You were lost and now you are found. Des was right about this. Like that song says."

"'Amazing Grace'?"

"That is the one." She turned and squared her shoulders. "And now it is my solemn duty to stir some life into my dead shit of a son."

"I think he's still with my father." Lucy pointed over to her family home.

"Oh?" Donna shrugged. "I will wait for him inside."

Her eyes twinkled at Lucy from beneath her red cap. "It makes him crazy when I do that."

"You're not bringing that dog into my house." Richard appeared suddenly at the end of the porch to Lucy's house.

Lucy's heart gave an odd, little leap as he strode toward them.

He hesitated slightly when he saw her, but didn't break stride. "Lucy"—he nodded a greeting—"I'll call you."

Donna opened his front door and walked in. Rasputin shot through her legs into the warmth of the house.

"I don't know why I bother," Lucy heard him sigh as he strode after his mother.

"Because you're a good man," Lucy murmured to herself. "The very best sort of man."

Chapter Twelve

Lucy was wrenched out of sleep. The sound of shouting echoed off the walls and she groaned. She blinked sleepily and fumbled for her phone to check the time.

"God in heaven." She dropped her head back onto the pillows. It was not even five-thirty in the morning.

No prizes for guessing who was doing the yelling. Couldn't the old bastard wait until a decent hour before he started bellowing? Or better yet, could he not yell? Two days in a row was the outside of enough. Her mom had said nothing about Richard's visit and he hadn't called.

She'd barely managed two hours of sleep the night before. Between Donna and Richard, her mind had buzzed too loudly for sleep. Her eyes felt gritty and her head pounded out a dull rhythm. Carl was, clearly, not feeling fatigued, if the volume the old bastard was putting out was any indication. No, Carl was in fighting form. Just as he went to bed at nine-thirty, come what may, he rose at six, every morning, and saw no reason why the rest of the world couldn't rise with him.

Lucy remembered outraged neighbors, year after year, complaining about Carl's gardening habits. Neighbors tend to lose their sense of humor about snow blowers going off at six-thirty on a Sunday. She was partially convinced the bylaw banning the use of leaf blowers for most of the year was thanks to her father.

"Don't give me that," Carl said, cranking up the volume. His voice drifted up from the kitchen, vitriol dripping from every syllable. There was an unfortunate theme to her father. Carl fighting with the neighbors, Carl arguing with the postman, Carl yelling at the garbage collectors, always Carl, generating drama wherever he went and wallowing in the aftereffects. It made her sick.

Throwing back the covers, she stepped out of bed.

"I know exactly what you're doing," Carl yelled.

Lynne replied, her tone conciliatory. Lucy didn't need to hear exactly what she was saying. She'd heard it a million times before.

"You think I'm too far gone to realize, but I've got news for you, you stupid woman."

Lucy balled her hands into fists and forced a breath through her clenched teeth. Oh yes, Carl was an expert at name-calling. He never bothered to edit his words before they came out of his mouth. It was all about his sense of self-entitlement. Carl was angry and that made everyone else his scapegoat. The injustice of it burned her up.

"You're an evil bitch."

And Lucy saw red. She was down the stairs before she could stop herself.

"Stop it." Her voice cracked through the kitchen, the moment her feet hit the tiled floor. Carl and Lynne spun to look at her. "That's enough." Her voice

shook slightly with the effort not to scream back at
Carl. "You can't speak to her like that."

"Lucy," Lynne squeaked and her eyes grew round.
"What are you doing up?"

"I can speak to her any way I damn well please."
Carl rounded on Lucy, his eyes bulging.

"Would you like some breakfast?" Lynne asked with
an edge of desperation. Lucy turned to snap at her
mother, mouth open, ready to snarl. She stopped.

Lynne cowered over by the fridge, looking like a
rabbit in headlights.

It gave Lucy the split second she needed to regain
her control.

"You're upset, Dad." This was not vintage Carl. So,
she didn't need to react like vintage Lucy. This was an
old, sick man and he needed her compassion more
than her bitterness. "But that doesn't give you the
right to call people names."

Carl opened his mouth to argue and then snapped
it shut again. He eyed Lucy warily as she stepped closer
toward him. "What are you upset about?"

"What do you care?" He crossed his arms over his
chest like a small, petulant boy. "You are just like her."
He thrust his chin in Lynne's direction. "You want to
lock me away. You had that doctor boyfriend of yours
come here so they could lock me away."

"Richard was concerned about you," Lucy explained.

Lynne stared at her in round-eyed amazement.

Lucy was pretty amazed at how she was handling
this herself as well. "We're all concerned about you."

"Not you." Carl's voice quavered. "You don't care
about me. You left."

"I know." Lucy was surprised his words still had the
power to hurt her. "But I didn't leave because I didn't

care." She thought about saying more, but decided against it.

Carl watched her, his eyes narrowed as thoughts raced through his head. "What do you want here?" he demanded suddenly.

"I want to make peace." Lucy shrugged. "To try and fix what I broke and make peace."

"Hah." Carl pointed at her triumphantly. "You see"—he glared at his wife—"I told you. She said it. She wants to fix things. You know what that means, don't you?" He stalked a few steps closer to Lynne.

Her mother held her ground, but seemed to shrink into herself.

"What do you think that means, Dad?" Lucy drew his attention back to her.

"It means you want to fix me. Like a dog needs fixing. You want to have me put away. In a cage where I can't get out." Lucy didn't try to follow his convoluted logic. He gave a strange little chuckle, like some moustache-twirling villain. Carl fastened a reptilian gaze on Lucy. "But you won't win," he taunted her. "You won't win because I win. I'm the winner. I'm always the winner. I got rid of you before, didn't I?"

It hurt and Carl could see it. His triumphant smile almost ripped Lucy's composure in two. "I'm going to bed," he announced gleefully and strode from the room.

Lucy watched him clomp up the stairs before turning back to her mom. Lynne had picked up a cleaning rag and attacked the front of the cupboards.

"Mom?"

Lynne dropped the rag onto the countertop. "I can't do this, Lucy." She planted her hands on the counter and looked at Lucy. "All this talk of change is upsetting him. It's not right."

"He's sick, Mom." Lucy took the stool on the opposite side of the counter from where Lynne stood.

"He's old," Lynne snapped back at her. "He's old and he's tired. You young people can't understand that, but it's how it is."

"Nobody is trying to force you to do anything," Lucy explained slowly. "But he's getting worse and you must have given some thought to the alternatives."

"Is this about selling the house again?" Lynne snatched up her rag and launched another offensive at the cupboard doors. "I told you, I don't know if I want to sell. This is my home."

"Mom." Lucy felt her patience starting to slide and hauled back on it harshly. "If you don't want to sell, then don't sell, but it's insane to keep going on like this. Dad is tired, you're tired, and this house is huge."

"I was born here," Lynne protested without looking up.

"Okay, so scrap selling the house, but what about another solution?"

"What do you mean?" Lynne fired back with a suspicious speed. Her head snapped up and she peered at Lucy over the top of the counter.

"If he gets much worse," Lucy suggested, "you are going to need some help with him."

"Are you talking about one of those home helpers?"

"Yes, there are those," she prevaricated. "I understand they are very good, but there are other options."

"Like what?" Lynne was still bristling.

"Like a facility that caters specifically to people with needs like Dad's. A place where they will know exactly what to do with him and how to make him comfortable."

"You mean a home?" Lynne reeled back, scandalized. "Lucy," her mom gasped at her. She leapt up and started polishing the counter.

"It's not as bad as it sounds." Lucy's gaze had to chase her mother around the counter. "Dad might have special needs you are not able to fulfill."

Lynne burst into mocking laughter and Lucy did a quick double take. "You've been talking to Richard," Lynne accused her.

"No, I—"

"Nine years ago you walked out on that boy and ripped his heart right out of his body and you're not even back in town a week and you have him dancing to your tune again." Lynne shook her head and sighed. "You and your way with men."

Lucy opened her mouth to protest, but Lynne wasn't listening. She had stopped that creepy laughter, which was a relief. She looked at Lucy and shook her head. "You're up to your old ways again, Lu Lu." The words slithered down her spine like ice and Lucy forgot what she was going to say.

"But I am wise to you now," Lynne chided her gently. "I am going to see how your father is." She walked toward the kitchen door, but stopped and turned around. "We can't have all that nonsense again, Lu Lu. I love you, but I am not going to enable your behavior. I've been reading about you alcoholics."

Richard felt like he must be the only person up and about at this time on a snowy Sunday morning. His excuse was he was going for a run. All the sensible people in the world were happily tucked up under their covers. Perhaps they were tucked around someone.

A sense of loneliness hit him. This morning he wanted nothing more than a warm temptation luring him back to bed. The only problem was his fantasy smelled like cinnamon and traces of L'Eau d'Issey and she walked as if ZZ Top's "Legs" was her mobile soundtrack. The sooner Ashley got over her shit and moved back in, the better they would all be. The thought filled him with a curious sense of unease.

Time to run. He really didn't feel like it anymore. But, driven by the frustration of his collapsing marriage, an iron-man triathlon had sounded like a great idea. He'd had several months to regret that impulse. Despite that, the training had given him something to focus on, besides his failure as a husband.

Richard put his glass down in the sink with a decisive clunk. Now his training would help him exorcise a blond demon from his system. He was about to move away from the window when he saw the flicker of movement. That was no squirrel.

He peered through the bare branches separating his property from the Flint house. In the summer, the straggly stand of trees was a fecund thicket of silver birch. Now the branches rose like graceful ghosts against the snow. And they harbored a fugitive.

Someone was hunkered down in the old fort. Years ago, Lucy and Ashley had built that fort amongst the birch trees. Ashley had shown it to him when they first bought this house. With his genius powers of deductive reasoning, Richard realized Lucy must be in there.

"What the hell?" It was Lucy. She was sitting on an

upended log of wood. And she looked like she was crying.

"Screw it. What kind of dork goes running in minus twenty anyway?" Richard reached for two coffee cups and filled them from the machine. He grabbed his coat as he left. He was back two seconds later.

"Damn, why don't men think to buy Kleenex?" He shrugged and grabbed a drying cloth.

Lucy was so absorbed in her own private misery she heard nothing until he spoke.

"I'm afraid I don't know the password."

She looked up and for the first time that morning, her face split into a smile. He certainly didn't need the password and even less so when he came bearing a steaming mug of pure heaven. Lucy drank in the sight of him and stopped. He was wearing some kind of Lycra tight things.

"You planning a pas de deux?" She motioned to his muscular legs.

"Ha, ha." He handed her one of the mugs.

Lucy groaned her appreciation as the aromatic waft touched her nostrils. Sweet God in Heaven, he'd even put cream into it. If this wasn't love, it damn well should be.

"I was on my way for a run when I saw you out here."

"What the hell are you doing going for a run?"

"What the hell are you doing sitting out here in an old children's fort?"

Lucy shook her head at him. "I asked you first."

"I'm in training. Your turn."

"I'm in mourning."

"Is that why you look like crap? No offense."

Lucy let out a shocked little gasp of laughter. "I am so taking offense at that."

"Hmmm?" Richard crouched down at her side. He tilted forward and reached out with one hand to catch a tear from her cheek. His knees bracketed the side of her leg from hip to knee.

Lucy grew suddenly light-headed. He was awfully close. It would be laughably easy to lean slightly to her left. She would tuck her face into that sweet spot between his neck and his shoulder. His chest would be broad and impenetrable beneath her cheek. She would feel the warmth of his body as his arms closed around her. And everything would be all right.

"Lucy?" He frowned at her. Clueless as to what was going through her mind. "What are you doing out here in your pajamas?" He looked down at her legs and then turned his head to the side and looked some more. "Is that SpongeBob SquarePants?"

"Yes."

"And Patrick?"

"Yup."

"This is pretty desperate stuff, Luce." He took a sip of his coffee and nudged her cup to her lips. Lucy sipped obediently and cradled her hands around the warm ceramic. "Sitting out here in the snow in your Patrick pants and crying."

"What do you recommend?" Lucy gave a watery chuckle.

"A good, stiff shot of—" He stopped suddenly and looked stricken.

"I tried that." Lucy took another sip of the coffee. "It didn't work so well for me."

"Shit, Lucy, I'm sorry."

"Forget it." Lucy waved a hand dismissively. "I'm not going to go flying off on a five-day bender because somebody makes a remark." She sniffed and he handed her a dishcloth. Lucy took it with a laugh. She scrubbed her face with the cloth. "I'm feeling sorry for myself."

"So you decided freezing your ass off would be a suitable fate?"

He surprised a snort of laughter out of her. "No, I was getting some space. Dad is bad this morning."

"Yeah." He exhaled softly. "I tried having a talk with your mother yesterday. She doesn't seem to want to hear it."

"I know," Lucy said, shrugging. "Every time I try to get her thinking about making any sort of choices, she digs in her heels."

"Lucy"—he rapped her knee gently—"are you sure your mom wants to do something about this?"

"Nope." Lucy sipped her coffee and sighed. "She sounded so desperate on the phone. I thought if I came here, I could help her, be here for her to lean on, like I should have done all these years."

He took a sip of his coffee. "People have to want you to help them for that to work."

"Now you sound like Mads." Lucy laughed softly. "My sponsor," she told him when he gave her a questioning look. "She is always saying stuff like that to me."

He opened his mouth to speak and then shut it again. He'd done that before and she suddenly wanted to know.

"What?"

"Nothing." He shrugged, not at all convincingly, and Lucy continued to glare at him.

"What was it like?" he asked suddenly. "Getting sober."

"Pretty hellish," Lucy answered, grimacing. "But the worst part is staying sober. Being here"—she motioned to the house behind them—"brings all the stuff up again, all the reasons why I drank." He waited for her to say more. "Having to face up to all the stuff I did. What a total screwup I was. That's the hard part."

"You weren't that bad." He tried, but Lucy gave a snort of laugher.

"I was a nightmare."

"Okay," he said, grinning sheepishly. "There were certain parts of your past behavior that still make me want to break out into a cold sweat."

"Is that all?" Lucy said a little breathlessly as they skirted closer to dangerous territory.

"It wasn't all bad." His voice deepened slightly or perhaps it was her imagination, but Lucy forgot how to form a sentence. Not when he looked at her with those summer-sky eyes gentle on her face. She had been sure she'd banished that look from his eyes forever.

"You look tired." He reached out a finger and gently traced the dark patches under her eyes.

Lucy forgot to breathe. His touch against her skin was blissful.

His eyes grew dark and he didn't rush to take his fingers away, but traced the line of her cheekbone to the edge of her mouth. His focus narrowed onto the small spot occupied by his index finger.

"I'm not sleeping too well," she admitted.

"Don't be too hard on yourself, Lucy. I think if you look fast, you'll see that even we are becoming friends again." The blue of his eyes grew hotter, more intense. "Or something."

He felt it too. Lucy knew he did. The flame between them flared into life too bright and too hot for him not to be part of it. With a soft sound of something close to regret, he dropped his finger and took a sip of his coffee. It was a diversionary tactic, but it gave Lucy a chance to release the breath she'd been holding.

"I should go in," she murmured and got to her feet.

He stood with her.

Like this, they were mere inches apart, but neither of them increased the distance. They were close enough to touch. If he moved one arm, he could draw her closer against him. His eyes drifted over her face like a touch and flickered across her mouth. The frigid air grew heavier and lambent with forbidden thoughts and desires.

"So what happens now, Lucy Flint?" The loaded question hung heavily between them.

"Now," she said softly. "I finish doing what I came here to do, fix what I can, and go back to Seattle. And I try not to fuck up any more than I have already."

Chapter Thirteen

"Lucy?" She could hear by her mom's tone that something was wrong. She had been in the process of dealing with some of the accumulated clutter in her bedroom. It made her feel as if she were making some sort of progress. "Can you come down?" Her mother's voice rose at the end of the sentence. Something was very definitely up.

"Coming," she called. It couldn't be Carl; he was safely ensconced in his new chair and watching some TV show at an ear-splitting level.

Lucy got to her feet. She had been sitting for so long, her knees creaked as she stood. She trotted down the stairs and stopped.

Ashley stood in the hallway, but not looking anything like her memories of the other woman. Dressed in a severely cut black skirt and a silk blouse, she looked sleek and commanding. It was a little intimidating. Ashley's puppy fat had redistributed itself over her body into enough lush curves to make a forties pinup gnash her teeth. Next to Richard, this was the meeting she'd dreaded most. Hell really did have no fury like Ashley scorned.

"Hi." Lucy sounded like her mom as she greeted the other woman.

Ashley subjected her to the same minute scrutiny.

"Lucy." Her voice was the same, with a lacing of steel through its honeyed tones. There was nothing reassuring about the tone. Ashley didn't seem to have softened toward her in the least.

"Look who it is?" Lynne chirruped enthusiastically. "It's Ashley, Lucy. She's come to see you."

"Thanks, Mom." Lucy took the remaining stairs at a slower pace. The air between her and Ashley was so thick it clung to the inside of her throat. There was so much to be said, and yet none of it came to mind.

Lynne stood uncertainly between them, ringing her hands over and over like a dishcloth.

"Would you like something to drink?" Her mother peered anxiously at Ashley.

"No, thank you." Ashley gave Lynne a tight smile. "This will not take long. I came to see Lucy."

"Isn't that nice," Lynne said.

"Yes, Mom." Lucy moved past her mother. Ashley stood eye to eye with her, thanks to a nosebleed pair of red heels. Lucy motioned toward the living room. "Shall we?"

Damn, awkward didn't even cover this. Ashley stayed right on her heels as Lucy led the way.

They stopped just inside the room and Lucy motioned toward a chair.

Ashley shook her head. "I am not staying long." Her eyes narrowed slightly in an expression Lucy recognized. Mentally she got ready. Here it came. "I had to see for myself that it was actually you."

"Yes." Lucy cleared her throat. "My dad hasn't been too well. I am here to help my mother."

"Really?" Ashley's red mouth puckered up into a

tight bow. "I find the timing very interesting." She crossed her arms over her chest. "Richard and I are separated and Lucy Flint comes back to town."

"One thing has nothing to do with the other," Lucy said. She had a good sense where this was going. "I came back to help my mother. I didn't even know about you and Richard until I got here."

Ashley's mouth split into a derisive smile. "Of course you didn't," she drawled. "And I would believe you, Lucy. Except we both know that I know you a whole lot better than that."

Ashley had her there. They had been friends for so long. Long enough for everything to have gone so horribly wrong. Lucy was well aware what her part was in the ugly mess they'd made of their friendship.

"Used to know me." Lucy bit back the surge of hot denial. Losing her temper would not help this situation. "You and I haven't spoken in over ten years."

"Since you made it your mission to take Richard away from me." Ashley's nostrils flared slightly.

"I was in love with Richard," Lucy replied.

"Bullshit." Ashley's composure cracked a teeny bit, her eyes narrowed viciously at Lucy. "I had something and you wanted it. Like everything else I had."

It was such a one-sided view of the situation, but Lucy kept silent. This could deteriorate into a kindergarten scrap faster than she could blink. She was not going to go there.

"And now you are back to do the same again." Ashley took a step forward. The heel of her shoe resounded against the wooden floor. "I thought Brooke must be talking shit when she told me, but here you are." Long, lacquered fingernails swept Lucy from top to toe. "Here to do what you always do."

"I am not here to cause trouble." If she said it enough, Ashley might just let this go.

"I don't care what you say, Lucy." Ashley shook her head angrily. "I know what you are and I know what you want here." She took another step until they were almost nose to nose. The musky scent of Ashley's perfume filled the tiny space between them. "So, I am here to tell you, not this time, Lucy. You will not get away with your shit again."

"I am no—"

"You can't have Richard and you can't come back to town and mess with everybody's life again. I am giving you this warning." Ashley raised one of her red-tipped fingers. "And I will warn you only once. If you insist on staying here, fine, I can't stop you. But if you go near Richard, you will be very sorry."

Lucy was momentarily taken aback. "Threats, Ashley?" This was like being trapped in a soap opera.

"One warning." Ashley's eyes could burn a hole in her chest.

Lucy could see she was deadly serious. Some demon made her ask. "Or what?"

Ashley gave a reluctant huff of laughter. "I know things about you, Lucy."

"Shit, Ashley," Lucy said, shrugging. "I didn't exactly make a secret of my behavior. The whole of Willow Park knows things about me."

"All of it?" the other woman drawled.

The skin at the back of Lucy's neck prickled. Ashley was very sure of herself.

Ashley's smile turned predatory as she watched Lucy's face. "That's what I thought," she murmured.

Lucy watched her turn and stalk out of the room. Her mind cycled rapidly, so many mistakes and so many dirty little secrets. They all crowded around her brain and demanded to be heard. Lucy took a deep breath. She couldn't go there. She was not that girl anymore.

Ashley stuffed her arms into her coat. A smug smile tilted the corners of her bright, red mouth. Lucy had come home with some vague idea that she might be able to deliver an amends to Ashley. There would be no such conversation with Ashley. It made her sad. It also pissed her off. Ashley could give as good as she got. And she had. The door shut behind the other woman on an ominous bang.

"That was nice of her to visit." Her mom slipped into the room, worrying her fingers together.

Lucy murmured something noncommittal and escaped upstairs. She suddenly felt like she needed to take a shower. She needed to get rid of all that anger aimed her way.

"Ashley?" Richard blinked at his wife stupidly. He was sitting in the kitchen going through some admin when she let herself in. It irked him and it shouldn't have. This was Ashley's house too. He was the one who wanted her to come back to it.

She looked good as she slunk into the kitchen. Ashley had that way of moving like a pampered house cat, all voluptuous and slithery.

"Hello, Richard." She bent and kissed him on the cheek. Her perfume surrounded him. It was such a familiar Ashley smell that it made his chest ache a bit. She slid into the seat opposite him. "So, are you busy?"

"No." He pushed his laptop away from him. It was not like Ashley to drop by and shoot the shit. He studied her, searching for a clue. Since the day she'd walked out, Ashley tended to only communicate with him through her lawyer. It was one of the things that drove him batshit crazy. He knew if he could talk to her face to face, then he could get her to see things his way. Yet, here she was, sitting opposite him and not looking like she was going anywhere in a hurry and he couldn't think of a damn thing to say to her. "How are you?" It was so lame he almost cringed.

"I am good, Richard." She purred the *ch* sound through his name, like his mother did and she wasn't even French. "Busy getting ready for the San Francisco opening."

"That's great," he muttered. It wasn't great at all, but it seemed the right thing to say. It wasn't that he wasn't pleased for her success. He was proud as hell of what she'd achieved. It's that Ashley's stores had become all she cared about, until her marriage seemed a nasty intrusion on her working life.

"You hate my stores." She pulled a face at him.

"No, I don't," he answered truthfully. "I hate the way they took over our lives."

"Richard," she growled at him and rolled her eyes. "We are not going to have this argument again, are we?"

"I don't know, Ashley." He sat back and folded his arms over his chest. "Are we?"

Shit, it annoyed him when she dismissed him like that. This entire separation crap was about her career. He'd suggested they start a family and Ashley had gone into rapid retreat. She was getting her career started and she didn't want to be tied down.

He got that. He knew how hard it was to build something up from the ground. But it hadn't ended there. He had suggested they wait and that's when the kicker had come. Ashley didn't want to wait, because

Ashley didn't want children at all. It turned out Ashley didn't want to be married either.

Annoyance turned her brown eyes hard like onyx. Surprisingly, she had no blistering comeback for him. Something here was a bit off. Ashley appearing in his kitchen was one thing, but Ashley not rising to the bait was just plain weird. And then he got it.

"You're here because of Lucy." He knew he'd guessed right the minute he saw her mouth tighten and her chin thrust out toward him. He had no idea why he said it, but the words seemed to come right out of his mouth. "Aren't we all getting a bit old to be hanging on to our old grudges?"

"What the fuck does that mean?" she snarled and there was the girl he knew and loved.

Richard shrugged and kept it light. Lucy was a trip wire where Ashley was concerned. As far as strategy went, pissing her off now would be an epic fail. He softened his tone. "It means that it's history now. Lucy is here to help her mother."

"You've seen her?" Ashley's eyes narrowed.

"Of course I've seen her," he snapped, a bit exasperated. "I am her father's doctor."

"And now it's all let's forgive and forget?" Ashley's eyes glittered dangerously.

"It's not that, babe." He leaned across the table and took her hand. He needed to diffuse the situation before Ashley went into full-on meltdown. "I think she's changed."

"Don't be so fucking stupid." She jerked her hand against his grasp. Richard tightened his grip. "People like Lucy don't change."

He opened his mouth to argue and then snapped it shut. He'd said the same thing to Lucy only a couple of days ago. Lucy did seem to have changed. There was a maturity about her now, but he sure as shit was not going to tell Ashley that.

"I don't want to talk about Lucy." He changed tack quickly. Under his thumb, her ring finger was bare. He gently stroked the empty place where his ring had rested all these years. His gut tightened, but he kept it out of his voice. You got nowhere by going head to head with Ashley. "You're here, like I've been asking you to be, and I want to talk about us."

"Actually," she said, simmering right down again. That was the thing about Ashley, she got mad fast, but she cooled down as fast. "That is why I am here. I thought we could talk."

Richard felt his heart clench and miss a beat. She was here and she was listening. This was his chance to make his wife see that their marriage was worth saving. He shoved aside the tiny niggle in the back of his mind. This is what he wanted.

Chapter Fourteen

Lucy let herself out into the bright morning sunlight. Her eyes watered slightly against the bounce of light off the snow and she dug in her purse for her sunglasses. She took a deep pull on the fresh morning air.

"Hey, Lucy, wait up."

Just about forever if you wanted me to. The thought popped into her head, surprising her as she turned and watched Richard leap and slide his way through snow and ice toward her.

"*Luce?*"

"*Yes, Richie Rich?*"

"*You know you're my one, right?*"

"*Your one?*"

"*My one and only.*"

"*Wow, that's pretty major.*"

"*Isn't it, though?*"

"*You might have to keep reminding me that I'm your one.*"

"*Can do, Luce.*"

* * *

"Are you listening?" Richard frowned down at her. He seemed tense, not like he'd been the last time she'd seen him. Lucy wondered if Ashley had been paying more visits than the one to her.

"I'm sorry." Lucy tucked away the past with a light laugh. "I guess I'm not."

"Are you going somewhere?"

"I'm off to fetch the milk." Lucy tucked her hands into her coat. "It's about the only thing my mother will let me do for her."

Richard looked over her shoulder at the house. "I'll walk with you." He jerked his head in the direction of the house. "You know, Lynne still hasn't called me. I have been getting some information together for her."

"I know." Lucy sighed softly. It didn't surprise her at all. "I'm not sure she's ready." They trudged on in silence. "You may have been right," she said. "Maybe I did push her into this."

Richard stopped dead.

Lucy walked on a few steps before she realized that he was no longer with her. "What?"

A look of utter bemusement crossed his face. "Did Lucy Flint admit she might be wrong about something?"

"Don't be a dick, Richard." She laughed and turned to walk on a bit farther.

He caught up with her and matched his longer strides to hers. "Actually, I wanted to ask you something." Richard broke the silence. "Ashley came to see me the other day."

There you have it, then. Lucy's chest constricted. She wondered if that had been before or after Ashley had delivered her little ultimatum.

"Oh?" She kept all expression off her face.

"Yeah," he said, shrugging his broad shoulders. "We talked, it was good."

"Hmm." Lucy so did not want to be talking about Ashley, but Ashley was still Richard's wife. "Ashley is well?" Lucy stole a glance at Richard.

He stared straight ahead like a man with something on his mind. "She's great, better than ever."

He didn't look all that happy about it and Lucy stayed quiet.

"We must have sat up until three in the morning, talking and catching up," he said.

Lucy slid a bit on the ice and Richard caught her. Even through all the layers of winter padding, she was aware of his hand on her elbow.

"That's what I wanted to talk to you about," he said, and his face grew taut.

Lucy's gut clenched; this was drifting straight into that place angels fear to tread. "Really?" She tugged her elbow out of his light clasp and quickened her pace. "Richard, I have to say, I really am not comfortable talking about this."

"Ah." The silence stretched out uncomfortably between them. The air loaded to capacity and Lucy had a sick feeling he was only getting started. "I don't see how we can avoid it, Lucy."

She almost laughed out loud at that one. "Very easily," she replied. "I help with my dad, go back to Seattle, and we never have to talk about any of this again." And that should have been the end of it, but this was Richard Hunter she was dealing with: persistent, determined, and stubborn to his core. He was going somewhere with this and nobody was going to get in his way.

"Come on, Lucy." He pulled her to a stop. "I need

to ask you to do something for me. It's to do with that task you were talking about the other day."

"What?" The nasty feeling took up residence in the pit of her stomach.

"I want you to talk to Ashley." The impact of what he'd said took a moment to catch up with her. The breath rushed out of her lungs in a large plume of vapor.

"What did you say?" She couldn't have heard that right.

"I want you to talk to Ashley."

A laugh of disbelief burst out of her. "That's so not a good idea, Richard." She shook her head at him. "I am the last person on the planet Ashley wants to talk to, especially about you."

His gaze stayed locked on her. He was serious and he wasn't shifting from his position.

The bubble of incredulity expanded in her chest. "You can't be serious about this, Richard. It's the dumbest thing I've ever heard."

His eyes narrowed at her in irritation and he hastily closed the distance between them. "No, it's not," he insisted, his eyes blazed blue flame. "One of the things she said last night got me thinking. Ashley has this theory that she and I settled when we got married. Now, she wants more out of life and she is telling me I want more too." He gave a bitter laugh and shook his head. "She thinks I should find what I had with you. Actually, she thinks I have never felt about anyone the way I felt about you."

"Richard, I really have nothing—"

"Fuck." He dropped his head forward and Lucy caught the woodsy scent of his shampoo. "Of course, I don't feel like that anymore. We were kids, it was a kids' kind of love."

Lucy bit down hard on her back teeth. She barely stopped the flinch in time.

"We were crazy and wild about each other, but that's not how mature and rational people fall in love." He was not being deliberately cruel, but it took pieces out of her bit by bit anyway. "I mean"—his tone gentled slightly—"I don't think it's in me to lose myself in another person like that again and, frankly, who the hell wants to? I am sure you agree?"

No, Lucy wanted to yell. She had spent most of her adult life searching for the same kind of love. She wanted it with every part of her. She could say none of that to him, so she walked on a few steps.

"You are the best person to do this." He followed her again. "You are the only one who can tell her there is no more 'us.'" He caught her by the elbow. "I need you to tell her we are well and truly finished, because it is bullshit. I am not still hung up on you, Lucy. I am not."

"You tell her." Lucy yanked away from him. It shouldn't hurt so much to hear spoken what she already knew.

"I have told her," he insisted. "She uses you as the main reason she won't come back to me." He pursued her and there was no mistaking the anger in his voice or the sharp tension etched along his jawline. "I can't lose my marriage, Lucy. I refuse to. I got married for better or for worse and I am going to stay that way."

"Ashley hates me." Her voice was strangely dead. "I'm sorry, Richard, but I can't do it."

"You mean you won't do it." He grabbed his cap from his head and bunched it into his gloved fist. "But you could make her see reason. You could do that for me."

Words failed her and she shook her head in denial.

His hands fastened on her upper arms and Lucy looked up reflexively. His eyes raged at her, full of the frustration of a man who was watching his carefully constructed world crumble at his feet. "You could make her listen to you."

Lucy shook her head mutely, but his grip tightened as if he could somehow force her to see his point of view. "If you told her there will never be anything between us again, then she would listen and maybe we could get back together again." And then he went for the kill. "You owe me this much, Lucy."

He spoke it softly enough, but it roared through her like a storm. Lucy felt everything in her still. Her heart stopped beating and her lungs caught halfway through her gasp of shock. *Breath in, breath out, Lucy— breathe in, breathe out.*

"I need you to do this."

He was drowning, she could see it, and he was reaching out to her. Using any weapon at his disposal, rightly or wrongly, fairly or unfairly, he was going to do this.

"I can't," she whispered, the misery rising up to choke her. She walked away quickly.

"So, this is how much you've changed?" he called after her. Lucy didn't turn. She did not want him to see how deeply his words cut. "You come back here with all sorts of good stories and words. Yet I ask you to do this one thing for me and you say no."

She wanted to turn and tell him all about Ashley's visit, but she couldn't do that. Richard wanted his marriage back and she was not going to cause any more conflict between them. It was not what she was here to do.

* * *

"Wow." Mads went momentarily speechless. Lucy knew it wouldn't last long. No matter how much she wished it to. "That is seriously fucked up, Lucy."

"Tell me something I don't know." She flopped back onto her bed and stared at the ceiling. The faded marks where Day-Glo stars had once littered the ceiling stared back at her.

"What was he thinking?" Mads sighed.

"He's desperate," Lucy replied. If she turned her head she could catch a glimpse of Richard's bedroom window. "You know, Mads, I thought I was going to come here and look at Richard and be able to say good-bye. I expected to look at him and see the shadow of the boy I was in love with and be able to walk away, happy it was all settled and the chapter was closed."

"You were that naïve?"

"So you anticipated this?" Lucy couldn't keep the acid out of her tone. "Some kind of warning would have been nice."

"Come on, Lucy." Mads wouldn't let her have a good wallow. "Get real and give yourself a break. You've been in love with this man since you were eighteen. There would be something seriously wrong with you if you got to Willow Park and all of a sudden it's some kind of faded memory. Of course you were going to feel stuff."

Lucy nodded her head in agreement, as if Mads were in the room with her. A shadow flitted in the dim recesses of the room across from hers. Richard was home. She turned her head away. No more looking out of windows and aching. "Mads, what if it's not just stuff? What if it's not some sort of nostalgia?"

"What are you saying, Lucy Locket?"

"I don't know what I'm saying." Lucy dragged in a deep breath. "This place screws with my head."

"When are you coming home?" Mads asked, concern etched into her voice. "I think it's time to get you out of there. You about done?"

"Nope." She sighed again. "I have to try and sort out something with my mother and then I can come home."

"How's that going?"

"Shit. She keeps dodging the subject."

Mads heaved another large sigh. "That is also fucked up. Are you sure she wants things to change?"

"Not you, too." Lucy stared at the unresponsive ceiling. "Richard said the same thing."

"Well?"

"No, I'm not sure, but how can anyone be happy living with this bastard?"

"I think you wouldn't be happy living with that bastard."

"Too true." Lucy simmered down a bit. "I don't see how she can continue to live like this and if she wants out, I have to try and help her."

"Get it done and come back, Lucy, as soon as you can. I'm worried about you in that situation."

Lucy was worried about herself too, so it wasn't too hard to agree.

Chapter Fifteen

Lucy looked around her bedroom and sighed.
Enough. It was like a graveyard to her lost youth.
She constructed the cardboard packing box. Since
yesterday morning, Richard was back to being aloof
with her. She should have told him about Ashley's
visit, then maybe he would understand, but it felt
sneaky and divisive. She needed to do something.
Sorting her room felt like something she could change,
an action she was able to take.

Her mother hadn't thrown away a damn thing. She
wouldn't be entirely surprised to find some moldy,
half-eaten piece of pizza lovingly tucked away in
Lynne's obsessive orderliness. FOOD THAT LUCY LEFT
UNDER HER BED would be the label of the box and it
might fit right here between LUCY'S DANCE SHOES and
LUCY'S ARTS AND CRAFTS. The museum of Lucy took up
most of her old bedroom. It had long ago spilled out
of the wardrobe and crept out from beneath the bed
to take up floor space.

Her mom had balked at the idea of throwing anything away and it was only by promising her mother
she would have the final say that Lucy finally got

permission to start sorting. The house was full of piles like this and they cried out to be gotten rid of. It was all perfectly orderly, but it would be the first thing a Realtor would insist on. When they got around to actually calling one. That, however, was a battle for another day. Lucy still hadn't managed to get Lynne to even let a Realtor through the door.

Lucy pulled one of the plastic packing crates toward her and pried off the lid. The smell of cedar rose from the clothing within.

"What have you got there?" Lynne appeared in the door with a tea tray.

Lucy consulted the neatly stenciled label on the front of the box. "HALLOWEEN COSTUMES," she confirmed.

"You aren't going to throw those away, are you?"

Lucy eyed the plate piled with date squares on the tray. Lynne's homemade date squares were as close to heaven on earth as she could imagine. If she stayed here much longer, she was going to have to dig out clothes in a larger size.

Lucy opened the box in front of her. All the costumes were neatly packed, still in the plastic wrapping from the dry cleaner. They were in order from the most recent to her very first Halloween. A spider, if she remembered correctly. Every one painstakingly and lovingly made by Lynne.

Whatever she wanted to be, Lynne would make it happen. Crafting the most exquisite costumes for her ultimately ungrateful offspring to lead the candy charge around Willow Park. And lead it she had. With Ashley firmly to her right, Lucy had made sure she owned Halloween.

"These are beautiful, Mom." She took out the top one, carefully opening the plastic. Glenn Close had made an awesome Cruella De Vil and Lucy had made an even better one. Not for Lucy, one of those store-bought, cheap costumes. "But I think we should let them go," Lucy said over her shoulder. Lynne was sitting on her bed, watching the proceedings, but not wanting to take part.

"Oh no, Lucy. Those are beautiful. You said so."

"Yes, they are," Lucy agreed quietly. "And it's a shame to let them grow old and faded in this box. Imagine how much joy these can give to another kid?"

"But those are yours," Lynne protested.

"I don't think I will be wearing this one anytime soon." Lucy held up a pint-size rendering of a bear. "And if they are mine, then I elect to give them to some other kids who can enjoy them."

Lynne looked mulish.

"You went to all that work, Mom. It's wasted in this box."

"Do what you like. They are yours." *Rip my heart out and stamp all over it, open a main artery and laugh as I bleed.* Lynne clattered around with tea mugs and side plates.

Lucy almost caved and put the box back onto the stack. Lynne had worked so hard to please her. There were three boxes of costumes. Some years, Lucy had been unable to make up her mind and Lynne had whipped up another minor miracle. God, but she had been a little shit.

Lucy held up a perfect mermaid tail in glittery blue fabric that she'd never worn. "Hell, Mom, look at all the work in this." The tail was encrusted with tiny jewels and beads that made it glitter and move like scales. "It must have taken you hours."

"It did." Lynne smiled mistily at the costume.

"And I never even wore it." Lucy put the costume

back in the box. "What a waste. You should have told me no when I changed my mind."

"Oh, Lucy." Lynne fluttered a hand at her. "You were never very good at hearing no." She gave a small, indulgent laugh. "I wanted to make you happy, Lu Lu."

Lucy forced a smile, but her chest tightened. She'd grown up hearing that phrase. All her mother ever wanted was to make the people around her happy. Inside, Lucy writhed and twisted impotently. The sensation of being stuck in cotton candy took over again. It was sweet and appeared harmless, but every instinct insisted on fight or flight.

Lynne slumped in a miserable huddle on the bed. She looked as if Lucy were tearing off pieces of her and putting them out in the hallway to be disposed of. Lucy felt like the worst kind of bitch.

"It's just stuff, Mom," Lucy tried to explain gently. "The important part is the memories and the time we shared."

Lynne's spine snapped to attention. "It is not just stuff." Her voice shook slightly. "It's important to me." Lynne got to her feet and smoothed the coverlet where she had been sitting.

"I didn't mean it that way, Mom." Lucy kept her tone soothing. "I think it's time to let go of baggage and move forward."

Lynne shook her head and frowned as she looked around the bedroom, her eyes scanning every small detail. "You want to walk away from the past, because you don't like what you see there. I don't feel the same."

"But it's gone. It's in the past." Lucy teetered on a verbal tightrope.

"I treasure the past, every single moment." Lynne dabbed at her eyes. "This room represents some of the happiest times of my life and now you want to throw it away like garbage."

"I didn't say it was garbage." Lucy blinked at Lynne in amazement. Lynne, who would make a new costume on Lucy's smallest whim, wanted to die on the hill of old costumes and faded memories. And the memories were not that good. Not from where Lucy was standing. "And I don't want to walk away from the past. I want to make peace with it."

"What does that even mean?" Lynne tossed her hand in the air in exasperation. "Things weren't so bad for you here. You wanted something and you got it. I loved you. I gave you everything. And now you say you want to make peace with it, like it was some dreadful time, like one of those people you read about or see on television."

"It's not that simple." Lucy searched for a way to explain.

Her mother stood with her shoulders hunched like a wounded thing and Lucy's heart squeezed in her chest. It was as if they were looking at two different versions of the past and Lucy had no idea how to say what she wanted to say without causing more hurt. Again, that choking feeling grabbed the muscles in her throat.

Words failed her and she watched as Lynne straightened the scatter pillows on top of her bed. Heart-shaped pillows, beautifully sewn for her by Lynne. It was a perfect pink, white, and red bower of a bed for a teenage princess. Everything in this room was for a princess, everything her secret heart could desire, made by Lynne for Lucy. A little tendril of truth broke away and floated to the surface of her mind. She had stayed away because of Carl, certainly.

But she had also stayed away because of Lynne and this, the burden of her constant ingratitude.

"It's not that simple," Lucy repeated, more quietly this time.

"Yes, it is that simple," Lynne tucked her hands into the opposite wrists of her cardigan, like a child. "You were loved and you had everything. I don't understand any of this."

"Mom—" And Lucy stopped short. She didn't have the right words to explain. Not without breaking her mother in two and she shut her mouth again. "It's to do with me being an alcoholic." It was such a cop-out she nearly winced at herself.

"What the hell are you doing?" Carl appeared in the doorway.

He looked like hell. His pajamas hung about his frame and were dirty and stained. Knowing Lynne, it must have been a battle of monumental proportions for Carl to still be wearing soiled clothing. His face was unshaven and gray, straggly beard dotted his chin and cheeks. All about his head, his hair stood up like a mad scientist's. He looked certifiable, glaring balefully at her from bloodshot eyes.

"What are you trying to do?" His eyes darted over the small pile of plastic crates. "What is all this stuff? This is mine, isn't it? You are throwing my stuff away." Her father had grown old and pitiful and Lucy's heart contracted painfully.

"Carl." Lynne uttered his name as a sort of animal moan, but he ignored her and focused his feverish gaze back on Lucy.

"What are you doing with my things? These are my things."

"They are old Halloween costumes of mine," Lucy said gently. She got up and stepped out into the hall.

His hard, accusing eyes followed her movements as she bent and opened the nearest crate. "See, Dad?" She held up the mermaid. "Old Halloween costumes."

"You're trying to get rid of me, aren't you?"

"What is it, Dad? What are you saying?" Lucy threw a quick glance at Lynne, but her mother wrung her hands and sent her a plea with her eyes. "Nobody's trying to get rid of you, Dad."

"You lie." Spittle collected around the corners of his mouth and his eyes narrowed viciously. "You can't lie to me." He took a few steps toward her and Lucy retreated. "I know why you are here. I've heard you talking and talking. Trying to get rid of me."

Lynne shook her head frantically in denial and Lucy took a deep, careful breath. "Dad." She gestured toward the open box. "Take a look. These are boxes of my old Halloween costumes. I thought I might take them to the Salvation Army."

"And where will you take me?"

"Pardon?"

"I heard you, whispering to her." He jerked his head in Lynne's direction. "Saying things about me so that she wants to get rid of me too."

"Carl?" Lynne covered her mouth with her hand. "How can you say such things? Lucy is your daughter, she only wants what is best for you. We're a family, we take care of each other."

Lynne threw Lucy for a loop with that one. *No*, she wanted to shout. *We were never that family.*

"Shut up," Carl said, rounding on Lynne.

Lucy swallowed the quick, sharp rush of anger and she clenched her fists together. It did no good to strike out in reaction. *Keep it cool, think, Lucy, don't react, think.*

"I don't want to hear your lies." Carl turned his venom back on Lucy.

It was easier when he picked on her and Lucy relaxed her fists. Lynne retreated into a wounded silence and Lucy stepped between Carl and the open doorway to give Lynne a moment to recover.

"You think you can get rid of me." His feverish eyes tracked every move she made. "But I'll get rid of you first. You can't come back here. We don't want you here."

It shouldn't have hurt, but it did, like a rusty blade to the gut. Lucy knew this about her father. Yes, he was sick and losing his wits, but he had never wanted her, never wanted a girl. She had spent her entire youth trying to be the boy he wanted. It had been a wasted effort. She kept her face blank. He would never see the marks he made with his cruel words. It was a habit so ingrained Lucy didn't even have to try. The mask descended over her features like a curtain.

"That's not true." Lynne bustled around her and confronted Carl. "We do want her here. You miss her when she's away."

"Miss her?" Carl jeered. "Miss the drama and the tears and the performances? Don't be stupid, woman. You were always blind to what she was, but I saw right through you." He turned back to Lucy, his face flushed. "I see right through to the rotten core of you and I know you."

"No, Dad, you don't." Lucy didn't know much, but this she knew for sure. Her father didn't even have a clue. Even now in his illness-driven malice, she was a stranger to him. And for once, Lucy was glad of it. This way, his power to hurt her was limited.

"You are not my daughter." He pointed a shaking hand at her, like some caricature of a patrician father.

"Oh, I am that." Lucy's face twisted into a rictus of a smile. "I don't think either of us is delighted about it, but we can't change the facts now."

"Get out." Carl stumbled toward her.

Lucy backed away. Carl looked wild and out of control and her gut clenched nervously.

His mouth worked feverishly, his eyes had lost their focus. "Get out of my house."

"Lucy." Lynne's eyes were wide in her face. "He doesn't know what he is saying."

"I think he does." Lucy's control teetered precariously. The malice on Carl's face sent loud alarms screaming through her brain.

Carl moved closer until he was almost upon her. Lucy stepped back toward the stairs, but he kept coming. "I don't want you here." His jaw split into a manic grin. "I never wanted you here."

"Carl!" Her mom was sobbing, but Lucy was aware of the stairs right behind her and she kept her eyes locked on her father.

"OUT," Carl bellowed, his fetid breath hitting her face in a damp, nauseating wave. His face contorted with rage. Her father's features wavered in front of her eyes, misty and unsubstantial. *No,* a voice whimpered in the back of her mind, *not again.*

She looked over to her mother, desperately trying to anchor the growing fear.

Lynne had both hands clapped over her mouth, her eyes wide with horror.

Carl's hand shot out and gripped her arm. Lucy tried to wriggle free, but he was stronger than he looked and he gave her a shove toward the stairs. *I always win,* his eyes glittered at her. His eyes loomed larger and larger in front of her. It was there, the desire to hurt and to punish. A voice screamed in her mind and Lucy's breathing quickened.

The ground beneath her foot was suddenly not there. Lucy slipped down three stairs before she grabbed the balustrade and stopped her fall. Her arm wrenched in the socket as she clutched the wood beneath her desperate fingers. The stair beneath her feet felt insubstantial and treacherous. Her heart pounded loudly in her ears, her knees had turned to rubber as she clung to the banister and watched him take two steps toward her. Lynne screamed, but Lucy could barely make out the words. Her mind skewed desperately back to another place and another man. She couldn't breathe. She was choking. Her vision flickered black around the edges.

Run! Lucy turned, her feet taking the stairs two at a time. She didn't stop for a coat, but hurtled through the front door, her heart pounding so loudly she could hear nothing else. *Get away,* the blood pounded in her ears. *Run, Lucy, run.*

The air hit her like a slap in the face, but Lucy barely felt it. The pavement was icy beneath her feet as she scrambled. Her footing went out from under her and she hit the ground with a bone-jarring thud. She tasted the coppery tang of blood in her mouth, but she didn't stop. She crawled back to her feet. She must escape.

A large form materialized out of the dark in front of her and Lucy screamed. The form moved and she brought her hands up to shield her head.

Chapter Sixteen

"Lucy?"

Hands on her arms, confining her and stopping her from getting away. Not this time. She wouldn't let it happen again. She was stronger now. Lucy kicked out. Her foot slipped again on the ice and she almost fell.

"Lucy, stop."

The hands prevented her from falling. Strong arms enfolded her against a hard chest. She wrenched her head free. She couldn't breathe.

"Lucy, don't make me shake you, baby."

Richard.

Her mind did another dizzying whirl and she stopped. Her breath caught in her throat and her head dropped forward onto his chest. She smelled sweat and Richard and she dragged the comfort into her lungs.

"What the fuck happened?" he asked.

She heard her mother's voice, but Lucy couldn't frame the sound into words. Beneath her ear, his heartbeat pounded slow and sure. Richard spoke again, a deep rumble through the breadth of his chest. She felt numb. She was aware of her feet moving, being steadily propelled forward. The cold crept around the edges of her perception and she shivered. Her teeth chattered in her head.

Lucy looked up.

Richard's face was set and grim. The details started to drop into place. He led her, half-carried her, toward his house. Lucy's chest constricted. She'd totally freaked out and she'd done it right in front of Richard. She wanted to run and hide, but his hold on her was firm and unrelenting.

"I'm okay now." Her voice sounded stronger than she felt.

"Bullshit." He marched her up the porch and through the front door. Lucy found herself in his kitchen again, being gently, but firmly, shoved into a chair. "Stay there," he said. His face was streaked with perspiration. Lucy took in the workout gear, the sweat making it cling to his body. He must have been out running again.

"Richard." She cleared her throat. "I really am fine."

His mouth tightened and he shook his head. "Stay there." His voice brooked no argument. "I am going to see what I can do for your mom, but you stay there."

Her mother. Lucy shot out of her chair as she realized she'd left Lynne there with that crazy old bastard.

Richard stepped right in front of her. "Sit."

Lucy's knees folded beneath her.

"I'm going over to see what's happening, but you need to stay right here."

The door slammed behind him and Lucy felt the silence in the kitchen press down on her. She propped her elbows on the table. Her hands were still shaking. Fuck. She had totally and completely lost it.

She hadn't done that in years. It was this place. Being here was going to drive her out of her fucking mind.

She wanted a drink, but she knew she wouldn't have one. The need to run and keep running had her halfway out of her chair. She could leave while Richard was still in there with her parents. She could get in her car and drive, but where?

Lucy shook her head and sat down again. She knew she wasn't going to do that either. Her knee ached and she bent to examine it. Her jeans were ripped and blood seeped out, staining the fabric around the tear. She must have done that when she fell. When she fell running out of the house like a crazy woman. Carefully she tugged the sides of the rip apart to assess the damage. It wasn't a deep cut, more of a bad graze.

She wondered what Richard was doing over at her house. With a groan she dropped her forehead onto the table. Way to go convincing him she was the new and improved Lucy. She'd dragged him into another one of those scenes he hated so much. She should never have come back here. It had seemed so right when she and Mads talked it over. It was going to shit so fast it made her head spin. Tears pricked the back of her eyelids and she raked in a hard breath. She couldn't cry, she couldn't.

Time dragged by, but Lucy focused on her breathing. The faint scent of almonds rose from the wood beneath her face and she grabbed onto that small detail. Drawing in the calming air and letting the ball in her chest unravel as she breathed out again.

She heard the door open and she sat up.

Richard stalked into the kitchen, his face carved into grim lines. The silence stretched between them as he walked over to the faucet and poured a glass of water. He brought it over to the table and set it in front of her.

"Is my mother all right?"

"She's fine," he said curtly. "I had to give your dad something to calm him down." He ran an impatient hand through his hair. "I have to take a shower and then we'll talk."

It was the last thing she wanted to do and Lucy started to rise to her feet. One look made her sink back down again.

"I should go," she protested.

"No." Richard had a look on his face that promised questions, questions she really did not want to answer.

"I won't be long," he said and left the kitchen.

She was alone with her lunatic thoughts again. She glanced around her for distraction. The kitchen was as immaculate as ever.

He must have had the world's fastest shower, because he was back in the kitchen before she had time to formulate a cohesive set of answers. He was in another pair of disreputable track pants and a T-shirt, his hair wet and slicked back against his head. He didn't speak, but knelt in front of her. Lucy wondered what he was doing, before she felt his hand grasp her calf as he peered at her knee.

"It's nothing," she said, dismissing the scratch.

Richard didn't seem to hear her as he examined the wound carefully.

Lucy wriggled beneath his clasp. He really was making too much of it. "I've had worse."

He sucked in a deep breath and looked at her. "That was my next question."

"It's nothing, Richard." She shifted her leg out of the warm hold of his hand. "My dad got aggressive with me and I had a meltdown."

"You're lying, Lucy." He got up and moved back to the counter. He found some swabs and a tube of antiseptic ointment. He put warm water in a bowl and came back to where she sat.

Lucy hissed in a sharp breath as he cleaned the scrape. He kept his head bent. His hair was drying, curling up slightly at the edges. Lucy wanted to reach out and touch the softness of those curls. Richard had always kept his hair short because he hated those curls. He worked in silence, smoothing ointment over her wound.

"Do you think I'll live?" She tried to lighten the mood.

Richard grunted and rose fluidly to his feet and sat opposite her. His eyes searched her face intently.

"Your dad is getting worse, you know?" He clasped his hands together in front of him on the table. Richard had long, elegant fingers and Lucy stared at them. "I recommended a center I know. It's nearby and he can stay as an outpatient or live in. I'll write up my assessment and send it to Lynne in the morning. I tried to talk to your mother tonight, but she's very upset."

"No kidding?" Lucy huffed. "I've never seen him like that. He was like a complete stranger." They were drifting closer to that place she did not want to go. Lucy talked to fill the silence. "I mean, you know he's never been the most charming man around, but nothing like this."

"Lucy?" he cut across her babbling. She snapped her mouth shut. "Your dad is sick and we can do something about that, but I want to know what the fuck happened to you out there."

"I told you—"

"Lucy." He leaned forward. "What happened?"

His eyes bored into the back of her head. He was

not going to back down and Lucy sighed. She so did not want to go there.

"It was a while ago." She dropped her eyes and pressed the palms of her hands into her eyes. She hated talking about this. "I'm over it." *Which is why you went apeshit tonight,* her mind whispered. Lucy gave a short laugh and looked at him.

She could see the same thought in his eyes.

"For the most part, I'm over it." She drew a shaky breath.

He watched and waited.

"I don't know what happened." She shrugged and clasped her hands together on the table. Two inches separated her hands from Richard's and she realized she'd unconsciously mimicked his pose. "My dad started to get aggressive and suddenly I'm right back there." She met his gaze and held it. Concern darkened his eyes to indigo. "Something like tonight hasn't happened in a really long time."

"Who was this guy? Jason?"

Lucy almost laughed at that. "No," she said hastily. "Jason had lots of charming quirks, mostly around not being able to keep his dick in his pants, but he never hurt me. Not physically."

Richard looked down at his hands for a long while. He stretched his fingers out until they touched hers. The smallest brush with the very tips of his fingers, but the warmth spread over her entire hand. Her fingers relaxed and he slid his between hers and tangled them lightly together.

"No matter how angry I was," he spoke at last, "I would never have wished that on you."

"Me neither." Lucy shrugged. "But it's a strange thing, because in the end it was what got me sober.

I had to go that low before I could claw my way up again."

His fingers tightened around hers. "How low?" His voice was a soft growl.

"I'm not going to get into the details with you."

Richard's face tightened.

He was not happy about that, but Lucy shook her head. The details were unimportant anyway. "His name was Peter and he was fun and exciting and he never judged me on how much I drank. Not such a nice guy as it turns out. A bit too quick with his fists."

Richard drew in a soft, harsh breath.

Lucy smiled ruefully. "He wasn't nearly as ready to put up with my shit and my drama as you were."

"Lucy?" His voice was so tender it almost undid her control.

Lucy pulled away. She couldn't risk the touch, not with her soul laid bare. "Peter put me in the hospital in the end."

Richard closed his eyes as if hearing the words pained him.

"That's where Mads found me and dragged me back into the land of the living."

"Mads?"

"My sponsor." Lucy smiled. Mads, her sponsor, life-line, and biggest nag.

"Luce?" Richard's eyes were unguarded and stripped bare of pretense. "You shouldn't have had to go through that shit."

"No," Lucy agreed, unable to look away from his stark honesty. "But I was drinking and so was Peter. He was a mean drunk."

"I wish I'd known. I—"

"What?" Lucy cut him off. "There was nothing

anyone could do. It was my battle and I had to fight it alone."

"I'm sorry." He took her hand again. "I'm sorry you got hurt." He raised her hand slowly and pressed his mouth into the palm. His lips were warm against her skin.

Lucy's fingers folded over the place he'd kissed as if she could hold the warmth in.

"I never thought of you as being in trouble." He frowned down at her hand.

"I know that." Lucy blinked at his bent head. "None of this is your fault. It's all on me and I can live with that."

Richard absorbed that in silence for a long while.

"I shouldn't have asked you to talk to Ashley." He spoke so suddenly, Lucy started slightly.

"No, you shouldn't," she agreed.

Richard gave her a wry smile.

It tugged at something deep within her. "Ashley doesn't want to hear it from me. I could only make things worse for you."

"I was reaching," he said, shrugging one shoulder.

"Reach in another direction," she suggested and he gave a short bark of laughter.

"So, you won't talk to Ashley and we're good?"

"Or something?" Lucy agreed. She tugged her hand out of his light clasp. "I should go home."

"You're going back there?" His forehead creased into a frown.

"My mom is there." Lucy didn't want to go back into that house, but her alternatives were not looking huge right now. "You said you had him calmed down?"

Richard nodded.

"And I know he's sick." She spoke with a lot more confidence than she felt. "He's never done anything like this before."

"You could stay here?" Richard suggested, but Lucy could see him regret the suggestion even before it had hit the air.

"No, I couldn't." She shook her head and got slowly to her feet. Her knee felt sore and bruised, but not even sore enough for a decent limp.

"Lucy?" Unspoken thoughts and feelings crowded into the small space between them. He wanted to touch her, she could read the intention in his eyes, but she couldn't let him. It would shatter what little composure she'd managed to regain.

He reached for her, but Lucy stepped away. His hand dropped back to his side. "I'll walk you home and make sure everything is all right."

Chapter Seventeen

Carl was already sleeping when Lynne let them back into the house. Her mother's face was drawn and pale. Her eyes searched Lucy's face, but neither of them had much to say. In the end, Lucy gave her mom a quick hug and went back upstairs. She could hear the low murmur of Richard's voice and then the door shut.

Silence descended over the house and Lucy let out a huge breath. It was still early in Seattle and she desperately needed to talk to Mads.

Lucy woke the next morning feeling wrung out, but resolved. Mads had wanted to hop on the next flight when she heard the story. Lucy knew the feeling. Her head and her emotions were in a dangerous place. She had barely managed to stop Mads from flying to the rescue, but they had agreed on one thing. It was time to do what she had come here to do and get out. She would focus on her list of amends and get it done. She couldn't even think about her mother or Carl. It was too big for her right now. The possibility of failure jeered at her.

She found Lynne, as per usual, in the kitchen. It

was past Carl's breakfast time, so Lynne was eating her own meal and making one of her neat lists of things to do for the day.

Lucy was almost dizzy with the relief of not having to deal with her father right now.

"Good morning." Lynne looked up when Lucy entered.

"Lu Lu?" Lynne's voice wobbled. "Are you all right?"

"I'm fine, Mom." Lucy managed a fairly convincing smile.

Lynne looked partially relieved, but worry lurked in her faded eyes. "Your father is not himself." Her mother frowned and picked at the edge of her list with her fingernail. "He would never hurt you if he was. You know that don't you, Lu Lu?"

"Sure, Mom." Lucy eased onto one of the stools in front of the counter. Her shoulder was stiff from where she had grabbed the staircase and her knee felt bruised and sore this morning. "But he is getting worse."

"Only since you came," Lynne said. She must have realized what she was saying, because her eyes grew huge. "Not that I am saying any of this is your fault." Lynne leapt to her feet and started pulling things out of the refrigerator. "I know he's been difficult, but I have never seen him do anything like he did last night."

Eggs, milk, and cheese hit the counter. Lynne whirled and clattered through her pot collection beneath the counter. "I spoke to Richard and he says he can give your father something that will help him not to get so angry." Lynne cracked eggs into the pan. "He said that things will be fine if Carl takes his medication."

"Richard said that?" Lucy wished her mother would

stop scraping the metal fork against the bottom of the pan. It was making her teeth ache.

"Not exactly," Lynne murmured quickly. "But I am sure it will." The fork kept scraping against the pan as Lynne's voice grew higher. "And if you were to try to stay away from him, everything will be fine again."

Lucy opened her mouth to argue.

Lynne grated cheese into the eggs, her hands moving so fast they were almost a blur.

Lucy studied her mother's face. It was set and determined. "You know there are alternatives?" she said instead.

"I can't talk about those now." Lynne's lips quivered and she pressed them together in a white line. "I don't even want to think about those."

"Then what am I doing here, Mom?" Lucy stared at her mother helplessly.

"You're here for a visit," Lynne stated with flat determination. "And when you go home, Carl will settle down and we will go back to how we were before."

"But, Mom," Lucy said, struggling to find the right words, "you were not happy about things before. You called me and told me that Dad was sick. That's why I came here."

"Is it?" Lynne's eyes were sharp and keen as she looked at Lucy.

"Why else?" Lucy blinked at her mother, absolutely floored.

"Because that is not what people are saying." Lynne turned away and grabbed a plate from the cupboard.

Lucy could guess what people were saying.

Lynne scraped the contents of the pan onto the plate. She put it in front of Lucy with a fork.

Lucy stared at the eggs, her stomach rebelled, and

she took the fork from her mother and laid it beside the plate. "What are they saying?"

"It doesn't matter." Lynne put the kettle on. "You know, Lucy"—Lynne didn't turn around—"when you go back to Seattle, your father and I will still live in this community."

"Yes, I know." Lucy started to get a glimmer of where this was going. The smell of the eggs turned her stomach and Lucy pushed the plate away.

"And I know that a whole lot of gossip would upset your father more. He is so very fragile right now." Lynne made a face and poured water over a tea bag. "I want you to keep that in mind."

Carl's grip on her arm had been anything but fragile. Her mother was blithely ignoring the possibility that it could be her next time Carl went over the edge. Okay, she got that her reaction had been extreme and had very little to do with Carl, but Lynne was floating in a cloud of denial right now.

Lynne had moved on to something else and that was what she was gnawing at this morning. There were times, and this was one of them, when Lucy fervently wished they could dispense with the bloody rituals of preparation and Lynne could get to what was on her mind. But that was not her mother's way and Lucy sat patiently through the preparation of tea. She accepted her mug with thanks and waited.

"I am not saying I believe what people are saying," Lynne assured her, but she was frowning down at the counter. "But I do think that Richard is awfully protective of you. And the way you ran over there last night will give people lots of fodder for gossip."

"So, they're talking about me and Richard?" Lucy felt the old, familiar surge of rebellion.

"What did you expect?" Lynne blinked at her.

"You come back, after all this time. Richard and Ashley are separated. People are bound to put two and two together."

"Mom," Lucy said, hauling back on the desire to swear at the lot of them, "you know they are reaching the wrong conclusion, right?"

"Of course I do." Lynne waved her hand through the air, but she sounded a little too fervent.

Doubt gnawed at the edges of Lucy's mind. It had not occurred to her that her mother might think she was back for the same reasons as Ashley and, apparently, most of Willow Park thought she was back.

"Richard happened to be running past last night." She didn't want to explain herself. She wanted to hotly declare her innocence and then rush out and do something to really make them talk. "We needed help and he gave it to us."

"I know that," Lynne hastened to assure her, but Lucy was far from convinced. "I am telling you what people are saying and that you should be careful."

"Okay." Lucy watched as Lynne started cleaning the pan. Last night and Carl were already swept under the rug, as far as Lynne was concerned. Anger darkened the edges of Lucy's vision as she stared at the congealing plate of eggs. She wanted to hurl it across the kitchen and storm out. The stool scraped loudly against the floor as she stood. "I think I'll take a walk."

"But, Lucy?" Lynne protested from behind her. "You haven't eaten a thing."

"I'm not hungry." Lucy shoved her arms into the sleeves of her coat and hunted for her boots. She had never wanted to yell at her mother more.

"Are you getting sick?"

Lucy yanked open the door. Cold air took some of the burn out of her cheeks. She closed it behind her.

Chapter Eighteen

Richard watched from his kitchen window as Lucy climbed the front steps to her parents' house. This was becoming a stupid habit. He couldn't drag his eyes away, though.

Her long legs ate up the distance as she strode toward the door.

He should be thinking about Ashley. His ex-wife. The thought popped into his head, taking him by surprise. Just like that, his brain had moved her into the past.

Granted, it was difficult to make sense of anything with ZZ Top pounding through his brain. Lucy's coat came to midthigh, but he could picture her prime ass that sat on top of those legs. Jesus, if she had any idea what she did to his blood pressure she would . . . His thoughts ground to a halt. What would she do?

He reached inside for his familiar line of defense, but stopped.

She stood in front of the door, struggling to put her key in the lock. The porch light gilded her crop of unruly, sexy-as-hell curls. She looked like a tousled, naughty angel and the thought didn't quite go all the way to scaring the shit out of him.

This was not good. She was burning her way back into his brain. He couldn't get the idea of some asshole using her as a punching bag out of his head. His hands tightened into fists by his sides. He wanted ten minutes alone with that guy. Ten minutes to show him what happened to fuckers who hit women. Anger pushed at his control, raw and primal in its intensity. He drew in a deep, steadying breath.

A light went on in the house and then off again. He imagined Lucy taking off her coat and climbing the stairs. With a soft curse he got moving. He'd spent so much of his time watching Lucy. God help him, but even now, he never got tired of it. He could drink her in constantly. It was as if the image of her was etched into his brain and he needed to keep updating it.

This felt like all sorts of trouble. The awareness dogged his footsteps every waking moment and chased him into sleep. Lucy, always Lucy and he didn't want it to be. There was no going back. The past was the past. You can't heat old coffee, as his dad used to say. Except, and this was the kicker, this particular cup had never gotten cold.

That kiss, the other night, still haunted him and the need to repeat his mistake got harder to ignore. Every time he had seen her since, his memory forced him back there. He hadn't forgotten a thing about her. Not the way she smelled, or tasted, or how he was always one move away from reaching out and grabbing on to all that magic that made up Lucy. His treacherous brain had merely been storing the information all these years in a secret compartment. Lucy had ripped it open.

Now, Richard could not get the lid to shut.

He glanced at his watch. Ashley would still be up. He needed to get his wife back. Then he would stop thinking about Lucy. When he was with Ashley, thoughts of Lucy slithered away and he was left in peace again.

If a text message could seethe, then this one did. Lucy frowned down at her phone.

Need to c u now

She wondered how Richard had gotten hold of her cell number and then remembered giving it to his receptionist when she went to his office with Lynne.

It's late, can w8 till morning?

She waited. It didn't take long.

No

Lucy stared at the text. She had seen him get into his car earlier and drive off. She had also taken note of when his car came back. It was getting pathetic. Who was she kidding? She was becoming a stalker. Her phone vibrated again.

Now or I am coming over there

Everything ok?

I need you

And that was all it took to get her up and out of bed. She pulled on a pair of track pants. No need to get dressed up or anything, but she took the time to brush her teeth before she snuck downstairs. Old habits can be good friends and she knew exactly which stairs creaked and where to walk. She slipped out of the house, the icy air scraping down through her windpipe like sandpaper. It was a cold, clear night. It should have been a dark and stormy one instead, because this was so not a good idea. But those three little words blinked up at her from her screen and she was lost.

His door opened before she reached the front porch. He jerked her inside without ceremony.

"What's up?"

His face was frozen into grim lines. "We need to talk."

As a general rule, those four words prefaced almost every piece of bad news she'd ever heard.

Richard's eyes were glacial and a muscle worked in the side of his jaw.

Lucy had the sneaking suspicion she wasn't going to like hearing them this time either.

She shrugged out of her coat and toed off her boots. All the time under the looming, fulminating cloud of male, repressed rage. It came off him in waves as he impatiently tossed her coat at a hook. It missed and fell to the ground with a soft sigh. Richard uttered a guttural growl and stalked away into the house. His heels ricocheted across the hard wood as he went.

Lucy watched him and raised her eyebrows. He was not happy, not at all. She bent and picked up the coat, hanging it carefully. It gave her a moment to gather her thoughts. She tried to think if she'd done anything to cause his current temper, but she hadn't seen him since the other night.

She trailed him into the kitchen.

"You're upset?"

He threw her a *no shit* look. Richard never exploded. His temper eked out of him in a series of carefully placed depth charges, deadly and designed to do maximum damage. Right now, he was about as angry as she'd ever seen him.

"I've been to see Ashley." He wrenched the fridge door open. Bottles clanked together under the force of his ire. He glared into the lighted opening, as if he were waiting for inspiration to strike. He leaned forward and came back with a beer for himself and a soda for Lucy. The can hit the counter with a clatter.

"It didn't go as you expected it to?" Lucy empathized with the crumpled can of soda.

He made a sound like a strangled laugh and tipped his head back. The beer disappeared down his throat. The bottle was empty when he slammed it back down on the countertop.

"You going to drink that?" He jerked his head at the can of soda.

"I don't think so."

The can got tossed into the back of the fridge. It must have hit something, because there was a dull thud before Richard slammed the door shut. He had another beer in his hand. He twisted off the cap and sent it skittering over the granite.

"Richard?" Lucy watched the way his eyebrows lowered over his eyes. "You want to tell me what this is all about?"

He took a long pull on his beer and made that strange laugh noise again. "You."

"What?" She blinked at him.

"You," he growled. "This is all about you." He raised his beer again.

Lucy reached over and caught his arm. Muscle bunched beneath her fingertips. "That doesn't work so well." She met his stormy eyes. "Take it from me."

He looked down at her hand on his arm. "Nine fucking years later and it's still all about you, Lucy Flint."

This was getting repetitive. Lucy dropped her hand. Her fingers still felt warm from where she'd touched him. "Is there a reason I'm over here?"

"Yup."

Lucy waited, but he kept staring moodily at the counter.

"Care to share it?" she prompted.

His shoulders slumped, as if he suddenly ran out of fight. "Actually, I have no idea why I asked you to come over here." He shrugged and raised his head. "I was so angry after I saw Ashley and I wanted to see you."

"What happened with Ashley?" Lucy knew the happy little skip of her heart was way premature. There was a lot more to this.

"She wants a divorce." The words fanned the angry spark in his eyes back into life.

Lucy was a little confused. She thought Ashley had wanted that all along. So, she waited for him to say more. It didn't take too long.

"I thought when she came over here the other day to talk, it meant she was going to give us a chance. Apparently, I was wrong." He went for his beer again and Lucy left it alone. *Hell!* She'd be drinking if that were an option for her.

"Why did she come, then?" Lucy could make a fairly accurate guess, but she wanted to see if he could do the same. Richard was too chivalrous for his own good sometimes. She had certainly taken shameless advantage in her time.

"Because of you." He swore softly around the lip of his beer. "I thought she was going to reconsider, maybe give us a chance, but Ashley wanted to make sure I was not getting too friendly with you." He was silent for a moment. "She doesn't want me, but she'd die before she let you have me." He grunted softly. "I tried to explain that you and I, we were over, but it doesn't matter to her." His eyes cut back to her, intent and keen in their focus. "And she doesn't believe me."

Lucy struggled to hold his stare. There was so much conflict in his blue eyes, it made her want to touch him and soothe some of it away. Except, she was the cause of most of it. Again. Shit, she didn't even have to try to screw up his life.

"I'm sorry," she murmured.

"You're sorry?" He gaped at her. "Oh man, Lucy. That is unbelievable, because this time you have nothing to be sorry for."

"Being here," she said, shrugging. "My being here has made your life more difficult."

"Yeah," he said, nodding slowly as his expression grew contemplative. "But that's not your fault. I'm the dickhead who can't seem to get it straight in his head. I'm sitting with Ashley, trying to explain how this thing between you and me is all over and then it hits me." He shook his head slowly. "It hits me that it's not over and what chance do I have of convincing anyone else of that, when I know I'm lying."

Lucy opened her mouth to say something, anything, but the words weren't there. The truth hung in the kitchen between them. The air around them crackled with possibilities.

"What a fucking mess." He stalked away suddenly, leaving a vacuum where so much intense, turbulent energy had been. "I don't get it." His hands went up in the air as if he could wrench the answers from the heavens. "Tell me why, Lucy? What is so goddamned awful about being with me?"

The rapid subject change threw her at first. Then she got it and Lucy's heart contracted. This had to be hell on any man, to have lost not one, but the two women you have loved. "There's nothing awful about being with you."

"Then tell me," he demanded as his eyes raked over her. "I'm one of the good guys. I'm a doctor, for Christ's sake. Every girl wants a doctor."

"I can't speak for Ashley." Lucy's legs felt rubbery and she leaned against the counter behind her for support.

"Then don't." He yanked out a chair and threw himself into it. "Speak for you."

"I told you why." Lucy felt as if her voice were an entity separate from the rest of her. "I was broken and hurting and I couldn't allow myself to be loved. I wanted to prove that everybody was right about me. I was no good and not worth anything. So, I did. I destroyed the one thing that was good and wonderful in my life."

"Why didn't you stay? We could have fixed it."

"No; Richard." Lucy shook her head. Behind her breastbone she could feel the old hurt gather and swell. "I am the only one who could fix it. It took me six years to figure that out and another three to start putting the pieces back together again. And I can say with absolute certainty that it was not you."

"Great," he jeered. He sprung out of his chair, eating

up the ground between them until he loomed dark and dangerous in front of her.

Lucy's heart leapt into her throat, but she held her ground. He would never hurt her, at least, not physically.

"The old it's-not-you-it's-me kiss-off. Ashley said the same thing." He was right in her face, but Lucy didn't move.

She could see the turmoil in his eyes. It was like a taste of gunpowder in the air.

"She says she married me as some kind of ultimate win against you." Ashley had apparently spared him nothing. Lucy felt the hurt climb into her throat and she tried to swallow it back down again. "She said she never really loved me, but that I was a good husband and we were content together. Now, content is not good enough. You getting all this?"

Lucy's mouth was too dry to speak, so she nodded.

His breath was hot and moist against her face and he smelled of malt and hops. The counter dug into her butt as she pressed herself away from him. She wanted to bring up her hands to put between them, but he moved closer, caging her with his body. His arms rested besides her hips, his knuckles white with his grip on the wood.

"Ashley thinks this is all about you, Lucy Flint," he spoke directly into her ear. He surrounded her. His arms kept her prisoner. The heat from his body wrapped around her and his breath fanned the skin of her neck. Part of her was frightened at his suppressed fury, but she couldn't deny he excited her at the same time. Her legs felt weak and she sank against the counter. Desire surged hot and strong through her. It washed over her in waves that she couldn't fight anymore.

"She says that it has always been you, for me."

Lucy made a soft, needy gasp as he pressed closer. She sensed the wildness in him and it sizzled and crackled through her body in a live circuit. Her breathing came short and quick. Her core tightened with need, pulling at her reason and demanding that she submit to the tug of fierce, reckless passion. She wanted to rip away any pretense of civility and feel.

"You know what I think?" His voice against her skin tormented her.

Her head reeled with the attempt to keep her focus sharp. It was too much for her. Her body vibrated like a tuning fork with his proximity and her thoughts tangled and tripped over her base needs. Somewhere deep inside a voice was warning her, but Richard drowned out the sound with his hot, hard body and the smell of man.

Lucy shook her head. She had no words, only the need to press herself a half inch closer until her flesh touched his. Her breasts felt heavy and swollen. Her nipples rasped against the front of her shirt. She had underestimated the strength of this thing that hissed and snapped between them. Desire fisted in her belly and moved lower. There had always been only him for her, but she dared not say the words. They jammed up in her throat and so she shook her head again. Small skeins of her hair caught on the roughness of his chin. Every inch of her being sought the contact.

"I think." He didn't brush the tiny connection of her hair away. His voice was tumescent with what he didn't say and she dared not. "I think it always comes down to you, Lucy. What is it about you that imprints every facet of my life?"

Harsh, hot breath fanned her cheek. "From the moment I saw you, you have cursed me." Lucy wanted to howl her denial. "I can still remember it like it was this morning." He breathed through his nose, inhaling the scent of her and Lucy's head tilted to give him access. A silent offering that she didn't want to control.

His head dipped in response until she felt the brush of his breath against the curve of her neck.

A small whimper escaped her at the graze of his mouth against her skin. It was barely a touch, but she felt it right through to her center. Her fingers dug into the countertop and she battled through the fog to hear what he was saying.

"You were standing next to Ashley, talking to her. She was supposed to be my girlfriend, but it was you I was watching. I stood there and stared. I must have stood like that for ten minutes. You didn't know that, did you?"

Lucy shook her head again.

His beard rasped lightly against her cheek. "And then you turned to me and it was like being punched. I couldn't breathe, Lucy. I swear to God, I stopped breathing. You were so unbelievably beautiful and I wanted you so much. I was rock hard, Lucy, and I was standing half a room away from you." He pushed toward her and Lucy felt the jutting pressure of his erection.

She moaned softly as her body flooded with answering moisture.

His mouth was beside hers and Lucy's entire being locked on the spot where they nearly connected. All she had to do was turn her head a quarter inch to the right and she could feel his mouth on hers. The need almost overwhelmed the fear, but the fear was greater. Terrified he would move away and even more terrified he wouldn't. So she stayed, her body locked in a stasis of longing and desire. Trembling, out of control, and bereft of will and choices, paralyzed by her longing.

"Ashley says you have always been first, but she has no idea. Does she, Lucy?" Her name was breathed across her bottom lip. "She thinks she knows, but she has no idea how it was for us." He released the counter suddenly to clasp her face between his palms and Lucy allowed him to pull her gaze from his mouth to his eyes.

It was all there, the impotent fury that he was helpless against her. It mirrored her desperation so fully. Lucy had no idea that she was crying until she felt his thumbs roughly push the moisture from her cheeks. He cradled her face between his hands, his fingers buried deep within her hair and pressing lightly against her scalp.

"Every flash of your eyes . . ." His voice dropped deeper and grew ragged with his breathing. "Every smile . . ." He touched the corner of her mouth and dragged his thumb across her bottom lip.

Lucy could taste the salty moisture of her tears.

"Every time you said my name or laughed. I watched you like I could never get enough of you. And I couldn't. I could never have enough of you. Even when I was buried inside you, with these legs wrapped around me, as close to you as I could get, it still wasn't enough. What is it about you, Lucy Flint?" He lowered his head toward her, but the battle still raged in his eyes. "And it was the same for you, Lucy. I can't be wrong about that."

It was a plea and she heard it. "You aren't wrong."

So soft she barely heard her own voice, but he heard it and he closed the breath of space between them and touched his mouth to hers, tentatively, at first, as if he was not sure this was really happening.

Need exploded in Lucy and she made a stifled, animal sound and pressed her mouth fully against his.

For a heartbeat, he didn't move, but his entire body tensed like a coil. Then the grip on her scalp tightened and he tugged her closer to him, more fully into the kiss.

Their mouths opened to each other greedily, tongues, lips, and teeth, all tasting, inhaling, devouring the essence of each other with a hunger that raged through her. For Lucy it was like coming alive again.

His kiss bruised, but Lucy pressed even closer, moaning her need in low murmurs into his mouth. He drank her desire thirstily, taking her mouth and plundering. Trying to sate something stronger than either of them. Against her body, he was hard and unyielding and it thrilled her.

The taste of him was heady. It was familiar and not at all the same. She pushed deeper into the kiss, as if she could satisfy her need like this.

It wasn't enough for either of them and she felt his hand, hard and demanding against her hips, pulling her against him, rubbing his rigid cock against the juncture of her thighs.

This was Richard, her body exalted and he was harder, stronger, and bigger than she remembered. But the smell of him was the same and the way they fit together, so incredibly, achingly familiar.

His hips moved against her, his erection full and swelling against her female flesh and Lucy responded. Moving against him as the thrust of his hips and tongue became more insistent.

He pressed into her, bending her over backward.

He released her head only to lift her hips onto the counter behind her. Parting her thighs and pressing forward, dominating her with his body and his mouth until Lucy felt the hard press of unyielding wood beneath her back.

His body pressed down onto hers.

She gripped his back, holding him in place with her thighs around his hips and her arms around his neck. He was hard where she was wet and wanting. The rough texture of his big hands against the skin of her waist made Lucy cry out into his mouth.

"I need to touch you." He pulled away enough to watch his hand disappear beneath the hem of her shirt, riding the gentle rise of her ribcage.

Lucy arched into his touch. It burned against her skin until his palm closed over her breast.

He captured her moan in his mouth. Taking possession of her mouth and the full, aching mound of her breast in one devastating movement.

There was no hesitation in his possession. No tentative exploration, but a certainty of his ability to drive them both mindless with pleasure; the awkward apology of a boy's touch had been replaced by a sure, slow hand of a man.

The thought beamed through the haze of lust.

In that split second between one heartbeat and the next, Lucy saw herself, spread like a sacrificial offering across the countertop, her body straining against his, her heart and her soul on offer with it. And just like that, it wasn't enough. The lust he offered was not enough. She reached desperately for that thought, beating back the need to ignore everything and submit.

She craved the closeness and the oblivion, but she wanted more.

It took him a moment to sense her withdrawal and then he raised his head. His eyes were feverish and his face flushed as he stared down at her. "Lucy?"

The question was there and with nearly every fiber of her being she wanted to answer yes, to give him permission to take her body.

"Not like this," she whispered instead.

He frowned and recoiled away from her as if she'd slapped him. "Jesus, Lucy." She winced as his voice shot across the kitchen. "Are you playing games with me?"

"No games." She pulled her shirt down with shaking hands and tried to wriggle off the counter. It was undignified and her cheeks flushed with embarrassment. Her position a powerful reminder of what had nearly happened here. What she still wanted to happen. "I'm not playing games."

He watched her with hot, angry eyes.

Lucy could see the rigid grip he exerted on his control.

"I was right there with you. And I want this," she said, gesturing toward the two of them. "But not like this. Not in anger." She took a shallow, shaky breath. "Don't make love to me in anger."

He stayed where he was, frozen to the spot as the desire receded and reality tiptoed unwelcome fingers through his brain.

Lucy watched it all happen, the disbelief, then the shock, and, finally, the regret. And inside, she died a little bit right there. He would have had sex with her and he would have regretted it. Her tattered dignity was not quite enough of a consolation, but it was all she had.

"Come to me because you want me, Richard." She drew even with him as she made for the front door. "Don't use the attraction between us to ease your anger and your hurt."

Still he didn't move and Lucy let herself out of the house.

Chapter Nineteen

Richard was grumpy, but he didn't give a shit as he slammed his car door and stalked toward his office. The heat hit him like a wave as he opened the door. A Chinook packed full of the assembled smells and sounds of the gathered humanity.

As one they looked up when he walked in, their faces reflecting largely divergent levels of patience. Most looked like they were bending the needle toward *Where the hell have you been? I have a life, which does not include sitting here getting old in your waiting room.* He couldn't blame them.

He was late. Horribly and irrevocably late and he would have the unmitigated delight of taking it on the chin for the rest of the day.

Lucy was back in town and his life was, once again, sliding to hell in a handbasket. She had that effect on things. Lucy arrived with her pet avatars of chaos and disruption and the three of them played knick-knack paddywhack all over his head.

Actually, it wasn't entirely her fault this time. True, trying to get to sleep with a raging hard-on had not helped. He'd overslept and then spent a frustrating two hours trying to get Lynne to make a decision. His entire time in Lynne's kitchen his one eye had kept creeping toward the stair to see if Lucy would join them. She hadn't and it was ridiculous how much that pissed him off.

Ah, shit. Richard caught sight of his first patient.

Brad-Leigh blinked back at him, two slimy trails of snot glued to the four-year-old's top lip. He hoped his nurse, Carmen, had remembered to restock the examination rooms with Kleenex.

"There you are." Carmen rolled her eyes at him. "You decided to take the day off, or what?" Richard threw her the look.

"Brooke," he said, nodding a greeting to the boy's mother and passing her a Kleenex. He suppressed the desire to shudder. He was a doctor, for the love of God. Blood, gore, throw-up and, yes, even Brad-Leigh's snot was all in a day's work. "Sorry I'm late. I will just be a minute."

Brooke twittered something, but Richard didn't hear her. He was already on the move toward his office.

Carmen glared at him from over the top of her reading glasses as he sidled past her desk. Richard was sure the woman wouldn't be in such a perpetually pissy mood if she conceded defeat and went two doors down to the opticians and got a decent prescription.

"Perhaps there is a reason you are late, hmm?" Carmen's sneer had all heads snapping in his direction.

"Give me a couple of minutes and then send in Brooke and Brad-Leigh." He kept up his professional face.

"You're very behind," she called after him, unnecessarily. "It is going to be a very long day." Again, with the unsolicited and obvious, Richard didn't deign to reply, but threw Carmen another look of complete, icy disdain. As per usual, she was unimpressed and merely glared right back.

"You have snow on your pants," deadpanned his middle-aged nemesis.

Richard made it into his office, barely taking the time to put on his lab coat, before he heard Brad-Leigh and his snot trundling down the corridor toward one of the three patient rooms. He winced at the unmistakable clatter of Brad-Leigh discovering the tray of instruments. Brooke's voice rose in the usual token, and unconvincing, reprimand.

Richard took a deep breath. It was in everybody's best interest to get Brad-Leigh and his mother out of the office.

"Good morning." He smiled at Brooke and turned his attention to Brad-Leigh. Brad-Leigh didn't move. He looked at Richard. "What seems to be the problem?"

Richard barely listened as Brooke went through a long list of complaints on Brad-Leigh's part. He quietly got on with his examination. Given free rein, Brooke would have her oldest child stricken with the bubonic plague and allergic to everything from mites to the greater Chicago area.

Brad-Leigh kept his pale eyes fixed on Richard's face. Another trail of snot hovered menacingly around Brad-Leigh's nostrils and Richard hastily grabbed another Kleenex. Brad-Leigh obediently blew his nose.

Richard finished his examination. Brad-Leigh had a cold. The same cold he'd had two days ago when Brooke had brought him in and the same cold he would have two days from now until the virus ran its course.

"Well, Brooke, he doesn't have a temperature and his lungs sound good. Just keep him quiet. You can use some Tempra or something like that if you think he's uncomfortable. Make sure he gets lots of rest and fluids."

"Shouldn't he have an antibiotic?" Brooke's face screwed up intently as she looked over his shoulder at her son.

"It's probably for the best to hold off on those for the moment." Richard snapped off his latex gloves and reached for his candy jar.

Brad-Leigh's expression grew animated for the first time since he'd arrived.

"I suppose you've seen her?" Here it came. Richard felt that unmistakable slide of his day from bad to hideous. Brooke watched him with the same intensity as she would a car wreck.

"Hmm?" He feigned disinterest as he made some notes on Brad-Leigh's already bulging chart.

"I can't believe she had the cheek to come back here." Brooke leaned toward him, inviting him into her bitterness.

"Who?" He peered over the edge of the file at her with his practiced, vague expression. The *you put what, where?* expression every family practitioner needs. It worked for exes back in town, too.

"Lucy Flint." Brooke straightened up, her eyebrows all but disappearing into her fiery hairline. "I ran into her the other day at the store."

"Oh." Richard closed Brad-Leigh's chart. Brooke looked at him expectantly, thick as a tick with the drama. He really, really hated this shit. "Yes, I've seen her." *And touched her and kissed her and put my hands on her. And I want to do it again.* "She's staying at her parents' house, which, as you know, is right next door."

Brooke visibly deflated and he got a certain child-ish satisfaction.

Brad-Leigh came to the rescue. Tired of waiting around as adults discussed a subject that wasn't him, he headed for a tray of gleaming, sharp surgical instruments. It got Brooke's immediate attention.

Richard moved behind his desk, confident nobody could or would see that beneath his neutral expression his heart thundered. If he had his way, it was going nowhere near his sleeve. He only needed to learn that lesson once and that had happened when Lucy Flint had blown out of town . . . with Brooke's boyfriend. Richard felt a brief moment of camaraderie with the other woman. He could still hear the murmurs of pity following him around the neighborhood. It must have been the same for Brooke.

"Keep Brad-Leigh quiet and if he's not better in a week, bring him back to see me." He smiled at her kindly. He stopped short of patting Brad-Leigh on the head and palmed another Kleenex instead.

"How did you think she looked?" Brooke's eyes narrowed in the corners and one started a slight tic. "I thought she looked older. I remember her as being better looking, don't you?" *Nope.* He tried his best not to think about how breathtakingly, mind-numbingly gorgeous Lucy still was. Richard kept his eyes on Brooke's.

The woman's face was alight with malice and his brief flash of goodwill disappeared. Perhaps Jason hadn't taken much convincing to disappear with Lucy.

Richard sighed. It was beneath him to have such a thought. It was probably another by-product of his shitty morning.

"Oh, she's grown her hair, hasn't she?" Like he hadn't noticed? He could still feel the silk of her mane between his fingers. "It looks good."

"Maaaa." Brad-Leigh strained to reach a set of clamps.

Brooke produced a candy bar from her purse and looked at Richard sharply, as if sensing all was not as it appeared.

Richard looked back at her.

Brad-Leigh went for the candy.

"Ashley knows she is here," Brooke stated smugly.

"I wonder who told her that?" he murmured and raised a brow at Brooke.

"I did." She puffed up with self-importance. Subtlety was lost on Brooke. "I told her straightaway. It was my duty as a friend."

Richard barely stopped himself from snorting. Ashley couldn't stand the other woman. He'd heard more than one scathing diatribe on Brooke.

"Was there anything else?" he asked.

"Are you all right?" Brooke cooed. She wouldn't be Brooke if she left the boil unlanced.

"I am fine, Brooke," he assured her with convincing calm. "Lucy is back in town, I am fine. Are we done here?" He indicated the waiting room outside. "Because, as you are aware, I was late and I have other patients waiting."

"Oh." Brooke visibly shrank before him. "Well, that's good then." She gathered up her son. "I still think she is looking her age. It must be all the wild living."

Brooke paused expectantly in the doorway, waiting for him to take up the conversational gambit.

"Take care." Richard left the room and was well on his way toward the second treatment room before he let out his breath. He hadn't even realized he was holding it.

"Good morning, Mr. Crawley," he greeted his elderly patient. "I am sorry you have had to wait so long. How's the back?"

"So, Doctor, two women, huh?" The old man's eyebrows shot up expectantly. "Lucky young dog. Which one are you going to take? Normally I wouldn't ask, but the wife and I have a little side bet going."

"Richie Rich?"

"Babe?"

"What's our song?"

"We don't have one but every time I see you, I have ZZ Top playing in my head."

"That is not romantic."

"You mean 'Legs' is not considered a classic love ballad?"

Christ. Richard stared at the chart in front of him, willing the squiggles to make sense. He had to find a way to get past this.

Chapter Twenty

"You know what I am going to say, don't you, girl?"

"I know, Mads." Lucy was exhausted, but Mads worked nights and Lucy knew she was up and about and it was still two hours earlier in Seattle. Unrequited desire, Lucy discovered, was about as pleasant as unrequited love.

"I had the feeling it was only a matter of time." Again, there didn't seem to be much point in denying it, so Lucy sighed and hung on for more. "It really doesn't make any difference what I say, Lucy, because you know this and it still isn't helping. So, all I can tell you is, get this out of your system, scratch your itch . . . whatever and then come home and we will put the pieces back together again."

"Maybe he won't be back." Lucy couldn't even pretend to be wishful about that.

Mads chuckled. "Honey, not even you believe that. You are as much tangled into his system as he is in yours. I can quote the Big Book to you until the cows come home. I can tell you the way it is and how it should be, but it isn't going to make one bit of difference. You guys are on a collision course to finish this thing."

"And then what?"

"I haven't a clue." Mads laughed again. "Damn, but I miss you, Lucy Locket."

"I miss you, too, Maddy Mads."

"Question? Totally off the record and asking as your girlfriend and not your sponsor."

"Uh-huh."

"What if the magic thing happens and all of a sudden Richard wants you back and it's all green for go and love in la-la land again. What happens then, Lucy?"

Lucy didn't even have to think about that response. "Then I stay here and make it happen."

"You know I hate to be cold?"

"You'll survive."

"I despise snow."

"It's pretty."

"And I have never been to Chicago."

"Then it's about time you did."

"Okay, babe, from your lips to God's ear."

Lucy hung up the phone. It rang again almost immediately.

"Lucy?" And her heart kind of sank. His tone radiated disapproval and disappointment. For a dizzy moment, she almost pretended to be her voice mail.

"Hey, Elliot," she said, keeping her tone deliberately chipper. "How are you?"

"Not so good, in fact," he responded with a touch of severity. Elliot was in no mood to be deterred or distracted. "I have been waiting for you to call. I was worried about you."

"I've had a lot to do here, Elliot. It's been a rather difficult time."

"I understand." The firm rebuke whipped out the phone. "But you could have found five minutes to let me know you were still breathing. A text message would have been all right, a call even better."

And he had her there. "I appreciate that, Elliot, but I didn't promise to call you and there has been rather a lot happening since I left."

"But you've been gone for so long, I've had to resort to phoning your sponsor to know you're alive."

Lucy took a breath. This was the thing with Elliot and it was entirely her fault. He was so used to rescuing her and it was so comfortable to let him. She had got it this way, because she set it up this way. Thanks for that one, Dr. Phil.

The key was to keep it logical and calm. It didn't do any good to lose your temper with Elliot. He was at his strongest when she lost it. "We talked about this before I left. I am here to settle things and get some answers."

"And that means you can't call?"

"It means"—Lucy sucked in her breath—"that I am concentrating on what I am doing here."

A loaded silence stretched out over the telephone and Lucy thought for a second they might have been cut off. It didn't occur to her Elliot had hung up. He would never, ever do anything so crass and childish. Elliot was always and under all circumstances a civilized man. And she should know. She had certainly pushed him over the years.

"I understand."

Damn. Shit and damn. Now Elliot's feelings were hurt. Lucy tried to backtrack. "I don't think you do, Elliot. I can't move on with the rest of my life until I get this stuff settled."

"Oh, get off it," Elliot snapped with uncharacteristic anger. "We both know why you are really there."

"Don't do this, Elliot." Lucy closed her eyes as if she could shut out the world.

"I don't think I have any choice left to me." He was seriously pissed now. Elliot's British accent always got more clipped when he was upset. "I have been waiting on tenterhooks to hear if some girlish peccadillo with a teenage stud is going to stop you from committing to us or not."

"Don't patronize me. This has never been about Richard. Well, not only about Richard. I came here for my mother." Lucy refused to let him get under her skin. Elliot was hurting and she knew it. They'd first met when she was only twenty-five. For the past five years they'd drifted in and out of a relationship that felt more like a mentor/student thing than a romance.

Now she was sober and Elliot wanted to know if they could, finally, move on to a better place. They'd kept the relationship more or less platonic for the past year. And although Elliot had dated other women in that time, Lucy had always known he was waiting.

Always waiting for her to be ready. He'd been good to her. At times he'd been the only thing standing between her and the results of her own stupidity. That's why she'd been putting off calling him and saying what she knew had to be said. The truth was right there, staring her in the face. Last night and what had almost happened in Richard's kitchen had put to bed any lingering doubts. She was never going to be ready. Not for Elliot, anyway.

"You're right," he responded. Always so reasonable at times it made her want to scream. "That was poorly done of me."

"Don't apologize, Elliot," Lucy whispered softly into the phone. "Just, don't."

There was another long silence and Lucy could hear him putting the pieces together. "So, Lucy, are you going to give me an answer?"

She owed him that much and so much more. It was Elliot who had given her her first glimpses of sobriety. Elliot who picked her up after Peter had left her in pieces. The same man she'd left Elliot for and not once had he reproached her. Until that last time, when he had issued an ultimatum, which ended up saving her life.

He really didn't deserve her. He deserved so much more.

"I . . ." The words that would end his waiting wouldn't come. Lucy cleared her throat and tried again. "Elliot, I really don't know how to say this."

How did you tell a man after all this, you didn't love him? How did you tell someone the collection of painful memories between you was part of the past and not your future? Lucy felt like she wanted to be sick. She was such a shit to be doing this.

"I don't think." She tried again.

"Jesus, Lucy." Elliot's voice was hoarse with emotion over the phone. "Don't be so bloody stupid."

There was no way to tell him it wasn't stupidity. It was instinct. It was the sense she was finally in a place where she recognized what she needed. And part of her was starting to see that, despite her sins, this was what she deserved. And what she deserved was not what he had to offer. How did you tell a man he wasn't . . . Richard?

"Five sodding years," Elliot rasped, and Lucy's chest constricted. The burden of his patience made it

impossible to keep her head up. She had known all
this time what he wanted and what he waited for and
she'd avoided dealing with it. "Five bloody, sodding
years and this is all I get."

"I am so sorry, Elliot." It was so absurdly inadequate. "I wish—"

"Oh, please. Don't you dare," he snarled at her.
"Don't you treat me like some bloody consolation
prize. I think we both know I am worth a whole lot
more than that."

"You are, Elliot, you really are. And I cannot tell
you how much you mean to me."

"Christ, Lucy, is this the best you've got? A whole
mouthful of limp platitudes and bullshit."

"I've hurt you and I have no idea how to make that
better."

"Really?" His accent could have cut glass. The
consonants bounced off the phone like clean strikes
off metal. "You could grow up, Lucy, and realize I am
the best thing that ever happened to you. You could
stop pining for some childhood dream and see real
life isn't like that. Real life is about real people making
a commitment to something and making it work. Real
life is about what we have, Lucy."

"I'm sorry," she muttered miserably. There was no
point in arguing with him. She had nothing to tell
him, but the inkling that she could one day, somehow,
have the dream come true. There was a grand passion
out there for her, a huge slice of heaven that was hers
for the taking.

It was unlikely it would be Richard. But surely,
somewhere, there was someone like him. Somewhere,
there was another love. Sometime in the future there
would be a chance to prove she could do it right this

time. But that opportunity was not with Elliot and it was time to cut them both loose.

"This thing with us, Elliot," she said, her voice trembling so much she had to clear her throat. "What we have, Elliot, is not what I want."

Another loaded silence and Lucy took a deep breath and then another. It was done and along with the guilt was a terrible sensation of relief. It was over.

"Out of curiosity, Lucy," he spat. "If I hadn't called you today, were you planning on taking another five years to tell me that, after everything, I still wasn't good enough for you?"

Lucy said nothing. Elliot was mouthing off in his anger and hurt and he had, at least, earned the right to do as much.

"Let me be clear about this," he carried on. "I don't want to be your friend, Lucy. I have enough friends and I don't need another one."

"I understand." She dearly hoped he might change his mind about that one day, but for the moment, and probably for a goodly while, it was better she kept a distance.

"And"—Elliot barely heard her—"this is the last time. We have been down this road three times before. This is it, Lucy. After this, I am not going to play the blasted fool for you anymore. You leave me this time and you stay gone. Are you clear about that?"

"I am clear, Elliot." A lifetime without Elliot seemed a long, long time, but she wasn't about to start trying to bargain with a wounded beast. Perhaps there would be time in the future for them to sit down and talk this through.

"No more desperate phone calls."

"I get that."

"No more rescues when you get yourself into shit so deep, you can't breathe anymore."

"I get it, Elliot."

There was silence again. Lucy could hear the rasp of his breathing on the other end of the line.

"Elliot?"

"Fuck you, Lucy. Just . . . fuck you."

The phone went dead in her ear. Lucy watched with a sort of detachment as she lowered her hands to her lap. They were shaking so badly she barely managed to put the phone safely beside her on the bed. It was done. For better or for worse, she and Elliot were done.

It hit her in a crash of panic that almost had her reaching for redial. She could still beg Elliot to be patient with her. She could ask him to wait for her. He was her safety net. Without Elliot in her life these five years past, Lucy was sure she would have ended up "working the track" with the crack whores.

She wrapped her arms tightly around her middle. The pain was staggering. He had been a decent man and a wonderful friend. He'd picked her up and dusted her off time and time again. Her phone was already in her hand. Ready to make the call and bring Elliot to the rescue.

She put the phone down again. He deserved more than to be someone's fallback position. Elliot deserved to be loved wholly, passionately, and freely. He didn't need to be Lucy Flint's charity case. Five years crashed over her like a wave. Her gratitude was genuine and sincere, but it wasn't love, not the sort of love he wanted.

Chapter Twenty-One

This had to be a new low. It was two in the morning, and she was listening to Adele crooning about lost love, and shoveling snow as if her life depended on it. Right now, it felt as if it did. Lucy wanted to crawl into her bed and cry, but she couldn't. Her tears were a dead weight, lodged behind her breastbone.

Lucy pushed the shovel into the fresh coat of about two inches on the walkway. If anyone saw her, they might think she'd lost her mind. Down the street a snow-clearing service backed a small plow out of a driveway. If Lynne heard anything, it would blend into the other sounds of the night. Lucy dearly hoped she was right. She couldn't face her mother right now.

A slight shift in the light was all the warning she got before a warm hand closed over hers. Lucy dropped her iPod and he reached out quickly and caught it. Adele sadistically launched into a heartrending chorus. *Tell me about it.* Lucy sniffled.

Richard's mouth moved, but all Lucy heard was Adele wailing away enthusiastically. His eyes were bluer than a clear sky and Lucy sank, came up for air, and then sunk all the way down to the bottom.

His mouth moved. He frowned, shook his head, and plucked the earphones from her ears. "These things will make you deaf."

"Is that your considered medical opinion?" She was proud she could still come out with the wisecracks. Given that she truly wanted to disgust Gloria Steinem and the girls and fling herself against his manly chest and have him sweep her away to the happily-ever-after place.

"What are you doing?" Prince Charming asked with a frown.

"You have to ask?" Lucy looked pointedly at her shovel.

"Lucy." His mouth tightened. "It's the middle of the night and you're shoveling snow?"

"Did I wake you?"

"Not with the shoveling." Richard pushed a hand through his hair, making it stand on end around his head. "You look like you need a friend," he said softly.

"Is that what you are?" Lucy heard her voice wobble dangerously and cleared her throat.

"Or something," he muttered, and took her arm. "Come on." He took the shovel from her hand and propped it against the side of the house. "Let's be sleepless together."

"Not a good idea." Lucy dug in her heels, but he tightened the grip on her arm and tugged her a few steps forward.

"I don't care," he said, and hauled her a few more steps. "I don't give a shit right now."

And just like that, Lucy realized she didn't give a shit, either.

He took her silence as agreement and kept her hand in his as he walked them through the silent garden to his house.

"Coffee?" he asked as he hung up his coat and reached over for hers to hang it beside his.

"No," Lucy answered, pulling a face. "I would like to sleep at some point."

The dim light of the entrance hall danced across the strong lines of his face. He cupped her chin and turned her face. "You've been crying."

"A bit," Lucy murmured.

His hand on her face was warm and gentle, but it sent a shaft of longing arcing through her body. She shifted away and dropped her head. Needing to move, she padded restlessly into the house.

"What is it?" He caught up with her on silent feet. "Is it last night?"

"Not really." She didn't have it in her to outright lie. "Something happened, earlier, and I . . ." She trailed off and followed him into the kitchen. She almost laughed. This kitchen had seen a lot of action since she'd been back in town.

"Tell me," Richard urged her softly.

"I hurt someone." She pulled out a seat and sat.

He went very still above her. "A man?"

Lucy nodded and looked down at the floor. His bare feet stuck out the bottom of his pants. He must have just pulled on his boots when he spotted her in her crazy wee-hour mania.

"A boyfriend?"

"Not really." Something in his tone made her look up. His gaze was trained intently on her face. The muscles of his jaw bunched.

"You sure you want to hear this?" Of all the things she and Richard could discuss, another man must be close to the top of the awkward list.

"No." His eyes bored into hers, as if he were trying

to see past her face and into the center of her. "Tell me anyway."

"His name is Elliot and he's a really good man." The pain in her chest unraveled slightly and she dared a bit more. "He's been amazing to me. He picked me up when I was at my lowest point and helped me get sober. He's one of the good guys."

"And?"

"He loves me and wants more from me. I don't feel the same."

Richard flinched, the slightest crease around the corner of his eyes.

"It isn't the same," she addressed the thoughts she could almost hear whirling around his brain. "Elliot is not you and I was always honest with him."

"Really?" His skepticism rubbed salt on an open wound.

"I never loved Elliot." Lucy hissed in a breath. "I never pretended to love him either. He . . ." She was making a mess of this. "Why don't I tell you the whole story and stop you from leaping to conclusions?"

She thought he might refuse and then his face relaxed slightly and he dragged out the chair beside her. "Why not?"

It was not exactly enthusiastic, but Richard was still listening.

"I met Elliot when I first went to Seattle," she said. "He was the perfect catch for me at that time. He had money, he was good looking and just that bit older to want to take care of me. I used him." She hated even admitting it. "Until I found something I liked more. I was drinking, heavily, and Elliot was a bit too grown up for me. Then I ran out of money, got scared, and went straight back to Elliot."

Lucy managed a dry laugh. "And he took me back.

He asked me to stop drinking and I did. I didn't stay for long," she said, shrugging. "I found someone more exciting, more like me, and I left him again."

"The prick with the fists?"

"That's the one." Lucy grimaced. "Then I got sober and Elliot has been waiting for me to get serious about him. He's been hanging around for me, all this time, and I had to let him go."

"Wow." Richard blew out a soft breath. He spun away from her and stood staring out the window into the dark. "There's a whole team of us. The men who never get over Lucy."

It stung like a slap. Lucy reeled back from the table and clambered to her feet. "That was a shitty thing to say."

"Yeah, I know." He dropped his head onto his chest. "I shouldn't have said it."

"I'm going home."

"Don't." His voice stopped her before she reached the kitchen door. "I'm mad at myself."

"That's just an excuse, Richard."

"You're right," he said, nodding. "And I'm sorry."

He looked at her across the length of the kitchen. The expression on his face softened. "I want you to stay."

Lucy's breath caught in her throat. "I don't want to be the enemy anymore."

"You're not." His voice grew hoarse, his blue eyes raw in their intensity. "Not anymore. And this guy, Elliot, he made his own choices. You're not responsible for him or even me, for that matter. You're our addiction, our drug of choice. So sexy and so beautiful and fragile and we're strapping on the armor before we've even formed the conscious thought. You're man candy, Lucy Flint."

"Man candy." Man, she wished that sounded like a good thing. Lucy gave a strangled laugh. "That's a new one."

"Not for me."

Everything in Lucy stilled, like the moment before the oncoming car broadsides you.

"Richard?" Lucy's breath caught in her throat and she struggled to swallow past the constriction.

"I'm not doing well at walking away from this insane thing between us." His gaze bored fierce and needy into her. "You're in my blood, under my skin, and I don't want to fight it anymore."

Neither of them moved. He waited for something and she had no idea what it was. The words were not there and Lucy shook her head.

"What is happening here?" Some rapidly fading piece of her tried to cling to wisdom.

"I don't know."

"You're lying."

"You're right, but I don't care."

His eyes heated as he moved closer.

Something caught fire inside her. *Oh God, this is actually happening? Richard wants me.* It got harder to breathe.

"I give up." He shifted closer, slowly, giving her every opportunity to back away.

And go where? When this was the place she wanted to be more than any other.

He was so close she could distinguish the tiny darker flecks of indigo in his eyes, feel the heat emanating off his body.

"Your call, Lucy." Dark, potent need laced his tone.

It tugged at Lucy. *Oh, God,* she wanted this. It pounded through her with each clamorous throb of her body.

He loomed over her, silent and waiting.

Unleashed tension crackled in the air between them.

Lucy's body knew what it needed, even if her mind was still trying to shout it down. "Is this a good idea?"

"Would it matter?" He called her bluff, lowering his mouth until the hot wash of his breath caressed her cheek. "I can't think of anything else. Since the moment I saw you standing in the snow, this is all I've been thinking about. I need to get inside you, Lucy, and I'm no good to anyone or anything until I do."

Okay.

It was a slow tango through the kitchen, marched to the sound of her pounding heart.

He advanced and she retreated, their eyes locked.

Lucy stopped thinking and let her body feel. And the dance continued, advance and retreat, pulse pounding and blood heating. He stepped forward and she went back, challenging him with her eyes, daring him to come and get her.

Lucy stumbled into the entrance hall. And still he came toward her.

Her back hit the wall and she stopped.

He kept coming.

Lucy grabbed the back of his head and tugged his mouth onto hers. *Perfect.* Only with Richard was it ever like this.

Heat burgeoned into wild fire between them.

The taste of him made her crazy as she pushed her tongue into his mouth.

He groaned low and rough, meeting each thrust of her tongue, feasting on her with lips and teeth, as if he couldn't get enough.

The wall was solid and unyielding behind her back as Richard shoved against her, his cock already hard and swollen against the front of her jeans. His obvious desire lit Lucy up from within and she wrapped her thigh around his hip, her body demanding what it needed from him.

He grabbed her ass, fastening around each globe and directing her slide against him.

Lucy whimpered and tugged at his hair as she ground against his erection. She couldn't get close enough, fast enough. Years, she'd waited years to feel like this again.

"Upstairs," he panted against her mouth. "Now."

His teeth nipped at her bottom lip, his hands already yanking her by the belt loops toward the stairs. "Bedroom," he growled, as he fused their mouths together again. He pulled away from her roughly. His breath labored and hectic spots of color stained his cheekbones as he grabbed her hand.

They took the stairs two at a time and Lucy didn't falter. She didn't notice the room or the bed until she was lying flat on it, with Richard pressing her deeper into the covers. The incredible heat of his body surrounded her and Lucy melted into him. She wrapped her thighs and arms around him, pulling him closer to her.

She wanted to hold him here forever.

He broke the kiss long enough to tug off her shirt and sweatshirt and send them sailing across the room.

Lucy wriggled up and grabbed his shirt. It disappeared in a tear of fabric and the ping of buttons across the floor. She reached out greedily for the feast of beautiful skin and muscle spread before her. *Hers.*

His breath hissed as she stroked his chest and slid her hands down over the ridges of his stomach.

"You're beautiful," she marveled, her hands feverishly tracing up over the swell of his laterals and over his back. Down the tightly packed muscle on either side of his spine she drew her palms, committing the feel of him to memory.

His breathing grew ragged as she stroked over his ass and raked her fingernails up his thighs. The waistband of his pants stopped her from exploring further. She slid her hand around to cup his erection straining at her through the fabric.

His cock jerked in her hand.

With her other hand she pulled his head back to hers.

He groaned and grabbed for her, eating into her mouth with his own as she worked the length and hardness of him in her hand.

Her fingers found the clasp and zipper and she eased him out. He was hot and smooth against her. He groaned into her mouth as she touched his bare skin. Gripping him firmly, she stroked down and up again.

He hissed and grabbed her hand and held it still on his flesh. "Shit, Lucy, you have to stop that."

No way. She wanted this and a whole lot more.

She tugged his pants and he reared back, hauling them down his legs and kicking them off.

Lucy sat up and pushed him over onto his back. He lay still for her as she studied him. His amazing body spread before her, just for her. It was a memory she wanted to last forever. As a younger man, he'd been beautiful and she'd forgotten nothing. As a man in his prime, he took her breath away.

"Come here." He sat up and slid one hand behind her head. His grip was light as his mouth found hers. His kiss had lost none of its intensity, but it was a leisurely exploration now, gentler as if he wanted to calm things down.

Lucy's pulse hammered the need for him through

her blood. She wanted to resist this new pace, but the taste of him acted like a drug as he made love to her mouth, slow and easy.

She gave up and let him lead.

He moaned his encouragement as his hands slid over the silk of her bra. Carefully, expectantly, he cupped the weight of her breasts in his palms. His thumb stroked across the feverish, aching peak of her nipple. Lucy pressed closer to him, arching her back to push her breasts into his caress.

"Lucy, baby, you're wearing way too many clothes," he murmured. He unclipped her bra, dragging the straps slowly down her arms. His eyes gleamed appreciatively as he pushed the last of the fabric away and his hands touched her bare skin.

"Shit, Lucy." His voice was rough and laden with barely contained desire. He reared up to fasten his mouth around one turgid nipple.

Lucy groaned, her fingers digging into his scalp to pull him closer. The heat was nearly unbearable as he drew her nipple into his mouth, running his teeth lightly over the sensitive flesh. He palmed the other breast, kneading the fullness as his thumb flicked over the peak.

She writhed against him, loving the feel of how hard he was against the juncture of her thighs.

He swapped breasts, suckling gently and then harder until she was arching against him, panting his name like a litany. Lucy had never thought her breasts particularly sensitive, but she could come from this alone.

"Richard!" His name was a gasp. "Please?"

"Still too many clothes." He flipped her over onto her back. His hands made short work of the clasp of her jeans. Grabbing the jeans and her panties, he tugged them off impatiently. He grabbed her by one ankle and lifted her leg slowly and reverently.

"These legs of yours drive me fucking crazy." He pressed a soft bite against her calf. He laid her leg back on the bed, sliding his palms from ankle to thigh on both of her legs until he reached the jut of her hipbone.

His hands slid over the ridge and onto the softer skin of her stomach, easing up her ribcage until he cupped her breasts again. "All of you drives me fucking crazy."

"Richard." Lucy shifted impatiently beneath him.

He moved over her until they lay chest-to-chest and toe-to-toe. Heat flared everywhere as naked flesh fused to naked flesh. He pressed nibbling, wet kisses along her neck and jaw, breathing in the scent of her deeply as he went. His hands shifted under her back until he cupped her ass again, pressing her against the jutting length of his cock.

It wasn't enough and Lucy's body writhed against him impatiently as his mouth moved to hers and continued its deep, relentless kisses. Heat uncoiled through her belly, feverish and restless.

"Please?" Her body ached for him.

"Tell me, Lucy," he whispered against her skin. "Tell me what you want."

"You." Lucy rolled her hips against him. "I want you, inside me, now."

His eyes flared hotter.

She almost came at the first touch of his fingers on her slick flesh. He slipped his fingers into her, circling the swollen nub with his thumb. Responding to the demands of her moans and her writhing, but never giving in completely.

Her thighs dropped open for him as he settled

between them. Soft, hot kisses down her ribcage almost made her weep with need. He pushed open her legs and blew against her slick, swollen flesh.

Lucy held her breath and then cried out as he fastened the heat of his mouth on her.

He tortured her with his mouth, sucking and licking and bringing her to the point of panting and crying with need. He took his time exploring and tasting the essence of her until Lucy wanted to scream. Her hands fastened in his hair, demanding his capitulation. And then he let her come, in one earth-shattering rush that began at her toes and constricted every muscle in her body.

She was dimly aware of him fumbling for a condom and putting it on. At that point she was glad he was thinking, because she was past it.

It had been a long time for Lucy and he was fully, gloriously aroused. Slowly and surely he eased into her, stretching her intimate passage to accommodate him.

He stopped when he was fully seated in her and propped his weight on his elbows. "Do you feel that?"

Lucy smiled and shifted beneath him. It was always like this with Richard. So right it made her want to cry.

She wrapped her legs behind his back and pulled him deeper. They were perfect together, like two pieces of a puzzle that fit seamlessly. For as long as she lived, Lucy wasn't sure she would ever again feel this intense sensation of right.

Lucy let him take her with him. After her last orgasm she was sure she was done, but already her core tightened. She moved with him, feeling the depth and hardness of each thrust, driving them both forward. Sweat slicked their skin as their bodies writhed and ground together until Lucy's climax quickened within her.

Richard pushed faster and deeper, his eyes locked with hers.

The stark intimacy caught in her throat. It was only her and Richard, together, as if crafted for each other.

He located the tight bundle of nerves screaming for his attention.

It didn't take much, she was more than ready and Lucy shattered into a thousand pieces.

He was right behind her. He gave a hoarse shout as he came with her, collapsing against her.

Hot tears pricked behind her eyelids. Lucy pressed her face into his shoulder, not wanting him to see how shaken she was. Perfect. One moment of intense, rapturous happiness that she had no words to express, only tears that she instinctively knew she couldn't shed.

Chapter Twenty-Two

Richard woke to unadulterated Lucy. And for a moment, he stopped and gloried in the rush of sensations. The smell of her was bone deep on him. That bit of sugar and spice that made him want to sit up and beg.

Her breath huffed heavy and moist against his neck. A spark of sensation shot from that point straight into his groin. He was already hard enough to tent the bedclothes and more blood rushed to answer the call of nature with each accelerating beat of his heart.

She lay half on his chest, her face buried against his neck and her thigh imprisoning him. He could have stayed like that forever.

Holy shit! The thought stopped the blood flow and just about stopped his heart.

Just sex, he'd promised himself, just sex and just this once, to get her out of his system. A carnal exorcism that would answer all the questions in his horny brain every time he looked at her. He had badly miscalculated. It had never, ever been just sex between them. It was so, so much worse now he knew how good they could be. And they had been unmitigated magic together.

Even better than when they were kids.

She was doing it again. Invading every facet of his being and Richard panicked. There was no other word for the heart-pounding rush of adrenaline that had him sliding out from under her and almost sprinting for the bathroom.

His reflection in the mirror stared back at him accusingly.

"You idiot," he told it. She had almost killed him when she left with Jason. Med school exams had kept him numb and too focused to feel for a few weeks and then it had all fallen apart. He still remembered weeping like a baby as his mother held him. The memory tightened his jaw and he reached for the familiar anger to sustain him.

It wasn't there. The anger was gone.

Fuck, fuck, fuck! Don't lose it, Richard.

The anger was an old friend; it pushed him forward when he wanted to run and hide. The anger had kept him alive for a while there and now it was gone. It was the vital wellspring from which he drew his formidable will. Just like that, it had disappeared.

Richard didn't even want to think what had taken its place. He only knew he needed to get Lucy and her warmth and light out of his bed and out of his house. He crept back into the bedroom.

She was still sleeping. Her beautiful hair tangled in a mass around his pillows. She looked like she belonged there.

Softly, he released his caught breath.

He needed time to get his shit together. He slipped into the hallway and made his way down the stairs to the kitchen. *What a fucking mess.* Coffee would get his head working again.

She didn't stir until he was back in the room with his peace offering. Watching Lucy wake up tested his resolve. She blinked into consciousness, like a sweet, sleepy kitten. Her face was all pink and rumpled from sleep and a soft smile played around the corners of her beautiful mouth.

He had never watched her wake up before. He had never watched any woman wake, not even his wife of seven years. Ashley hit the day running. She hated hanging around in the bed and would be up and moving before he'd cracked an eyelid. It had never bothered him. He had never thought anything missing until right now, watching Lucy unfold into wakefulness like a butterfly.

"Hi." Lucy's voice, husky with sleep, tugged at him. She rubbed her eyes before she spotted him sitting by the bedside.

He braced for what needed to be done and pushed the cup of coffee toward her.

Lucy gave him a huge, goofy smile and reached for the cup.

The sheet slipped giving him a glimpse of her breasts before she tugged it back up and restored her modesty. It was like bolting the barn door after somebody had blown the rest of the building away. The image of her was already seared into his being.

His body was not on board with his brain right then. *Forget about it,* whispered his treacherous libido. *You can deal with all that feeling crap later. Climb back into that bed and go and get some more of what we liked so much last night.*

"Mmm," she murmured appreciatively as she took a

sip from her mug. "And he makes a great cup of coffee." Her green eyes danced at him over the rim as she invited him to share the joke. And damn him if he didn't want to. Richard squashed the desire ruthlessly.

"I don't mean to be rude, but I have early-morning appointments."

Her eyes danced and her lips twitched. She thought he was joking.

Richard saw the exact moment she realized he wasn't and his gut twisted. The hurt that flashed momentarily through her beautiful face boomeranged right back at him. Christ, he was being deliberately cruel. The notion did not sit well at all, but he ignored the desire to retreat and clenched his jaw. This was for the greater good.

"What I mean is, I have to get going. You are welcome to stay, have a shower, and let yourself out, but I need to get to work."

She held up a hand to stop him and Richard tensed. Her face had lost all traces of honey and love now. "I think I understand what you mean." She put the cup carefully on the bedside table and frowned at it. "You want to tell me what's going on, Richard?"

"Nothing's going on." He avoided making eye contact. "I have a busy day ahead and—"

"Stop." Flash-fire emotion did an advance and retreat across her face.

"Ah, Lucy." He got to his feet quickly, discomfort twisting him around and around. "Let's not do this, all right?"

Her face remained set and impossible to read.

His confidence wavered. This was not the Lucy he remembered. No screaming and no tantrums, he could deal with those. He was an expert at meltdowns. Lucy looked at him from her adult, woman eyes and saw right through his bullshit. It was a terrifying experience.

He stumbled about for the right words to, at least, soothe her feelings. "Last night was amazing." *God. So lame.* Could he get any lamer than that? He felt his rear engine catch fire and the alarm started blaring at him. He was going down. "But it shouldn't have happened." *Mayday, Mayday.* Flames shot out behind him. "It was a mist—"

She exploded into action.

Richard hopped back.

"Don't you *dare*." She flung back the covers and leapt from the bed.

Curse him to hell and back, but he was not blind to the fact that she was naked. He wished to God he'd thought to put on something more substantial than a bath towel.

"Don't you dare say it was a mistake," she yelled at him as she hunted around for her clothes. "Don't you dare say that. It's such a damn cop-out."

"Lucy." He went for a reasonable tone, feeling like the world's dumbest ass. "It shouldn't have happened. It was a mistake."

"Mistake," she shrieked as she snatched up her panties from the floor beside the bed. Her breasts bounced and jiggled, distracting him, as she wriggled into her underwear. "A mistake is when you burn the roast or stub your toe on the furniture. That's a mistake. What happened between us has been in the cards since I first arrived back in town."

She rummaged around and located her bra. She covered her beautiful flesh, but it didn't help. His cock twitched and swelled. Richard lowered his hands and prayed she didn't notice.

"Shit." She hauled on her jeans. "You and I have

never gotten out of each other's systems. Me coming back here proved that. I'll tell you what happened, Richard." She spied her shirt and pounced. "You had time to think about it and now you're trying to back-pedal for all you're worth."

She'd managed to yank her T-shirt and sweatshirt over her head, but to his chagrin it didn't help lower the situation with the towel.

"You feel things for me and you don't bloody like it. But that does not negate what happened here." She made a furious motion with her hand to encompass the room. "What happened last night was no mistake. The fact that you regret it now doesn't change that."

She was all flushed and passionate with anger and it was like a red flag to his lust.

She dropped to her knees and ferretted under the bed. Her ass waved in the air at him as she dug around for her socks. Christ, he was a dog.

"Last night was incredible." She snatched a sock from the tumbled linens. "It was amazing and earth shattering and you felt it too. All three times. It was as intense as when we were kids, only this time the sex was as mind blowing as the buildup. You can't change that. No matter what bullshit you spout this morning."

She came up at groin level and, of course, she noticed. His cock stood front and center and begged to be noticed.

Her eyes narrowed like a rattler. "You have got to be kidding me."

He took a cautious step back and out of her reach.

"I can't help it." Now, he was whining like a kid.

"You're pathetic."

Richard winced, but he deserved that. He was pathetic.

"You wanted me badly enough to go for it yesterday.

You certainly weren't fighting it last night. Now, you wake up this morning and you know what, Richard, you're scared. I rocked your world and you're running scared."

She was bang on the money, but male pride demanded he defend his position. "I am not scared. I don't think it was a good idea."

"Your dick disagrees with you," she snapped back.

It was pointless to defend that and Richard stood there. Her footsteps clattered down the stairs. A silence and then the house shuddered as she slammed the front door behind her.

Carl was in the kitchen when she stormed into her house about two minutes later. He sat on a kitchen stool like an expectant spider and watched the door. He'd been waiting for her, no question.

Lucy was already bruised by her encounter with Richard. Later, she had a nasty suspicion she was going to feel a whole lot worse, but for now, anger sustained her. Oddly enough, a trip around the mulberry bush with her father seemed like just the thing to keep her mind off the boy next door.

"So, you're back." There was no mistaking the glee in his eyes or the smug satisfaction oozing from his mouth.

There didn't seem any point to replying, so Lucy picked up the kettle and put it on the gas. "Would you like some tea?"

"I've already had some," he said, grinning at her. "Just getting in?"

Again, was there any point to replying? She got the tea bags out and put one in a mug.

His eyes tracked every move she made.

She ran out of things to do with her hands, so she leaned her hips against the kitchen counter and folded her arms over her chest.

He stared right at her. "You had to do it, didn't you, Lucy?"

Lucy kept her expression neutral.

This was where she was supposed to ask what he meant. That would give him the opening to go on and on and on, in exquisite detail, about whatever bug he currently had up his ass. More games to make her morning complete. *Yay.*

All games made her sick. Men made her sick and men playing games made her want to throw up, right here and right now. She glared at the silent brick edifice next door.

Last night had not been a mistake. It had been fucking glorious. She never wanted it to end, but it had. With a great, big thump this morning. Richard had not behaved like Richard. Not the Richard she had in her mind, anyway. He'd been disappointingly human this morning when she needed a hero. Had he always worn shining armor in her version of him? Well, be that as it may, he'd certainly come tumbling off his white charger this morning.

Carl still watched her expectantly. It was laughable how low order his needling was right now. "Where's Mom?" she asked instead.

"Upstairs." He managed to sneer the word, not ready to let it go without another few good tries to get her all riled up. Richard was so many steps ahead of him. "Wondering where her precious girl has got to."

"Oh, really?" She was ice. She was cold. She was cool as a cucumber as the taunts bounced right off her. Goddamn it, she was titanium. She went to the kitchen door and called up, "Mom, I'm home. I'm making tea, do you want any?"

Lucy waited for an answer. Silence.

"She was worried about you." Carl played the guilt card. "She didn't sleep at all, but I am sure you didn't let that bother you at all."

"I'm thirty years old, Dad." Lucy saw his guilt and raised it.

"Does that mean you can't use a phone?"

"No." Lucy could feel the mud coming up around her ankles and starting to suck. "I am sorry for that and you are absolutely right. I should have called so you wouldn't worry."

"I didn't say I was worried, I said your mother was."

My mistake then. "I should have called to let Mom know I wouldn't be home."

Silence howled through the kitchen as she made her tea. When she was through being mad she was going to want to cry, but for now she would settle for the tea and a shower.

"Your mother didn't know where you were," Carl continued pedantically. "But I knew."

"Uh-huh." The sharp stain of tea spread through the water in her mug.

"You were with him." Carl jerked his head toward the house. "You couldn't stay away from him, could you?"

The answer to that one was painfully and pathetically obvious. She stared into her cup as the tea steeped.

"You were always like that when he was around. I used to watch you." Carl's voice twisted with malice. He leaned forward onto the counter, as if he could push the words at her more forcefully. "You were pathetic."

Lucy almost flinched and then it struck her that she didn't need to. The comment stung, but didn't wound. Where once that statement would have been a sword through her heart, today it was a bug bite. She looked at her father over the rim of her teacup. She saw a bitter, old man who would be right at all costs. A little part of her brain disconnected and shut down. Honesty compelled her to admit that where Richard Hunter was concerned, she was still a little pathetic.

Her lack of response seemed to challenge him to go even further. "I used to watch you when you were younger, panting after him all the time. He was Ashley's boyfriend, but that didn't stop you. No, that was what made you do it."

For the most part, true, Lucy thought as she sipped her tea.

"Now, he's her husband and you are still whoring yourself out to him."

Whoring seemed a little harsh, but that was Carl. Why go easy on someone when a sledgehammer would make your point more effectively?

"What is going on in here?" Lynne arrived in the doorway, armed and ready to join the battle.

Lucy felt numb as she kept her butt pressed against the counter and sipped her tea. It was like watching a show play out around her, as she stood in the center, there but not there, involved, but so totally detached.

The story always went a little something like this: Carl attacked, Lucy fought back, and Lynne flew right into the middle. They all had their preassigned roles in this melodrama and the lines really didn't change that much. Lucy was always bad and unworthy, Carl was always self-righteous and cruel, and Lynne was always the rescuer. What a sorry bunch they were. Lucy and Carl would get worse. Carl would turn on Lynne, now playing the role of victim, and Lucy would roar in as defender. Carl attacked, Lucy fought back, and Lynne flew right into the middle. Lucy bit back a sigh. It didn't matter one bit this morning.

She should have known better than to think last night had meant any more than scratching an itch. Richard had responded to a physical need, not an emotional one. Part of the blame was hers and her ridiculous expectations.

"Dad was expressing an opinion on my where-abouts last night," Lucy responded to her mother.

Lynne looked momentarily confused by the change in script, but even now Lucy could see her rallying. "What did you say to her?"

"I told her she behaved like a whore over that Richard Hunter and she always has."

"Carl." Lynne rounded on her spouse. "That is no way to talk to our daughter."

And like that they were back on track again.

"I'm going to have a shower." Lucy placed her mug into the dishwasher.

"He didn't mean it," wailed Lynne at her back.

"Oh, I think he did." Lucy straightened up and looked at her dad. "I think he meant every word. I think I have been pretty much a constant disappoint-ment to him since the day I wasn't born a boy."

Lynne looked ready to wade in, but Lucy cut her off. "But I don't care anymore."

God, it felt so good to say that. It felt even better to know it was true.

"I'm not a whore. I may have made some question-able decisions when I was younger, but I am not a whore and I am not worthless and I don't need anyone to tell me that."

As exit lines went, it was pretty much the bomb. Lucy used it to get herself out of the kitchen and up the stairs.

It occurred to her, as she turned the shower up to its hottest, that it had been a long time since Carl's opinion of her had been anything more than mildly annoying. The thing with Richard was going to hurt far longer. She'd gambled and lost.

Now, in the disappointing aftermath, she could see her own shattered hopes. That did not entirely take away her one night or make it meaningless. Only she had the power to do that. Lucy stepped under the hot water and let it wash over her.

It was over. After twelve years, it was finally over. It was time to grieve and then heal. Lucy was amazed she was being so together about all of this. She stepped slightly outside of herself and saw Lucy Flint coping with heartbreak and rotten fathers like she'd written the textbook.

That lasted for all of ten minutes. And then she started to cry. Apparently grieving had arrived with a vengeance.

Chapter Twenty-Three

"Hey."

"Hey yourself." Lucy had not expected this. Richard standing at her door, hot and sweaty in one of those silly, Lycra getups for cycling. His hair was all plastered to his head where his helmet had flattened it.

Her brain stuttered to a halt. She was not exactly thrilled to see him. Ah, jeez, Lucy almost sighed out loud. She was ecstatic to see him. She didn't want to be and she definitely knew she shouldn't be.

"So, um, this morning . . ." He ran a hand through his hair. It stuck straight up in the air like an antenna. "Not my proudest moment."

Lucy raised an eyebrow. Was she getting an apology or an explanation? Both? Neither? "You can say that again."

He smiled, but resisted the gag. "The thing is, Luce, I totally lost it. I woke up this morning with you in my bed and it felt so amazing. I panicked."

The panic thing sucked, but the middle bit really softened the blow.

"And now?" Lucy was softening, but not putty.

He was obviously ill at ease and fidgety in his own skin. It also helped to soothe the hurt a bit.

"Now . . ." He sighed and went at the hair again.

Lucy pressed her lips together as his hair channeled Bart Simpson.

"I haven't got a clue. I know I behaved like a dick this morning, but I was really hoping you could give me a free pass on that one."

"I probably owe you one or two of those," she admitted grudgingly.

"Maybe we can call it even?" he asked softly, tentatively.

"Okay." Lucy shivered in the cold wind whipping through the open door, but this felt more important. "So, we're even. What happens next?"

"Man, you're tough," he groaned softly. "I don't know, Lucy, but I do know that I am sick of fighting." He shifted his helmet from one hand to the other. The helmet she had given him. "I thought, maybe, you'd like to come to dinner."

"Dinner?" Lucy eyed him warily.

"At my house." He made an abrupt gesture in that direction with his helmet. "Not like a date or anything," he hurried on as she hesitated. "My mom is coming and Josh. I know they would both like to see you."

"I don't know, Richard." Things were only getting more entangled with Richard and this morning had cut right through to the heart of her. It seemed a bit masochistic to be lining herself up for more hurt. On the other hand, she wanted to go. She wanted to take every moment she could before she went back to Seattle.

"Do it for my mom," he coaxed, his eyes twinkling at her. "And Josh has been asking about you."

"Am I going to get an apology with dinner?" She could feel herself sliding straight into a hell of her own making.

"Do you want one?"

"What do you think?"

He ducked his head, but the tiny beginnings of a sheepish grin hovered around his mouth. "I think you want a bit of groveling."

"Well, then, look at the brain on you."

He looked up at her. "I can grovel."

"Really?" She pursed her lips and glared at him skeptically.

"I was married for seven years, I learned a thing or two." He held his hands out wide in supplication.

"Good."

"But I prefer not to do it on an empty stomach."

"Fair enough."

"So." He shifted the helmet again. "Dinner? Tonight?"

Inside Lucy, a tussle was going on. She didn't know if there would ever be a time when she wouldn't want to be with him and he was here on her doorstep asking. On the other hand, she'd spent this morning trying to put his behavior in perspective and move on. A sensible, mature adult would assure him she was not angry about this morning, but would politely decline his offer.

"Please, Luce," he said, reading the hesitation on her face. "I was a total dickhead and I would like to try and make it up to you."

"I'm not sure. I'll think about it." It was a token protest and she didn't think he was any more convinced than she was. "What time?"

"You'll come?" A huge grin of relief split his

face. He'd been really nervous. Lucy stared at him in amazement.

"Maybe."

"Be there at eight."

"I said maybe," she had to shout, because he was already on the move. She peered around the door-jamb to watch him sprint away from the house. He leapt the four steps to the driveway and slid a little on the pavement.

She closed the door slowly. Caution waited for her behind the door. *You should have said no,* it whispered to her. *You should have made him work a bit harder.* Yes, but where was the fun in that. A smile tilted the corners of her mouth upward. It would be good to see Donna and Josh.

"Lu Lu?" Her mother's voice drifted down the stairs. "Who was that?"

Lynne appeared at the top of the stairs wearing unhappy all over her face.

"It was Richard," Lucy replied, but she had the feeling her mother already knew that.

"Did he want to see me?" Lynne folded her arms and tucked her hands into the sleeves of her cardigan.

"No." Lucy drew a careful breath. "He came to invite me to dinner with his mother and Josh."

"Oh." Lynne loaded the syllable with meaning.

Richard saw them from his kitchen window. His mother and Lucy, chatting away like sorority sisters. Lucy had always fit right in with his family. This might be a stupid idea, inviting Lucy to dinner with his mother and brother. Ashley would have a shit fit if she heard about it. Richard shrugged off the thought. Ashley had made her decision. He waited for the crushing sense of failure to hit him. All he got was 'meh.'

Lucy's laugh reached him, muted by the window glass.

Were Lucy and Donna talking about him? He felt childish even thinking it, but he wanted an answer anyway.

He reached the front door before them.

Donna smiled up at him, happy to see him. "Look who I found?" She motioned to Lucy and her smile grew broader.

He was getting the maternal seal of approval. At thirty-two, it shouldn't matter anymore, but who was he kidding? He was Donna's boy through and through. He smiled back at his mother.

Richard turned to greet Lucy and his chest tightened. He forced himself to breathe. She was wearing makeup tonight, her green eyes all hot and smoky, drawing him deeper. There was something shiny on her mouth that made him want to suck on her bottom lip. He looked away quickly. Distraction offered itself up to him, trying to make itself invisible between his mother's ankles.

"What is that rat doing here?"

Rasputin gave him a reproachful doggy stare.

"Hush now, Richard." Donna disentangled the quivering mutt. "You are frightening Rasputin."

"And he is dripping on my floor." Richard jabbed his finger at the pool of melting snow surrounding the pitiful-looking creature.

"Then," Donna said, sticking her chin out. "You will fetch me a towel and I will clean it up. Honestly, Richard, the way you worry about your floors is like a middle-aged housewife."

"Those are real birch," he yelped in protest.

"And you are becoming a nag." Donna hung up her coat and got to work on the laces of her boots. She rose and sniffed the air. "What are you cooking for us?"

"Pasta." Richard was aware of Lucy hanging up her coat. He turned to take it from her and stopped. He nearly swallowed his tongue

She wore a black dress that ended several incredible inches above her knees. A pair of heels made her legs stretch on forever. Last night, he'd had those legs wrapped around him. Lust punched through him like a fist.

Lucy looked up and caught his stare. A blush of color crept over her cheeks.

He wanted to know what she was thinking. If it was anything near where his thoughts were going, this was going to be a long, long night.

"Oh, darling," Donna chattered away oblivious to the snap of sexual tension. She reached up and patted his cheek and Richard jerked his eyes away from Lucy. "You know how I adore pasta. How are you doing it?"

"Seafood, garlic," he said, shrugging, and turned back to the kitchen. He needed to get it together. His mother would see straight through him.

"So, *belle fille*"—Donna's arm slid around Lucy's waist—"you and my son have made friends."

"Or something." Richard said from up ahead.

Lucy choked back a laugh.

Donna rolled her eyes and made a shushing motion at his back. "It is good to see you."

Lucy dropped her head to hide her face. Donna made something burn bright and hopeful in her chest. A sense of belonging that she couldn't afford to acknowledge. This might have been a really big mistake, coming here tonight.

Donna gave her waist another squeeze before letting go and following Richard into the kitchen.

Lucy wondered what the rest of the house looked like. She had only seen this room. *And the bedroom,* whispered a naughty little voice in her mind.

The back door opened on a blast of cold night air and Lucy turned.

"Well, well, well, Lucy Flint, in the flesh."

Lucy found a veritable man-god shrugging out of his long black coat. Even from here, Lucy could see the coat was cashmere. Holy cow, but he looked good. Lucy gawped openly at him.

Joshua Hunter had been a fine-looking boy; as a man, he was ridiculously beautiful. He was well worth a second and a third look. The grin Josh threw her said he knew it, as well.

"Josh." Lucy responded to his grin with a shy smile. "How are you?"

"How do I look?" he shot back.

"Like a girl," Richard barked from the stove.

"Oh, please." Josh grinned back, undeterred. He looked down at his Paul Smith floral shirt and back up at Richard. "What do you know?"

Lucy's smile widened. When you looked like Josh Hunter, your ego was fairly bulletproof.

"Man." Josh turned back to her and gave her a bad-boy grin.

Oh, that grin should come with a health warning: hazardous to girl parts everywhere.

Josh's gaze swept her from top to toe and his eyes gleamed appreciatively. "You're looking good, Lucy."

"Liar. Great shirt." She giggled, and she never giggled. There was just something about Josh Hunter.

Josh grinned. "Come here, beautiful, and give me some sugar."

Without waiting for a response, he strode toward her and swept her right off her feet and into a monstrous hug. His body beneath that hug was tight and hard and Lucy was willing to bet it would be worth getting a look at him out of his fancy shirt.

She was laughing and breathless when he put her on her feet again. Thank God, despite his near godlike beauty, Josh Hunter had never done it for her.

"It's good to see you, Lucy." He held her at arm's length. "You and those legs." Laughter played in the depths of his eyes. Richard and Donna had blue eyes. Josh ramped it up all the way to indigo and surrounded them with lashes that had no business belonging to a man.

"Excuse me," Donna said, coming to her rescue before Josh could make her blush any more. "Am I invisible?"

Josh strode off in his mother's direction. "Hey, good looking." He gave Donna a noisy kiss on the cheek. "What's cooking?"

"Nothing." Donna tried for repressive, but her eyes, clearly, hadn't received the memo and twinkled back at him.

Lucy watched them and felt the familiar allure of this family wash over her. Josh was Donna's charmer. Richard was her rock, while Thomas was her baby. All three of them fine, beautiful men any mother would be proud of.

A pang of nostalgia had Lucy blinking rapidly to clear the tears prickling the back of her eyelids. She had loved spending time with the Hunters. They always felt like a real family. In the Hunter household, people were allowed to be themselves. When she was with them, Lucy never felt as if she were constantly failing some sort of bizarre test. She used to sit amongst all three boys and Des, letting the sounds of argument and laughter wash over her, and pretend she was one of them. For the first time, she felt the tangible loss of Des. She looked up and caught Donna watching her.

The older woman gave her a gentle smile, as if she understood what Lucy was thinking.

Richard opened a bottle of wine. He poured a glass for his mother and then Josh. He set a glass of sparkling water in front of her. She smiled her thanks and their eyes met. His eyes glowed hot at her.

"Great dress," he murmured, so quietly only she could hear him.

Lucy's pulse picked up the pace. She dragged her gaze away and watched him go to work on some onions and garlic, his long fingers working quickly and efficiently.

"So, Lucy?" Josh slid his arm around her waist and tugged her against his side. He smelled deliciously sinful. "Did you and Richard kiss and make up?"

"Jesus!" Richard glared at his brother.

"What?" Josh shrugged unrepentantly. "It was a bit of humor, Richard. Lighten up a little, would you?"

Richard growled and turned his attention back to his mother. He and Donna started a conversation, speaking in French so rapid Lucy lost track of what was being said.

"It's why he's the favorite," Josh said, as he jerked his head at Richard and Donna. "Because of the French. Clearly, I'm the better brother, but all he has to do is *parlez* a phrase or two and I'm dog meat."

"Then learn French," Lucy returned tartly.

"Ah, baby," Josh gave her the smolder. "I know all the French I need to."

"I bet you do." Lucy ruined the effect with a giggle.

"Would you give it a rest?" Richard growled at his brother suddenly.

Lucy looked up in surprise.

Josh blinked, recovered fast, and gave Richard a look loaded with challenge.

They never changed, these two. They could turn a clambake into a head-to-head challenge.

Richard shook his head and returned to his conversation with Donna.

Josh turned back to Lucy. "So, sexy lady, what have you been doing since you left? Last I heard you were working in New York." Josh leaned over the counter and grabbed his wine.

Richard worked at the stove. The smell of frying onions and garlic filled the kitchen.

"No, I gave up modeling," she replied.

"Damn," Josh murmured. "I almost had a full collection of your lingerie catalogues."

"Lucy's been in Seattle," Richard rumbled from beside the stove. Clearly, not only keeping his attention on his mother.

"Is that right?" said Josh with a motion to Lucy to tell him more.

"I'm working as a personal trainer at the moment," Lucy said.

"Hence that smokin' body," Josh said, winking.

"Until I can finish school."

"You went back to school?"

"You're studying?"

"School?"

All three Hunters turned on her at once. Lucy felt disconcerted to be the center of all that attention. Her eyes drifted to Richard. He had an expression on his face that made her little light glow brighter.

"I'm getting a masters in physiotherapy." Her cheeks heated.

"Lucy Flint," Donna shrieked and went all pink and sparkly.

For a moment, Lucy thought she might burst into a jig around the kitchen.

"I am so proud of you, I could kiss you." And then, that's exactly what she did. Donna grabbed Lucy's face between her palms and gave her a great smacking kiss on the forehead.

"I'm proud too," drawled Josh. "In fact, I am so proud I am going to have to kiss you." He was halfway to her before a feral noise from Richard's throat stopped him. Josh paused midreach, threw Lucy a look of unadulterated mischief, and planted one right on her mouth. "Was that good for you?" he asked as he stepped back.

"That's some lip action you got going on there, Josh." Lucy pretended to fan herself.

"Wanna see it again?" he leered back at her.

"No," snarled Richard before Lucy could come up with a quick reply.

"Jealous, Richard?" Josh taunted.

"I'm married," he spat back at his brother.

"Not anymore," Josh returned softly.

Lucy froze, but Donna pushed her way between them with a colander of shrimp. "You talk too much," she said to Josh, but left it at that.

The tension between the two men thickened in the air. Across from them, Richard was like a coiled spring. Josh stared back at him. Like old times, Lucy thought as she sipped her water.

Josh could never resist needling his brother and Richard took the bait every time.

"What's new with you, Ma?" Josh broke the eye lock and turned to Donna who was washing shrimp at the sink.

Richard snorted softly.

Donna glared at her oldest son and he stared back at her implacably.

Lucy looked from Donna to Richard. It had seemed like an innocuous enough question.

"Did I miss something?" Josh, obviously, felt the same.

"Did you tell him your great idea?" Richard raised an eyebrow.

Donna picked up her wineglass.

"What?" Josh demanded.

"I was going to tell him tonight." Donna shrugged. "But why don't you do the honors."

"Ma has decided to go and see her father," Richard announced.

"What?" Josh stared at his mother and then at Richard.

Donna shrugged and reached for a cloth to dry her hands. "It's time and he's sick. I want to make peace. Go home."

Lucy understood that and the look Donna gave her said that she knew it too.

"Cool." Josh dragged a chair out and sat down. "When did you decide this?"

"You think it's cool?" Richard crossed his arms over his chest in a gesture Lucy recognized well. Richard was gearing up to entrench himself. "You know what that shit put her through and all you can say is, 'cool'?"

"Jesus, Richard, she's old enough to take care of herself," Josh snapped back at his brother.

Richard tossed a wooden spoon onto the countertop. "I think she's being impulsive and hasn't thought this out."

"And I think she's earned the right to make up her own mind and do what she likes."

"I'm in the room," Donna reminded her sons. "And thank you for your support, Joshua, but I really don't need anyone's approval." She glanced up at Richard again. "I am old enough to make my own decisions and I need to do this. So I am going to. *Point final.*"

Richard and Joshua locked eyes across the kitchen.

"Your sauce is burning." Donna gave Richard a push. She threw Lucy a look loaded with exasperation. "Still they must butt heads, all the time."

"Richie Rich."

"Flower?"

"Would you fight off ravening hordes for me?"

"Ravening?"

"Yup."

"Hmm . . . couldn't I raven with them?"

Josh and Richard had one or two more skirmishes, but it didn't bother her. Donna ignored them and so did Lucy. Dinner was fun. Josh kept them laughing. And Richard? Lucy's thoughts stuttered to a halt.

Richard was silent, for the most part, but his eyes strayed back to her time and time again.

God, she was in so much trouble and happily tumbling deeper.

She didn't stay late.

"I'll walk you home." Josh got up to leave with her.

Richard tensed and opened his mouth to argue, but shut it again. His cheek moved against hers as Lucy thanked him for dinner and kissed him a polite good night.

Donna gave her a warm hug and made her promise to drop by and see her, soon.

"This is not necessary," she said as Josh pulled her arm through his and tugged her out into the cold. "I think I can find my own way home."

"Yeah," he said, grinning, "but my mother would kill me if I let a lady walk home alone."

He stopped at the stairs leading to her front door.

"It was good to see you again, Lucy." He leaned down and gave her a kiss on the cheek. "Listen." He straightened up and for once there was no mischief in his eyes. "I have a few friends in the program, so if you need a meeting, you let me know."

"Thanks," Lucy said, smiling. It was easy to forget Josh had a sweetness that ran all the way to the bone. He spent so much time hiding behind wit and charm it was easy to overlook the real man lurking inside. "It was good to see you, too." And she meant it.

Chapter Twenty-Four

It took Lucy a while to get away from Lynne and up to her bedroom. Her mother was waiting up for her and full to bursting with questions. There was only so much Lucy was prepared to share with her. It reminded Lucy of times in the past when Lynne had wanted to know everything about her day. Lapping up the details of her daughter's life, as if she could capture the moments for herself. It was invasive then, and now, it was just plain odd.

Lucy hung up her dress and slipped into her pajamas. She crept across the hallway from the bathroom and into her bedroom.

The light was on in Richard's house. Richard was clearly visible, silhouetted in the frame of his bathroom doorway. He must have stepped out of the shower.

Look away, whispered her better self, but very, very softly. *No fucking way,* roared back the rest of her and Lucy stood still.

"Shit," she breathed out loud. He was beautiful and she'd had her hands and mouth all over him the night before. "Don't go there," she tried to tell her fogged brain. "Let it go and move on."

Lucy ogled the tight line of his butt, perched temptingly above the hard swell of thighs. His lean waist swept up into the clean, wide lines of his shoulders. His arms rippled with muscle as he toweled himself dry. Pure, unadulterated lust rushed through her veins and she stood, fused to the spot. She remembered the feel of his hard body and the taste of his skin.

"Turn around," Lucy murmured under her breath. "Please, please turn around." God, this was reprehensible, but she wasn't going anywhere. Besides, she reasoned strongly, if he didn't want her to look, he should have closed the blinds to his bedroom.

He started to turn around and reality was like ice water down her neck. She ducked out of sight to the side of the window. And just in time.

She stayed where she was, contemplating her next move. She could stay down and belly-crawl to a safe distance. Or she could step in front of the window, as if she had come in to draw the drapes. Which, she had and, if he was still there, then she could pretend surprise—yank her bloody eyeballs away—and discreetly move out of sight.

She was mentally cataloguing her options when her cell vibrated in her hand. She almost dropped it and then scrambled to answer.

"Hello," she whispered hoarsely. God knows why? Richard could see her, but he didn't have supersonic hearing that could penetrate two sets of triple glazing.

"That's very rude, you know?" Richard's voice chased over her nerve endings. She went hot and then cold. "I am very sure there are all sorts of laws against peeping at the neighbors."

"Who is this, please?" Lucy brazened it out.

His deep chuckle told her it had been an epic fail. "Come to the window," he commanded softly.

"Are you dressed?"

"No, but you've seen it all before."

"It must have slipped my mind." Lucy went for nonchalance.

"Come to the window."

"At least put a towel on." Her insides melted.

"I have a towel on."

"Oh, okay." Lucy stepped out from behind the wall and he laughed.

He was wearing a towel, riding low on a set of narrow hips. It was like her own Old Spice commercial, only better and real and less than twenty feet away. He had his phone pressed to his ear and a small grin playing around the corners of his mouth. Damn, but she wanted to bite him. "Are you showing off?" Lucy accused.

"Maybe." His stab at humility really lacked conviction. "What do you think?" He flexed a bicep for her.

She thought it was rather yummy.

"Hmm?" She put her head on one side and studied him.

He grinned and posed through her perusal.

"It's very nice, Richard." And then she gave an apologetic wince. "But you used to have these cute, little skinny arms. And I really preferred them."

"Is that right?" he drawled, totally unconvinced.

"Oh, definitely," Lucy assured him. "And I really got off on your chicken chest back then. All these bulging pecs and ripped abs are so . . ." She made a business of searching for the right word. "They're so passé."

"So now you speak French, *chérie?*"

"I get by with a little bit here and there."

"Impress me with something," he challenged with a tilt of his jaw in her direction.

"Oh, I couldn't." Lucy batted her lashes furiously. "I am naturally modest. You, on the other hand . . ."

"Since when are you modest?" he snorted.

"I have changed in many ways."

"Yes, you have." And her insides grew warm and gooey. "So, you liked my skinny arms and turkey chest, hmm?"

"Chicken chest," Lucy corrected gravely. "You know how roosters have this bit that sticks out, but there's only bone there?"

"Uh-huh." His eyes narrowed at her over the distance separating them. "I never had a chicken chest."

"Sure you did," she assured him. "Like you had that cute, little potbelly."

He looked down over the corrugated skin of his abdomen.

Lucy wanted to touch so badly her hands started to sweat. Oh dear, this was not good. Her skin felt too tight for her body. She wondered if he could hear her accelerated breathing down the phone, or had any idea how hard her heart hammered against her breastbone.

"So, what have you got?" he shot back at her while she silently salivated. "I seem to recall from last night that you are still quite something."

"Quite something?" Lucy jeered and flapped her hand at him. "Smokin' and you know it."

"Yeah," he rumbled in a voice that shot straight into her pants. "I think I need a bit of a refresher," he suggested huskily.

Lucy's face baked. "Is this some puerile version of 'I'll show you mine, if you show me yours'?"

"Oh, yeah." He flashed another grin her way. "And you're looking at mine," he pointed out with another devil-spawn, sexy chuckle.

"Not all of it," Lucy said, and then winced.

His one hand went straight to the tucked edge of the towel. "You ready for this?"

"No," she yelped hurriedly and then lowered her voice. The last thing she needed was Lynne coming to check on her right now. "And it makes no difference, because I am still not showing."

"Coward," he taunted.

"Oh, please, that is so lame. As if I am going to start dropping my clothes because you called me a coward." She had to speak as loudly as she dared over the loud clucking noises he made.

"I can hope," he pointed out reasonably. "Actually"— and his expression grew truly evil genius—"I have thought of something else you can do to prove your sincerity."

"Don't even go there, buddy." She made a chopping motion with her hand.

"It was worth a try," he said, shrugging. "But come on, Luce, this is hardly fair. I am standing here in a towel."

"You called me and told me to come and look."

"I called you to tell you spying on your neighbor's bare ass was rude."

"Not when he's waving it in the window." She gave him her best repressive look. "Besides which, you are being an exhibitionist now."

He laughed without bothering to deny it. "So, the answer's still no?"

"'Fraid so."

"Even if I tell you it's only professional curiosity.

As a medical man, I would like to see the changes that age has wrought on a beautiful, young body."

"You are so full of shit."

"Right back at you, sweetheart," he said, winking.

"And on that note." Lucy managed to dredge up the self-possession to get away. "I am going to bed."

"Planning on sleeping naked?"

"Nope. Me, SpongeBob, and Patrick are staying together."

"You're not a team player, Lucy Flint."

"That's for damn sure," she snorted, and turned away from the window.

"You still have a great ass," he told her.

"You big flirt."

"My mother says I'm charming."

"Your mother has no idea." His chuckle made gooseflesh spread all over her. "Say good night, Richard."

She laughed and snapped off the light. She hung up on his long protest and slipped into bed. She didn't draw the drapes and she could still see him standing by the window.

Her cell phone vibrated and she picked it up.

"Still me." Richard's voice sent her pulse into overdrive.

"Oh, hi." Her voice came out all breathy and come hither. "What can I do for you, Doctor Hunter?"

"Um . . ." His voice was like hot chocolate and it sent shivers down her spine. "I've got this mental image giving me some trouble."

"What's that?" Lucy heard the dark, sweet promise in his voice and it flowed through her like honey.

"You in that black dress," he murmured. "I can't seem to get it out of my mind."

"Hmmm," Lucy purred into the phone. "What would you prescribe?"

"I was wondering if I should make a house call?"

Lucy almost melted into the mattress as hot pulses shot straight to her core. "You were?"

"Mmm." His murmur stroked her from the inside. "You looked a bit feverish to me earlier."

"Richard?"

"Yes."

"Is this a booty call?"

"I'm not sure. That would depend on whether or not you're coming."

"Not yet, I'm not."

He groaned softly. "Lucy, I am dying over here."

"I'll be right over."

"Shouldn't I come there?"

Always the gentleman. Lucy rolled her eyes. "Not unless you want to share the details with my mother in the morning."

"I'll stay naked."

"Good idea."

He was waiting for her by the time she slid and slipped her way across the icy sidewalk to his house. The door opened and he tugged her out of the biting wind.

"Oh, God, I officially have no pride," she muttered as he shoved her coat down her arms. "I answered a booty call."

He was still wearing only his towel, slung low on his hips, and Lucy drank him in.

His hair was wet from the shower and he smelled of soap and man.

Lucy's mouth watered. Not only did she have no pride, but she was a helpless slave to her sluttish tendencies.

Her coat hit the floor and his one hand slipped behind her neck, tugging her closer.

"Lucy." His voice was hoarse and rough in the near dark. The only light cast was the dim glow from the ambient city lights. "Could we not talk tonight?" It was not a request. His mouth sealed the demand on hers.

Lucy opened for his assault immediately and all thoughts of leaving disappeared.

His mouth devoured her in a rough slide and tangle of his tongue. As he consumed the taste of her, they were moving all the time deeper into the house. Under her palms, his chest was firm and beautiful and she spread her fingers wide.

She slid her hands down over his washboard stomach, glorying in the feel of him, moaning her pleasure into his voracious mouth. Her fingers found the tuck at the edge of his towel and pulled. The terry cloth dropped in a sibilant sigh to the floor and Lucy stepped over it.

He was fully, magnificently aroused and Lucy closed her hand around him.

He tensed and froze, absorbing the feel of her caressing his cock. He tugged his mouth away from hers. His eyes were heavy and laden with desire, burning into her with a ferocity that tugged between her legs. "Get up those stairs."

"Make me."

He was on her before she could blink. Lucy's world went ass over tip, quite literally, as he hoisted her effortlessly over his shoulder. He took the stairs two at a time while she squealed and laughed. She hit the bed still laughing. "Oh my, but you have learned a thing or two."

"You talk too much." He hauled her shirt over her head. She wasn't wearing a bra and his eyes feasted on her naked breasts. He reached out with both hands to cup them, before lowering his mouth to lavish attention on the peaks with his tongue and teeth. Pleasure rocketed through Lucy.

He helped her wriggle out of her flannel pajama bottoms, wrapping her legs around his hips to bring his erection against the cradle of her thighs. He was so hard she ached for him and pushed her hot, slick flesh against his hardness.

"I have to get inside you, now." He reached for protection as he spoke.

He drove into her in one sure, strong stroke that arched Lucy up off the bed. He took her hard, strong, and fast and Lucy clung on for the ride. Urging him on to more and more with her hips and her hands and her teeth against his shoulder. The climax built rapidly within her, plummeting her over the edge in a wild free fall that left her clinging to Richard as he emptied himself into her.

It took a while to come down. Lucy stayed perfectly still, glorying in the feel of his strong body over her and inside her. Eventually, one of them shifted and he rolled over onto his back. He kept one arm around her and tugged her over to lie on his chest.

"Jesus, Lucy," was all he said, his breathing still a bit rapid. "Did I hurt you?"

"No way."

"You make me crazy, you know that, right?"

"I think we make each other a bit crazy." Lucy got comfortable against him.

He shifted to accommodate her, his arm tightening around her waist to keep her safe.

Feeling like a guilty teenager all the way and cursing herself for it, Lucy opened the front door to Richard's house. She peered around the crack onto the deserted street. It was still pitch dark outside, a little before six. She had a few minutes to slip inside her house before Carl woke up. She was cutting it close, but she'd lain in bed for a few more precious moments, listening to the steady thud of Richard's heartbeat and glorying in the feel of him wrapped around her.

"How old are you?" She shook her head at herself as she crept down the walkway to her own house. The window to Richard's bedroom was still dark. She'd sneaked out before he was awake, a part of her not wanting him to wake up and do the same as last time. Last night was magical and she wanted to surf the high for a bit longer before reality came crashing down on her.

Chapter Twenty-Five

When she saw Lynne's face over breakfast, Lucy knew she'd made the right choice of discretion over valor the night before. Her mother wore a long-suffering expression that tugged at Lucy's guilt mechanism. An internal struggle kept her silent for a moment, but she lost the battle.

"What is it, Mom?" she asked. Carl was having his breakfast in bed and they would be undisturbed.

"Nothing." Lynne sniffed, and vigorously cracked eggs into a bowl.

"It must be something." Lucy strongly suspected she hadn't managed to get back this morning quite as secretly as she would have hoped.

"It really is none of my business." Lynne enthusiastically whisked the eggs in the bowl. At this rate, Lynne would be able to beat the air it was so thick. "Would you like scrambled or an omelet?"

If Lucy said poached, her mother would tip the entire lot into the trash and start again, without so much as a reproachful look. Lynne reserved her displeasure for much larger transgressions.

"Whatever you want to make is good with me."

The silence in the kitchen grew deeper as Lynne scrambled eggs. Lucy got up to make the toast. Lynne moved around the kitchen, her gestures quick and jerky as if she could barely contain them.

"Mom?"

Lynne pulled the pan of eggs from the heat.

"Mom, do you want to talk about something?" She had no idea how long she would still be in Willow Park. It seemed such a stupid waste of time to spend it like this. All she knew was what last night meant to her. Without knowing how much, if anything, it meant to Richard. She had no business building castles in the air.

"There is nothing to talk about." Lynne scraped eggs onto a plate and slid it beneath Lucy. The plate hit the counter with a solid clunk.

"You seem angry." Lucy fiddled with her fork. Her mother was not going to make this easy for her.

"I'm not angry." Lynne jerked her face away from Lucy's sight. "What have I to be angry about?"

"Oh, Mom." Lucy wanted to scream her frustration. "Can we not do this, just once, can we not do this?"

"Well then, Lucy, what would you like us to do?" Lynne turned and looked at her, her face rigid with disapproval.

"I would like it, if we could talk about whatever is making you angry and not do this . . . this." Lucy didn't really have the words and she waved her arms to encompass the two of them and the kitchen.

"Is that what you would like?" Lynne thrust her chin out belligerently and Lucy got the first inkling her mother was more than upset with her.

Lynne was angry. It didn't happen often, but when it did, it was noteworthy.

Unease flickered through Lucy as she studied her mother's implacable expression.

Lynne crossed her arms over her chest. "Because we spend a lot of time on what you would like. We talk about it all the time." Lynne's eyes narrowed into angry slits. "I have an idea. Let's talk about what I would like?"

"Okay?" Lucy answered carefully. Lynne burned on a long slow fuse, but when she reached the end—duck.

"What I would like is for you to stay away from Richard Hunter." It burst out of Lynne in a low, furious hiss of noise that was no less powerful for its quietness. "But you knew that, didn't you? And it didn't stop you. I know you were over there again last night."

"Mom . . ." She was thirty years old; she didn't have to account for her whereabouts.

"Haven't you done enough yet?" Lynne's face grew flushed. "You left so much wreckage behind you, you know, Lucy?"

"I am not trying to hurt anyone."

"And yet you do, anyway." Lynne uncrossed her arms and slapped her hands against the counter. "You come back talking about how you are a new person, but look at you." Lynne shook one hand at her. "You're the same. Doing the same things all over again."

"That's not true." Lucy was armored and ready for attack from Carl, but from Lynne, it found a raw nerve and scraped.

"People in this place have long memories," continued Lynne as if she hadn't spoken. "And not one of them has forgotten how it was. How you were. And now you are back and messing with a young man who has become a respected member of this community. A man who, as far as I know, is still married."

"I'm not messing with him, Mom. This is a mutual thing."

"I don't care about that." Lynne's lips thinned into a hard line. "It's wrong is what it is. It's wrong and you knew that, but you went ahead and did it anyway. Just like you used to do."

Lucy struggled to control her anger. The need to defend herself bubbled up in her throat, but she fought it. "You know, Mom, one of the things I have had to learn is to let go of the past."

Lynne rounded on her. "Isn't that wonderful for you. I wish we all had that convenient free pass you have."

"Mom?" Lucy blinked at Lynne. Free pass? Oh, that was a good one. Here, have a pass to rigorous and relentless honesty with yourself. Have fun with that. All you have to do is drag your sorry ass out of the shit that being an alcoholic landed it in.

"It would be nice if we could all say sorry and get a 'do-over.' But life doesn't work like that, Lucy. You don't get to do whatever you want and then say sorry and everything is all right again. There are consequences to your actions and you have to live with them. You made your bed, my girl, and now you get to lie on it."

"Mom." Lucy's gut churned. Her mother's anger was like a wave of hurt that hit her full frontal and traveled through her, striking most major organs on the way through. "Mom, I can't change the things I've done. I can only take responsibility for them, ask forgiveness, and move on."

"How very convenient," Lynne sneered at her and Lucy recoiled physically.

She'd always wondered how her mother quelled all the anger she must have built up over the years. Now she was beginning to see. It didn't dissipate. It seethed quietly until the floodgate could safely be opened.

"You get to move on and everyone else gets to live with the consequences. Goodness me, but I wish we could all be so lucky." Lynne gave a brittle little laugh.

"I understand there were consequences to my actions. I live with them too."

"No, you don't." Lynne actually raised her voice. "You swanned off to New York and then Seattle. You weren't here to see the way people laughed behind my back about my uncontrollable daughter. They pitied me. Do you know that? I could see it in their eyes."

"Mom, I—"

"Me, they pitied me, Lynne Redley Flint. God help me. Most of their fathers worked for mine. All these years, they have been waiting to see me fall. And it was my own daughter, my flesh and blood, who gave them what they wanted." Lynne took a shaky breath. "You were my pride and my joy, Lucy. I gave you everything. All I had inside me to give and then more and it wasn't enough for you. You had to go and be an alcoholic and then throw your body around like you were nothing more than cheap trash."

Lynne breathed heavily, her face flushed with her emotion. "And they laughed at me. I was so proud of you and you dragged both of us down. I don't understand any of this, Lucy. I don't understand it and I don't accept it."

Lucy sat there for a long moment. Slut, drunk, worthless, embarrassment—all names she had called herself.

It was a surreal experience to hear the voice in her head come out of someone else's mouth.

Only she hadn't stopped there. Her anger with herself had run way deeper and been far more damaging. As fast as the ugly accusations rose, they subsided again. She was none of those things, perhaps she never had been. An alcoholic, yes, but the rest of it was all pointless self-flagellation. Hearing it directed at her was oddly liberating. There were no harsher words that anyone could hurl at her than the ones she used to torment herself. Being an alcoholic was not a life sentence of shame and degradation. She was done with that.

Lynne, it appeared, was not done yet.

A year ago, Lucy had sat with her mother in her small apartment in Seattle and asked Lynne for her forgiveness. For all the pain and the humiliation and the disappointment. Until this moment, had her mother really been honest with her about anything?

They had cried and hugged and mopped each other up and when it was all over, they had agreed to move forward. Only one of them had moved forward.

Lynne had not forgotten and neither had she forgiven.

Lucy got slowly to her feet.

Lynne turned her back and got busy scrubbing at the kitchen counter. Her entire body vibrated with the movement of her vigorous cleaning.

Lucy felt a bit as if she were moving through a haze. There were so many thoughts clamoring for her attention she couldn't quite tease out one thought thread and follow it through.

Carl had been the demanding and judgmental

one, not Lynne. It was always Carl who pointed out her faults and her failures.

Lynne was the rock on which Lucy built her house. Lynne was the one who believed in her and understood her.

Lucy watched with helpless fascination as the foundation beneath her cracked and crumbled. Somehow she found her way up the stairs and into her bedroom.

All the clutter and detritus of her life was suddenly almost obscene. This was the web Lynne had woven around and through her for thirty years.

Carl had thundered and bullied her into submission. That, she had been able to stand against, toe to toe, and fight.

This was more insidious and far, far more effective.

She sank slowly onto her bed and looked around her. She had been fragmented for so long, it had become her normal. Inside were two Lucys. There was the girl plastered all over this room, a desperate creature trying to grow and develop and being prodded and pushed into a shape that was more pleasing to her creator.

And then there was this Lucy. The one who had finally emerged from the chrysalis, battered and bleeding, but determined to find her way out.

Lucy stood and went to the corkboard above the desk. Her younger self stared back at her. Green eyes wide, defiant, and determined, grabbing for life with the desperation of a drowning girl. Because in this house she had drowned and here she had not existed other than as an extension of Lynne or Carl.

With a shaking finger she traced the lines of her face in the picture. What a beautiful face it was. She studied the younger version of the features she saw in the mirror every morning. This girl was her and so agonizingly young. For all her faults, she was a child, a young girl, on the brink of womanhood, lost and desperate.

Lucy had spent so much of her life hating and despising this girl, the girl who did the bad things. This was a bad, bad girl and should be shut down and tucked into a corner.

Lucy unpinned a picture of her and Ashley. They must have been all of twelve, dressed in tattered shorts and T-shirts that read WILLOW PARK DAY CAMP. Ashley had her arm around her neck in a stranglehold and Lucy wore most of the popsicle in her hand all around her mouth.

She smiled at the girls. Just two young girls, not bad, evil girls who deliberately betrayed their fathers and broke their mothers' hearts, just two young girls laughing on a summer day.

She stepped closer to the other pictures.

There were more, later pictures. Lucy dressed up for a prom, all Lolita-like in an ice-pink, silk dress.

Not a bad girl at all, a young girl, growing and stretching and trying to find her way. A woman started to peer out cautiously from within the child, so delicate and fragile and so ready to take on all comers.

"Hello." Lucy touched a fingertip to her graduation photo.

Richard was there, standing behind her and beaming down at her. She mugged it up for the camera with her diploma and her cap.

"We know how to do better now," she said out loud, her voice a soft whisper in the silence of the room.

She turned back to the room and shrugged. What did it matter if Lynne wanted to cling to this stuff? The real Lucy was no longer in the past.

Chapter Twenty-Six

Brooke's house was not hard to find. In fact, it stuck out like a pair of dog's balls in a block of aging Willow Park grande dames. Brooke and Christopher must have had a special friend in town planning.

Gone was the red-face brick, beneath layers of stucco white, Moroccan-style plasterwork. All the old cottage pane windows had been removed and tortured into arches that appeared strangely out of proportion. An entire wing was tacked onto one side of the original house. It started under the eaves, went straight up, and then tapered into half an A-frame. A child with a set of building blocks had, clearly, been their architect.

Lucy took a deep breath. She was not here to judge.

"Lucy?" Brooke appeared on the front step beneath a soaring arch that had once been a square-fronted porch. Today, she was poured into shiny, black trousers. Her coat was bright red with the arms covered in zebra print, the heads of which opened their maws over her chest and shoulders. "Can I help you with something?"

Here goes. Lucy sucked in a breath and tried to calm the butterflies overrunning her stomach. She felt ready this morning to do this. Lucy had the feeling she would need all her newfound fortitude, because Brooke was not looking in the least welcoming. Not a shocker after the scene in the store, but not exactly encouraging, either.

"Actually"—Lucy tried to keep her smile warm and open—"I wondered if you had a minute?"

"What for?" Brooke folded her arms with a wide sweep of her zebra.

Lucy flinched. It was a fair question, but not one she had a short answer for and certainly not one she wanted to get into standing on the sidewalk. "It won't take long," she evaded neatly. "I need to come in for a bit."

Lucy shivered under the hostile rake of Brooke's eyes as the other woman studied her intently. It looked like Brooke might refuse and then she shrugged and motioned for Lucy to follow. The heels of Brooke's boots clipped sharply against the terra-cotta tiles as Lucy trailed her into the house.

Lucy stopped dead inside the door, shaken out of her purpose for an instant. A giant Versailles, crystal chandelier dominated the entrance hall. Colored crystals had replaced the clear ones and shed their jeweled tones all over the walls and floor.

"Spectacular, isn't it?" Brooke murmured from beside her. A rapt expression spread across her features. "Christopher had it specially made for our eighth anniversary."

Lucy turned to look at her in surprise.

Brooke's pale blue eyes dared Lucy to comment.

Lucy leaned over to take off her boots. It gave her a moment to collect her thoughts. Brooke must have worked fast, because nine years ago Lucy had left town with her then-boyfriend.

"Yes," Brooke said, having read her mind. "We have been married almost nine years."

Forget fast, Brooke must have had a meteoric courtship.

"We met, fell in love, and six weeks later, voila." She flashed a rock the size of Lucy's purse at her and tittered happily.

Voila, indeed.

Brooke wrestled free of the zebras to reveal more animal print beneath.

Lucy was no expert, but she thought this might be snow leopard. Or close enough. She shrugged out of her old black parka and Brooke hung it beside the door.

There was a definite order to the coat hooks. First, there was a man's jacket. Christopher, she guessed. The next hook was impaling the zebras and the following two were clearly for children, one blue and one pink.

Brooke examined her from head to toe, not missing a thing. Her eyes were of such a light blue that in some lights they appeared almost colorless. It could be a bit disconcerting, having those unfriendly orbs turned in your direction.

Lucy took a careful breath and smiled cautiously.

"We should sit." Brooke turned suddenly, leaving Lucy to follow in her wake.

Lucy took the opportunity to mentally run through the speech she and Mads had worked on. Her mind kept going blank. Now that she was here, in Brooke's home, the past throbbed alive and palpable between them. Lucy cursed herself for not trying to have this meeting on neutral ground. But it was a miracle Brooke had agreed to see her at all.

Lucy stopped a moment on the threshold of the living room. Blue, blue, and blue, everywhere you looked, from the sofas to the drapes to the carpet. So blue, it made the back of Lucy's eyeballs ache. And when it wasn't blue, it was gold and that, too, assaulted her eyes. A huge gas fireplace dominated one end of the room. Disembodied blue flames danced in eerie solitude above blue glass pebbles. The heat it put out was making Lucy's scalp itch already and she chose a seat farthest from the inferno. It seemed a fitting place from which to do penance.

"Lucy Flint." Brooke stood opposite her and stared. She shook her head at the peculiarity of it all. "Sitting here. Now."

"Brooke," Lucy began on a deep breath. It was time. "Thank you for seeing me."

Brooke shrugged one shoulder, as if it were a minor inconvenience. "I have no idea what this is about, Lucy." She settled onto one of the blue velour chairs near the fire. "But *I* have not forgotten how civilized people behave."

"Well, thank you." Lucy took a breath. "I think I should start out by telling you I am an alcoholic."

Brooke's eyes lit appreciatively. This was excellent fodder for the gossip canon.

Lucy grit her teeth and got on with it. "I have always had a problem with alcohol, but it took me until my late twenties to realize I was no longer in control of my drinking."

Brooke went a deeper shade of pink and a soft sheen of anticipation glowed on her skin.

"It was then I sought some help." It was getting harder now and Lucy took a moment to gather her thoughts. "I went to AA and they put me on their twelve-step program. I am now at step nine and that is about making amends to people who I have hurt or injured."

A small frown crossed Brooke's forehead and Lucy could sense the change in the other woman. She was not nearly as eager to hear what Lucy had to say anymore.

Lucy got to the meat of it. "Brooke, when I left Willow Park, with Jason, I can only imagine how much that must have hurt and I want you to know I regret it."

Brooke's face had gone a bit pasty looking.

Lucy could see the hurt no amount of bling could hide. It stared out of Brooke's face at her accusingly. The past was not a kind place for the other woman. "But even before Jason, I treated you very badly. I said and did things that were unkind and hurtful," Lucy said softly, not wanting to leave new wounds on top of old scars. This was not the purpose of her visit today, at all.

"You used to call me pudding," Brooke said in a dull, flat voice that hid more pain than Lucy cared to dwell on.

"I remember that, too," she said. "Brooke, I am here to tell you I realize how badly I hurt you and I am truly sorry for the pain I caused you. When I drank, I only focused on myself to the detriment of others. It is not an excuse for my behavior, but it is an explanation and one you deserve. My drinking was an illness that seeped into every area of my consciousness and caused me to behave in ways I am not proud of."

Brooke had gone completely still, but Lucy forged forward. "It has taken all this time to realize how much I injured you and I ask your forgiveness. You are under no obligation to give it, but I want you to know I am deeply and sincerely sorry for any hurt I caused you and if there is any way you can think of that I can make it up to you, you need only ask."

Lucy sat back in her chair and waited. Her heart pounded loudly in the stretched silence.

"Well." Brooke sat back suddenly. "Well," she said again. "You always drank too much." Brooke recovered some of her composure and her face lost the sickly pallor.

"Yes, I know." Brooke had not even seen her drinking at its worst. "I have never had any control when it came to alcohol, which is why I am where I am now."

"Hmm?" Brooke frowned again and worked at her bottom lip with her teeth as if she were weighing something carefully. "You have stopped drinking?"

"Yes."

"Forever?"

"That's how it works." Lucy nodded.

"And now you come back to Willow Park and say you're sorry. Sorry for all the things you have done and the people must forgive you. Just like that."

Lucy's mouth twisted ruefully. "I can't change the past, Brooke. I can only take ownership for what I did, beg your forgiveness, make it up if I can, and move on."

Brooke continued to sit there and stare at Lucy. "You are sorry?" Brooke drew the words out thoughtfully. "This is what you came here to say?" Her voice was not quite steady and her body was as tense as a drawn bowstring.

"I realize it probably seems inadequate when all is said and done," Lucy said, shrugging helplessly. "So, if there is anything I can do to prove my sincerity, I would happily do so."

Brooke gave a short bark of laughter and patted her hair self-consciously. Her hands were not quite steady. "You know what you can do for me, Lucy Flint?" She paused and turned to face Lucy.

Hot, angry tears glittered in her pale eyes and her jaw worked spasmodically as if she were reaching desperately for control. "You can give me back my beautiful party. The one I spent nearly a year planning and you ruined. You took it from me without a thought. Can you do that for me?"

"Brooke . . ." The blood drained from Lucy's face.

"You can give me back my boyfriend, the love of my life. You can give me back Jason." Brooke lurched forward suddenly until her face was mere inches away.

Lucy shrank back reflexively.

Brooke made no effort to conceal her anger and her bitterness. "Do you know how they laughed at me? They pitied me. They all looked at me and felt sorry for me. I crawled, Lucy Flint. I crawled through this town like a joke."

"I am so sorry."

Brooke was not listening to her. "I want you to crawl like I did. I want you to feel my shame. That's what you can do for me, Lucy Flint."

Lucy got unsteadily to her feet. Frantically, she searched for the right words, but her mind was blank. She tried to think what Mads would say, but she couldn't.

Brooke had risen to her feet as well.

"I can't go back and change things," Lucy stuttered, her heart racing. "I can only do things differently in the future."

"Yes, I heard. You can only say you're sorry and beg for forgiveness." Brooke cut her off again. "You haven't changed." Brooke stalked toward her, her voice low and menacing. "Nothing about you has changed. You come here, today, speaking about your regrets, but I saw you, Lucy, and I know that it's all more lies."

The hair on the back of Lucy's neck rose.

"I saw you sneaking out of Richard's house this morning."

Lucy went cold and then hot.

"You are doing what you always did, taking everybody else's man. He is married, Lucy, married to Ashley, but you never let that stop you. Never." Brooke made a slashing motion with her hand and Lucy stepped back.

"Forgive you?" Brooke's voice rose to a shriek. "I don't forgive you, Lucy Flint, not now and not ever. I wish on you all the pain and humiliation you caused me. I wish every scornful word you said to me and every single thing you did to hurt me back on you. Do you understand me? Do you hear me, Lucy Flint?"

Lucy had to get out of here. Brooke's malice poisoned the air until it became difficult to breathe. "I think I should go." Her feet carried her quickly to the door. Her mind registered only the need to escape.

Brooke had seen her this morning, which meant that the entire Willow Park community would know by the end of the day. Ashley would know, if she didn't already.

"Yes, you should go." Brooke scrambled after her. "You should go. You should get out of my house."

Her tirade gathered momentum as she followed Lucy out of the living room. "And you should get out of Illinois completely. Go back to Seattle. Leave here. We don't want you here. Not me, not Ashley, and not Richard, nor any of the others that you crapped on."

Somehow Lucy made it out the door. She was almost

running as she reached the sidewalk. Beneath her hastily pulled-on boots, her feet slid and slipped on the ice, but she didn't slow down. Her heart jumped in her throat. She thought she might be sick.

Brooke's hatred was a living thing pursuing her down the street.

She pulled out her cell with shaking hands and hit speed dial. It hurt more than she could have imagined. It hurt and it shamed her. She must have said something coherent, because the next thing she heard was Mads, firm and gentle.

"You have to breathe, Lucy, breathe."

She dragged air into her lungs obediently and somehow managed to push it out again. She told the story haltingly, not quite believing it, even as she recited the details.

"Okay, Lucy Locket," Mads spoke again, soothing her with that dark, velvet voice. "There are always one or two like that, but you have to let it go, Lucy Locket. Do you hear me?"

"I hear you," Lucy whispered into the phone.

"You breathe in and you breathe out and you let it go. She is not able to forgive you. It's sad and regrettable, but it's her choice and the reasons she can't are hers to own. Got that?"

"Yes," Lucy lied unconvincingly.

"You will." Mads chuckled softly. "You did the right thing, Lucy. Now let it go."

"Just like that?" Lucy gave a harsh bark of laughter.

"No," Mads returned quickly. "There's quite a bit more to it than that."

Chapter Twenty-Seven

"See there." Carmen nudged his arm and Richard's signature scrawled across the entire bottom half of the prescription he was writing. "Look, that's the one. The one I was telling out about."

Richard did not want to look, but he did anyway. A light silver Mercedes pulled up and parked in a slot right outside the windows to his waiting room. A man got out.

Richard studied him covertly while pretending to rewrite the prescription.

He had a tall, suave thing going on in his beautifully cut dress coat. Richard was willing to bet the coat came from London or New York. The man looked at the traffic and then crossed the street.

"He's from out West." Carmen gave him a look of great significance.

"Carmen," Richard said, going for a repressive tone. "I would imagine a lot of people are from out West." He shouldn't have bothered. Carmen was impervious to his frosty dignity.

"Yes, but they don't all ask for directions to the Flint house." Carmen raised her thin eyebrows up to her hairline. "I heard she had a boyfriend over there in Seattle. An older man with money."

"She told me she was done with him." Richard hadn't meant to say that out loud.

As one, the cluster of people waiting for him turned and looked at the stranger.

"But he's here." Carmen snaked her head back and forth like a mongoose taunting a cobra. "And that means he isn't done with her."

A murmur of agreement shot through the waiting room.

Richard—and his patients—watched as the man used the ATM and then picked his way carefully through the ice back to this side of the street. Even his snow boots looked expensive. They didn't even look like snow boots, for the love of God.

"He's going next door to the florist," Carmen reported and there was an excited twitter through the assembly.

Richard kept his attention on the patient chart in front of him.

A short while later, Carmen gasped. "He's got flowers," she hissed at the top of his head. "Roses."

A spattering of conversation broke out.

Out of the corner of his eye, Richard watched as the man deactivated the alarm and opened the door. What kind of poser rented a car like that? Carmen said he was older. He looked it. There was a definite tinge of gray in his hair. And Lucy hated roses. She said they were old-lady flowers. At least, that's what she used to say.

"What do you think he's doing here?" Carmen looked up at him expectantly.

"I have no idea." Richard closed the file with a smart snap and handed it to her.

Carmen glared at him. "But you're going to find out, right?"

"Find out what?" Richard felt like an insect with a pin stuck through the middle of it.

"What he's doing here!" Carmen yelled at him, as if he were the most obtuse being on the planet.

"No, I'm not," Richard yelled right back.

A collective gasp from their audience broke their deadlock.

Carmen snatched the file from his hands and stomped over to her computer. She mentioned something very uncomplimentary about his parentage as she stalked away.

Richard cast one more surreptitious glance out the window. The Mercedes disappeared over the railway tracks. Lucy lived on that side of the tracks.

And he was sure she still didn't like old-lady flowers.

A slither of fear snaked up his spine and Richard took a slow and careful breath.

"Ashley?" She was the last woman he'd expected to see this evening and, quite possibly, the most unwelcome. Soon to be ex-wives should be banned from visiting on days like these. There ought to be a law about it. He'd been behaving like a dickhead all day. Actually, since he had seen the man in the Mercedes. He wanted to call Lucy, but the bigger part of him was chicken shit. So, he stayed later at the office and pretended he was not hiding out.

"I see Carmen was not exaggerating." Ashley sashayed into his office and took a seat on the other side of the desk. She looked good. No, in fact, she looked great. She'd looked that way ever since she'd left him. It was not a welcome thought.

"What can I do for you?"

Ashley cocked her head on one side and studied him. "Carmen says you have been like a bear all day. I think she might be right."

"Ashley"—he used his most repressive tone—"it's been a long day. I don't want to fight. I want to go home and put my feet up."

"I don't want to fight either," she sniffed while Richard grew wary, "but I did want to talk to you."

"And you had to do this here?" He indicated his office with an irate wave of his hand. In truth, it wasn't the venue, so much as the implacable look on Ashley's face. It was the sort of look that warned him Ashley had an agenda and was willing to pursue it relentlessly. He didn't want to go twelve rounds with her. He wanted . . .

The things he wanted were so twisted in his head that he dared not unravel them for fear of what it all meant.

"You are never at home," Ashley said reasonably. "At least I knew I could catch you here and keep you here long enough to have a conversation."

"I have patients to see." He launched a last ditch attempt at escape.

"No, you don't." Ashley settled herself into a chair. "I am the last one. Even Carmen has gone home. She called me before she left."

Busted.

Ashley sat and looked at him.

Richard waited her out.

Patience was not Ashley's strong suit and she would get to why she was here. She barely lasted two minutes before she made a low noise of irritation in the back of her throat. "Are you going to tell me about it?"

"What?" Richard watched her carefully.

"Are you going to tell me about you and Lucy?"
Ashley's mouth twisted spitefully.

Shock held Richard immobile for a few life-saving
moments. He shouldn't have been surprised. You
couldn't do anything in Willow Park without somebody finding out. But, who would have told Ashley?
Certainly not Lucy or his mother or Josh. They might
fight, but they were still brothers.

"You haven't said anything, Richard." Ashley raised
one brow in an imperious arch. "Either you're wondering whether or not to lie, or you're wondering how
I found out? Don't strain yourself," she snapped.
"Brooke saw Lucy creeping out of our house."

There was his answer and Richard sat back in his
chair.

"How could you?" Ashley's voice vibrated with
anger. "How could you sleep with her, again? How
could you humiliate me like that?"

Richard was dimly aware he should be trying to talk
his way out of it, or explain. There was not much he
could say, however. He had, for sure, not slept with
Lucy to spite Ashley. In fact, Ashley had not even entered into his thought processes where Lucy was concerned. Ashley certainly would not want to hear that.

Which left the question as to why he had allowed
himself to fall back under Lucy's spell.

He almost laughed out loud. Allowed himself?
That was a good one. His resistance had been token,
at best.

Ashley was right. He had never gotten over Lucy.
Perhaps if she'd come back into town as the same
hell-raising terror she had been, he might have been
able to walk away. But Lucy had changed. She had
grown into the woman he had sensed in her all along.
The same woman his dad had always seen, lurking

beneath the surface of all that anger and rebellion. The woman was twice as heady and compelling as the girl had been. He'd not stood a chance.

Ashley saw none of this, because she was still at war with the Lucy who left town nine years ago. As she glared at him from across his desk, the thing that struck him the most forcibly was that it wasn't his infidelity that bothered Ashley. It would be a bit rich, having been separated for over a year. No, what was eating Ashley was the fact that it was Lucy he had been unfaithful with.

"I don't think I am the only one who never got over Lucy Flint," he suggested mildly.

Ashley flinched as if he'd struck her. She recovered quickly. Her eyes went like pitch and her mouth contorted into a snarl. Vitriol spewed out of her in a vicious diatribe that seemed to be endless.

Richard stopped listening to the words and watched Ashley's face instead. He had always known Lucy was a hot spot, but until this moment, he had underestimated how hot the flame burned.

Ashley took a pause for breath and Richard cut in quickly. "Is this why you came here today, Ashley?"

This scene was beneath both of them.

Her breathing grew ragged as she battled her formidable temper back under control. It took a moment and her color was still high. "No," she managed, her jaw tight. "I want you to sign the papers, Richard, so that I can file them." There was the slightest hesitation and then her voice grew brittle with determination. "Or I am going to have to get the lawyers involved in making it happen?"

"We discussed that. We both agreed it wasn't necessary." Richard tamped down on his surge of irritation. He didn't like being threatened.

"That was before one of us made it necessary." Her eyes narrowed. "It's been over a year and in the circumstances, I think it's fucking stupid to pretend this is still a marriage." She straightened in her chair and lifted her chin. "If I end up going to a lawyer, you can be sure I will drag your friend Lucy into this as well."

There was a heavy silence in his office. Richard heard the thud of his dead marriage hit the desk. It should have ripped him apart, but instead he felt numb, numb and relieved, as if someone had taken the trouble off his hands.

At some stage in the last year, the will to fight had dissipated. He'd been running on fumes and habit and now, this thing he'd been digging in his heels about was over. He was flogging the proverbial dead horse. And he was tired of it. It had taken Lucy, blasting her way back into his life, to bring into focus the half-life he'd been living.

Ashley got to her feet, straightening her fire-engine-red pencil skirt over her full hips. She picked up her purse. "It's all right to be scared, Richard. It's not all right to let that fear rule your life."

She had to get in her one more shot of psychobabble. She was right.

She walked away, her hips swaying as she went. Out of his life, it would seem.

Richard studied the faded print of the human anatomy on the wall. Everything around him was changing so fast. He seemed to be constantly running around trying to catch it and hold on tight. His mother was stretching her wings in alarming directions; Ashley was determined to toss away the training wheels, aka him and Lucy. His brain stuttered to a halt and his sense memory zoomed into the gap.

Lucy, cinnamon and Issey Miyake, jade eyes and soft, pouty lips. Lucy with the endless legs and the smart mouth. Lucy and her huge heart with her arms held wide to embrace all life had to offer. Lucy, of the silken skin and sweet, sultry sighs.

She scared him shitless. He was also really tired of being scared. He reached for the phone.

Donna answered on the second or third ring.

"*Maman?* If you still want to go and see your father, I thought I might come with you." He listened to her speak. "Why?" They always had to ask why. "Because it's Canada and I don't want you going there on your own."

Her response elicited the first smile he'd felt crack his face today. *"Au revoir, je t'aime aussi."*

Chapter Twenty-Eight

When the universe, fate or whatever, decided to kick your ass, it took aim and kept kicking. There was no avoiding the fact she'd traveled miles to end up where she started. Lucy looked at the silent phone in her hand. The center had called looking for her mother and then ended up speaking to her instead.

Lynne had never sent in the forms for Carl. She had never given them the doctor's recommendation. They had held a place for as long as they could, but places were at a premium and there were other people out there who needed care. The center had tried, several times, to get ahold of her mother, but Lynne never returned any of their calls.

"We're sorry, but we have had to give the place to another family," the center director told her.

Lucy assured the woman she understood. She carefully replaced the phone on its cradle. She was angry, but not entirely surprised. Some part of her had always suspected this is how it would end. If that weren't enough, all the signs were there. Mads had seen it, Richard had seen it. Hell. Even she'd seen it, but she hadn't wanted to acknowledge what was staring her in the face. She wanted to rescue Lynne. Who knew what Lynne wanted? Perhaps Lynne was as clueless as the rest of them?

She'd barely seen her mother since that last get-together in the kitchen. Lynne was avoiding her. Either making herself scarce or hiding, in plain sight, behind an endless supply of domestic detritus.

Lucy glared at the phone again and then got wearily to her feet. Frustration curdled in her stomach as she stood there for a moment more.

All of this, all the anguish and the soul searching, all of it felt like it was all for nothing right now. She was feeling sorry for herself, but by her reckoning, that scene with Brooke had earned her the right for a little wallow. So, yes, she was feeling sorry for herself and, no, she was not going to do anything about it for the moment. Later, she might decide to show up and man up, but not right now.

She blew out a large breath and went to find Lynne.

Lynne was in the basement. The place smelled faintly of the beer Carl used to brew years ago and of dust and damp. It was her least favorite place and Lynne spent hours down here, doing the laundry. A coat of paint wouldn't have killed anyone.

"Mom?"

"In here," Lynne chirped cheerfully. The walls were covered in vinyl wainscoting that was clinging on from the seventies. It kept company with mold-colored linoleum on the floor. On second thought, a coat of paint wouldn't have made any difference.

Lynne hauled sheets out of her ancient washer and stuffed them into an even older dryer. The things must still be coal powered.

"I spoke to Mrs. Rogers from the home."

Lynne stiffened immediately, but did not look up from what she was doing. "Oh?"

"She said she has been trying to get ahold of you."

"Hounding me is more like it." Lynne slammed the dryer lid down with a metallic clunk. "The woman has been calling nonstop. Don't you think she'd have gotten the hint by now?"

"Mom, she needed to talk to you, because she had a place for Dad."

Lynne's lips compressed and she bent to load more laundry into the machine.

"Mom?"

Lynne started shoving shirts into the machine. It was not like her mother not to carefully check labels.

"Mom?"

"What?" Lynne straightened suddenly and glared at her. "What do you want me to say to you? You are as bad as that woman on the phone. Always pushing and pushing to get me to do what you want me to do."

"Mom, I thought this was what *you* wanted."

"You thought, Lucy, you thought and you went ahead and dragged me off to see the doctor and started talking about selling the house and making me throw out stuff. You thought, Lucy, and then you charged straight in, without even asking." Lynne measured detergent into the dispenser.

A surge of anger speared through Lucy and she ground her teeth together to stop from blurting out hurtful, ugly words. "You're right, Mom." It cost her a molar to get that past her clenched teeth. "You never asked me to help sell the house or to find somewhere for Dad."

Lynne gave a vicious twist to the dials.

"But all my life you've needed me to stand between you and Dad."

"That is not true. I have never asked you to do anything of the sort." Lynne turned to her with wide eyes. Shock glimmered in their depths. But, there, right at the back, the tiniest flash of guilt. It disappeared as quickly as it had come and Lynne crossed her arms over her chest. "You can't blame this on me. This is what you do. You go rushing into everything impetuously without thinking about what anyone else wants or needs. It's the way you are. It's the way you always were and you can come back here talking about change, but I am not sure you even know the meaning of that word."

Shit, that hurt. "I have changed." Lucy dug her nails into her palms. "Whether you believe that or not, it's *my* truth." The anger simmered and spat near the surface and she took a deep breath, counted to ten, and then again backward. Serenity danced tantalizingly outside of her grasp as she stood and looked at her mother.

Lynne with her face set in bitter lines of disappointment. The years etched across her skin like a living journal.

"If you don't want to put Dad in a home, that's fine. If you want to live in this house for the rest of your life, that's fine too." Lucy met Lynne's glance head-on. "But you chose this, Mom. And, just like me, you're going to have to live with the consequences of the choices you make."

"Why are you talking to me like this?" Tears filled her mother's eyes.

Lucy's heart gave a sharp twist. She didn't want to hurt her mother. That was not what any of this was about. "It's okay, Mom," she said, finding her voice. "Mrs. Rogers only called to say the place has been filled."

Lynne fiddled with dryer dials and Lucy made her way back upstairs.

Chapter Twenty-Nine

It was not in Elliot's nature to walk away. Not when he'd decided he knew best. And she, more than anyone, should have known that. Lucy watched as Elliot made a lifelong slave of Lynne over a bunch of roses and some heavy-handed flattery.

Old-lady flowers, Lucy sniffed, as Lynne lovingly transferred them to a vase. Then she felt bad. Nobody, not even her, ever bought Lynne flowers.

Elliot was a master at the small, meaningful touches. He and Lynne had met before in Seattle a couple of times and Elliot worked the connection, slathering on the charm like axle grease. He was good at it too.

Even Carl seemed grudgingly impressed.

Lucy had to admit, Elliot presented well. He was tall and fit. His clothes were immaculate and elegant in a way that silently yelled expensive, but would never deign to be flashy. His heather-colored sweater was definitely cashmere, Lucy decided, as she watched him pick crumbs from the sleeve. His manners were impeccable and he had the ability to talk to anyone about anything and at any time.

Case in point. He sat in the kitchen with Lynne,

eating her mother's date squares, eulogizing about the taste and trying to cajole Lynne's secret out of her. *Crisco,* Lucy wanted to yell.

He'd arrived at the house shortly after dinner. There was no opportunity to talk to him though. Not with Lynne and him making up for lost time and chatting away like hens in a coop.

While she hovered around the background feeling, and, in all likelihood, looking like a sulky adolescent.

Lynne was already making noises about him not spending money on a hotel. Lucy would have told her not to bother. Elliot never went anywhere unless he was assured of at least an 800-thread count in his sheets.

She studied him while he nattered on to Lynne about the shocking state of the roads.

He was a good-looking man. His features aquiline and clean cut. His gray eyes were direct and confident and he carried himself with the effortless grace of one who understood his own worth. He was quite the catch. Apparently, the blood running through his veins was a touch blue as well. Not that Elliot would do anything so crass as mention such a fact, but a mutual acquaintance had felt no such reticence.

Despite that, Elliot was no trust-fund baby. He'd made his money in his twenties and early thirties, cashing in on the dot-com bubble before selling out at just the right time. While she tore up the neighborhood of Willow Park, Elliot had been busy buying and selling a fortune.

Since then he'd pretty much been doing what he wanted. Contemplating his navel, following Eckhart Tolle around for a while, and rescuing blond waifs with an unfortunate propensity for alcohol.

"What are you doing here, Elliot?" Lucy couldn't stand another swapped recipe.

"Lucy," Lynne chastised her, frowning at her over Elliot's shoulder. Her mother had barely said a word to her since their little heart-to-heart in the laundry. Elliot's arrival had given Lynne all the distraction she needed.

Elliot turned to her and she was caught in the tug of his attention. He had this way of looking at her that made her feel like she was locked in a tractor beam and being steadily towed along into the mother ship.

"It's all right, Lynne. She has the right to ask after our last conversation. And I did just turn up on your doorstep, uninvited and unannounced."

"I don't like a guest not to feel welcome in my home," Lynne said, twinkling at him.

"I doubt that's possible, Lynne."

Oh, please. Lucy wanted to throw up.

Elliot could sell sand in a desert when he turned it on. It was probably how he'd managed to make such a lot of money in such a short amount of time. It made Lucy want to gag.

The laughter in his gray eyes as he looked back at her told her he knew exactly what she was thinking and it amused the hell out of him.

"Perhaps we can go somewhere and talk?" he suggested reasonably.

"I don't think there is anything more to say, Elliot."

"Lucy," Lynne twittered anxiously. "The man has flown all this way to see you. The least you can do is hear him out."

"Boy, are my arms tired." He gave her a soft smile that invited her to share the old joke.

Lucy softened a touch.

He was a good man. He was just not the man for

her and the sooner they both realized that, the better. So, she would tell him again and again until he understood it.

"Come on then," she invited graciously. "We can talk upstairs. You can bring those with you, if you like." She indicated the date squares.

"Oh, I couldn't," he demurred unconvincingly. Who was Elliot kidding? He had one massive sweet tooth.

"Please." Lynne pushed the plate in his direction. "They will only go to waste if someone doesn't eat them."

He took the plate from Lynne with a killer smile and followed Lucy upstairs.

"You're angry with me," he said, as Lucy closed her bedroom door behind them.

Lucy took a deep breath. "I am not mad at you, Elliot. I don't really have any reason to be mad at you, but I'm not sure what you're doing here."

"Good God." He looked around him with avid fascination. "Is this some sort of macabre shrine to a still-living person?"

"It certainly feels that way," Lucy returned without thinking.

His gray eyes immediately went from transfixed to concerned and fastened on her face. "Are you all right?"

"I'm fine," she assured him quickly before she found herself being psychologically dissected. "Really, I'm doing fine. The room is a bit too much." She crossed her arms over her chest, knowing he would read the body language as defensive and not really giving a shit. "Why are you here, Elliot?"

He thrust his hands deep into his pant pockets and walked over to the desk. He peered forward to get a better look at the photos. "I thought, actually, I hoped, you might have changed your mind."

Lucy closed her eyes and dropped her head. Some tiny piece of her had actually held out the faint hope she wouldn't have to do this. *Wrong*.

She opened her eyes again and Elliot was watching her. "Have you?"

"No," she whispered softly. God help her, she really didn't want to hurt him. "I haven't."

"I was afraid of that." He looked perfectly relaxed, but a telltale muscle twitched in the side of his jaw.

"Then why did you come?" Lucy gentled her tone. Elliot wasn't the enemy.

"I love you," he said with a shrug. "It's a habit I can't seem to break."

The sting of tears burned behind her eyes. Life would be so much simpler if she felt the same. But she didn't and no amount of wishing it could make it so. "And I love you," she said. "Just not the way you want."

Elliot dropped his chin onto his chest and kept his eyes locked on the floor. His chest rose and fell as he drew in a long breath. "Because of him?" he asked.

"No, Elliot. Because of me."

Richard stopped in the act of flipping the light switch in his bedroom. He was about to have a shower to ease away some of the tension of a long day when he caught sight of the window in the opposite house.

Richard couldn't wrench his eyes away.

It wasn't really spying if you happened to look up and see something by accident. And if that thing captured your interest, it was only natural you would stop and take a closer look.

Lucy was clearly silhouetted in the window. And so was her Fancy Man with the flashy car.

There was nothing much to see, but pathetic bastard that he was, he stood and watched anyway.

They were talking. They were talking intensely. At least, Lucy talked intensely, waving her arms around and flapping her hands as she went.

Fancy Man stood and, for the most part, listened.

Richard had to offer the man a brief moment of brotherly empathy. She was talking. Talking, talking, talking. Couldn't she draw him a picture and be done with it?

Fancy Man got into the spirit of things and put in his two cents worth. He got ardent, his hand movements abrupt, as if he was trying to make his point carry more weight.

Lucy shook her head.

Richard stepped closer to the window. Was Lucy crying?

Something perilously close to rage shot through him. He reserved the right to make Lucy Flint cry. Richard stopped in midstride and midthought. What the hell did he mean by that?

Fancy Man was trying to calm Lucy down. Stepping toward her and touching her arm in a way that got more rage bubbling through Richard's system.

He didn't like the man's hands on Lucy. The fact the man had put them there before did not help matters. This was a man Lucy had been intimate with, maybe still could be intimate with, and the thought spiked his temper even further.

One of those out-of-body experiences he'd heard about hit him square in the jaw. He jumped back nine years in time. The fury was the same and so was the insane poison of jealousy flooding through his veins.

Another man had Lucy Flint.

Richard wanted to vomit and he forced his attention back to the present. The man with Lucy now was not Jason, but the cauldron within him still kept bubbling.

So, he stood there in his darkened bedroom and watched them. He couldn't hear a word they were saying, but they were still talking.

They both looked sad and frustrated.

Fancy Man shoved his hands in his pockets and his shoulders slumped. The poor bastard looked defeated.

Lucy swiped a hand over her cheeks. She was definitely crying.

Richard ached with the need to hold her and comfort her. But stronger than that was the impotent savagery that held him back. He could go over there right now and take her in his arms, except the blackness welling within him held him prisoner.

Fancy Man stepped forward and put his arms around Lucy.

She held herself stiff and resistant.

Fancy Man said something close to her ear and Lucy collapsed against him.

Fancy Man lowered his cheek to the top of her head. He looked like a man who'd lost the thing most precious to him.

If he'd lost Lucy, then Richard knew how he felt.

The mind-numbing, clawing pain that had almost consumed him alive was there in the room with him. He knew how the other man felt, because he'd been that man. He had given everything he had to Lucy.

He and the nameless man across the way, they had that in common.

Desperately, they had both tried to hold on to her. They thought they could make her love them. Stupid, starry-eyed dreamers, they believed if they loved her enough she would stay. They were comrades in arms, him and Fancy Man, battered, bruised, and confused, but still none the wiser.

Richard loosened the button on his shirt. It tightened and dug into his throat and he tugged at it roughly. The button popped and skittered across the floor and still he couldn't drag enough air into his lungs. It was happening again and all around him the earth gave a sickening lurch.

In the room, Fancy Man had his eyes pressed closed as if he were trying to stem tears.

Richard knew that face. He'd worn that face for a long time. His chest constricted again and breathing became harder. He recognized the signs of a panic attack.

He had to get out.

Chapter Thirty

Donna said nothing about finding her oldest son on her doorstep without a coat. Shivering and almost blue from the cold and wearing an expression as if he'd peered into the maw of hell.

Quietly Donna let him in. She poured him a stiff measure of whiskey and gave it to him, before digging in the linen closet for a couple of the boys' old things she had yet to part with. She put on the kettle and watched him as she went about making tea.

She had mothered three boys and she knew her men. Richard would talk when he was ready. Like she didn't know the problem already. Her oldest son had just hit the wall he'd been racing toward for most of his adult life.

"Ma?"

"Yes?"

"Why do you have to make all these changes in your life?"

Donna put her tea bag into the cup before answering. "Because I am still a young woman, Richard. I need to do those things I have always wanted to do, before it is too late. I loved your father, I've told you this before, but I spent a lot of my time making sure he was happy and letting my needs slide."

"I don't like it," he stated in such a pig-headed, definitive, Richard fashion, she had to snort with laughter. He'd done that since he was old enough to shake his little towhead and assert his will.

"I know you don't, *mon fils,* but it's not the changes I am making that are bothering you. You don't like change. Change frightens you."

"That's not true," he protested, and helped himself to another gentleman's measure. He did not drink, this boy of hers, and he was fit as well. He would be three sheets to the wind if he kept this up.

Donna had never seen Richard drunk. Once, when he was thirteen and he'd had one or two beers too many, but Des had dealt with that. Josh, she'd put to bed a time or two, Thomas a couple more than that, but Richard, never.

He hated to lose control and being drunk would do that to him. It might be an interesting experience. He worked his way through the second drink. The kettle whistled and she poured hot water over her tea bag.

He looked up at her suddenly and frowned. "It's true," he stated.

Donna stirred her tea and waited.

"You know, if you weren't my mother, I would be applauding what you're doing," he said, and gave a mirthless little laugh. "In fact, the other day a woman came to see me. She's going through a divorce and I'm giving her some help with depression. I told her to find something that makes her happy and do it. Something that makes only her happy."

"It was good advice." She smiled at him and blew on her tea.

"But I hate it when you do it." He waved his hand

at her. "I love your new hair and I hate it. I think your new clothes look great, but I want you to put the old ones on." He went for the whiskey bottle again.

A sandwich might help soak a bit of that up and she got to work, cutting thick slices of bread. Donna added cheese and sliced pickles to his bread. She opened a bag of potato chips and tipped half of them onto the plate next to the sandwich. The rest she kept for herself.

"Ashley came to see me today." He took a bite of the sandwich.

It wasn't exactly a surprise to Donna. She'd heard the story of Lucy leaving Richard's house from at least three different people.

"She wants me to sign the divorce papers," he mumbled.

"So sign them," Donna said, and shrugged. "You both deserve to be happy and hanging on to a dead marriage is not going to do that."

He took a bite, chewed, and swallowed.

Donna imagined his mind doing the same thing. Methodical, careful, and considered, that was her oldest son.

"I know that I am not"—he waved his hand a bit sloppily—"all in love and starry eyed about Ashley, but I married her, Ma, and that has to count for something."

"It does, Richard." Donna brought her tea and the rest of the chips to the table and sat opposite him. "It means a lot, but it has to mean a lot to both of you. Marriage is tough, Richard. It's not for the faint-hearted and it's not what you think it's going to be when you get married, all swept up in the romance and hopeful. It takes two people to really, really want to make it work."

"And Ashley?"

"She doesn't want it enough. And Richard?" Here Donna had to go gently and she crunched a chip before she stepped on hallowed ground. "I think she is right."

He drew in a sharp breath, but the whiskey must have softened him because he didn't cut up rough at her.

"I think you both deserve more than that warmed-up friendship you called a marriage."

"Ma," he said, looking thunderous.

"You hardly spent any time together, Richard. You had different interests from the start." Donna didn't want to even speculate what their sex life had been like, but she had never seen Richard look at Ashley with one tenth of the heat he gave Lucy. Which brought Donna around to the real reason Richard was tying one on in her kitchen. "You going to talk about her?"

He tipped another measure, this one a bit smaller, into his glass. "Nope." He shook his head mulishly. "I can't talk about her. You would think I would have been done talking about her years ago."

"Uh-huh."

"I am done with Lucy."

"You are?"

He frowned and shook his head vigorously. "I saw her with that man from Seattle tonight."

At last, the truth started to leak out and Donna waited. "He loves her, Ma. He really, really loves her and it's killing him that she doesn't love him back."

"You spoke to him?"

Richard shook his head. "I saw them, through the window. It was all over his face."

"Ah." Donna pushed the chips away, her appetite gone. "What does Lucy say?"

"She says she doesn't love him. She broke up with him because she can't love him the way he wants her to." He laced his fingers together around the glass, but didn't drink.

"It is not the same situation as you and Lucy."

"I know that," he said, and snapped back the whiskey. "I know that, but it still scares me."

"And why is that, *mon fils?*"

He frowned down at his hands. "Because he was me. I saw myself on his face."

"You saw yourself nine years ago, Richard." Donna gently cupped his fingers between her palms. "You are not that man and Lucy is not that girl."

He made a soft noise in the back of his throat. "Ma?"

"Yes, Richard." It amused her how quickly the alcohol hit him.

"I don't think I'm done with Lucy."

"Neither do I." Donna took a deep breath. "Neither does Josh. He could see how you looked at her that night she came to dinner."

Richard made a rude noise and refilled his glass. "I wanted to punch Josh when he came on to her."

"He wasn't coming on to her." Donna gave a weary sigh and moved the whiskey out of his reach. "Josh is a flirt. He flirts with all women. It's his thing."

"What is with that?" Richard demanded with a scowl.

"It's his way of hiding how sweet and sensitive he really is. He had the misfortune to be born with the soul of a stargazer behind the face of a player. People never see how quickly he can be hurt or how much he wants to be loved. All they see is what is on the outside."

Richard reared back in his seat and looked at her,

as if he were seeing her for the first time. "Whew! That's a bit deep, Ma."

Donna hid her smile behind her teacup.

"What about Thomas?"

"Thomas?" Donna smiled. "Thomas is my adventurer. There is always going to be another mountain for Thomas. He grew up in the shadow of first Des and then you and Josh. Between the three of you, there is nothing that you don't excel at. Thomas is the youngest and he is always scrambling to keep up. He always will."

"Hmph." He gave her that look again. The one that said he was not sure she wasn't an alien plant after they'd abducted his real mother. "And me?"

Donna laughed out loud. "You fear the thing that you desire the most. You hate that you want it so badly. You are scared you will get it and terrified you won't."

"Ah, come on," he protested with a frown. "That's a bit vague."

"You want clear?"

"Yes."

"You sure?"

He paused for a telling moment. "No."

"Tell me when you are. Or better yet"—Donna poured the next shot for him—"figure it out for yourself. Before it's too late."

"Ma!" They both jumped as the back door thudded open. "Have you seen, Rich . . . there you are." Josh blew into the room, not looking like his normal, laid-back self. "I've been looking for you. There is something you should see."

Chapter Thirty-One

Lucy quit. Her phone vibrated in her hand. Twelve missed calls. The screen lit up again with another call. It was Mads and Lucy stared at it and waited for it to go to voice mail. Through the wall the soft sound of Lynne's weeping came from the room next door. Lucy wished she could cry, but the tears were stuck somewhere in the middle of her.

The image on the computer screen burned into the back of her brain. It felt almost surreal. This was the sort of thing that happened to famous people. The e-mail, with the link, had dropped into her inbox about half an hour ago. It was one of those automatic notification e-mails, with no way to reply and no way to respond. She laughed softly. What would she say anyway? It was a little pointless to start protesting her innocence, not when the truth was there in black and white for anyone with a browser to see.

They were not bad pictures, considering how drunk Jason had been when he took them. It was not his finest work, but they were perfectly in focus and identifiable. There were only three pictures in the link. Lucy had no idea how many more there were, but she did have a vague recollection of Jason shooting spool after spool that night.

Lynne didn't own a computer, but a friend had been kind enough to rush right over with her laptop. Lucy stared at it now. She lay sprawled across an unmade bed, her eyes vacant, dark smears of old makeup beneath them. In the pictures, she looked wasted; wasted and grubby and completely naked. The e-mail had a long list of recipients. Just about everyone she knew. Richard was on that list. She'd noticed that much before she'd got stuck on the site with the pictures.

God. She'd been so stupid to even think there might be some kind of happily ever after out there for Lucy Flint.

She pushed the heels of her hands into her eyes. Exhaustion dragged at her neck muscles until it hurt to move her head. Her cell rang again. Elliot. She let it go to voice mail. It rang again and she glanced down. Another number lit up the screen and this one she didn't recognize at all. She let that one go the way of all the others. They would give up eventually.

Lucy stood up. She felt older than the wood floors that creaked beneath her feet. Carefully she closed the laptop. The pictures made her feel vaguely queasy.

"Lucy?" Lynne's voice rose querulously from the room beside hers.

Lucy walked straight into the bathroom and closed the door.

Her mother's footsteps crossed the floor toward the bathroom.

She stared at her face in the mirror, pale, tired with her mouth set in a grim line. It was the same face as the one in the pictures. Only she'd still had her short hair then. She touched the ends of her hair. Maybe she could cut it again.

"Lucy?" The handle rattled as Lynne tried to open the door.

Lucy kept staring at the face in the mirror. She had a few more lines on her face now, but all in all, not many. She probably looked better today than she had in those shots. Then, she had been partying hard and it was etched into the face in the photographs. Not that anyone would be looking at her face.

"What are we going to do, Lucy?" Lynne wailed from the other side of the door.

"I'm going out," Lucy said. She hadn't realized that was what she was going to do until the words came out of her mouth. And when they did, she knew that was exactly what she was going to do. She left her phone in the bedroom. She had nothing more to say.

She walked past her mother in silence. The weight of Lynne's reproachful stare pressed into her shoulders as she descended the stairs. "Why did you do it, Lu Lu?"

Lucy snorted beneath her breath. Why had she done anything back then? She did it because it felt like a good idea at the time. She was a bad girl and she wanted the world to know it.

"Where are you going?" Lynne came halfway down the stairs toward her.

She shrugged and hauled on her coat. Lucy had no idea where she was going, just out.

"Shit." Lucy hauled the frigid air into her lungs. It went down with claws all the way. It was so cold her eyes teared up immediately and then froze.

Lynne stood in the doorway, babbling about something, but Lucy tuned her out. It didn't matter anyway. She felt dead inside. There had been a brief moment, when she first followed the link, when she had felt shock and then rage. Then, it had all gone numb and she preferred it this way.

It was better this way, because nothing changed in the end. She had made all these huge life-changing decisions and done the demon confronting, but what for? What she had ended up with wasn't peace or serenity. What she ended up with was nothing. Or worse, a dirty, smutty visual reminder of a girl you had once been. You couldn't leave the past behind. You didn't get to walk away from that girl.

It didn't matter what she did.

Brooke was right. Lucy wanted to scoff at the idea of Brooke being right about anything, but there it was.

She would always be the girl in the pictures. It didn't matter what she did on the surface, down deep there was that girl and she could never outrun her or leave her behind. She would always be Lucy the drunk, Lucy the slut, dirty, grubby Lucy looking wasted and out of it. The soul-searching, the tears, the desperation, and the shame had all come to this. It didn't matter how much she grew or tried to change. Here in Willow Park everything was exactly the same. She was still the wild, out-of-control party girl who couldn't be trusted and wasn't worth shit. Hot breath formed icicles on the inside of her scarf.

She quickened her pace. The cold seeped through the toes of her cheap boots. She would need somewhere to get out of the cold.

Fucking pointless, all of it.

She'd sent Mads the link just after she'd received it. Mads had been trying to reach her ever since. Mads would only talk and talk and Lucy didn't want to hear it. She'd said all of those things to herself and they were nothing more than platitudes.

All the times she had clung perilously to her sobriety, fighting sometimes between one heartbeat and the next not to melt into the sweet, numbing oblivion of alcohol. And for what? For this? To stare into the face of Brooke's bitter rage? To go round and round in circles with her mother and her father? To face the sharp, searing regret that was Richard? And to come right back to where it all began—crazy Lu Lu, up to her old shit again.

Lucy stopped and breathed—first in and slowly out. She forced the hopelessness to recede slightly and she looked around her slowly, taking it all in.

Lucy had no idea how long she sat at the bar and watched the barman pour drinks for the people around her. She had been walking for so long, her feet had gone numb and she had ducked into the nearest place that offered relief from the bitter cold. Seeing where she found herself had almost made her laugh. She was like a homing pigeon.

The bar had changed, more trendy and upmarket now and none of the old faces were around. God, she'd run riot in this place. Been asked to leave more times than allowed to stay.

The barman looked at her again, silently asking what she wanted. She shook her head and he turned away again.

A body slid into place on the stool beside her.

She kept her eyes on the rows of bottles along the mirrored shelves. So many different ways to lose herself and drink away the pain. Her old friends Johnnie Walker and Smirnoff winked at her.

The man beside her smelled great, familiar.

Out of the corner of her eye, she saw him raise a hand for the barman.

The newcomer turned on his stool.

She could feel his eyes on her face. Lucy glanced at him.

Josh Hunter looked back at her. His hair was tousled from the wind and his cheeks reddened by the cold. He nodded a greeting. He turned again when the barman returned.

The barman put two glasses of whiskey on the counter in front of them.

Lucy looked at the whiskey and looked at Josh.

Josh shrugged. "Your choice, Lucy."

The familiar peaty scent of the liquor taunted her nose. It gleamed amber in the light from the bar. In that glass lay the path to sweet oblivion. All she had to do was reach over and take it.

Beside her, Josh raised his glass and downed it in one shot.

Lucy stared at her glass. Her hand twitched beside it, but she didn't touch it. "You've seen the pictures?"

"Yup." He motioned to the barman again. "And, in case you're wondering, so has Richard."

She still felt like ice inside, but a small shard broke away with a sharp jab to her chest. The glass beckoned to her. *Take me,* it whispered. *Drink me, and it will all go away in one sweet rush of alcohol through your system.*

"What are you going to do, Lucy?" Josh sipped his second whiskey. He jerked his head in the direction of her untouched glass. "I'll stay here and get drunk with you, if you like. I'll even carry you home when you're done, without trying to get into your pants."

"They're everywhere," she whispered, her voice hoarse and strained.

"Yup," Josh said, nodding. "I have managed to get the domain taken down and we can get them barred, but that won't stop all the downloads that have already happened. Or the hundred horny men who will e-mail them to their friends."

"At what point are you going to start helping?" The glass in front of her seemed to swell in size, the heavenly smell grew stronger.

"I have already helped you." Josh grabbed her hand from the bar and held it between his. "I've done what I can, Lucy, but you know what the Internet is. Once something is out there, it's out there and we can mitigate the damage going forward, but there is no stopping this."

"Do you know who did it?"

"We do." Josh pressed her hand. "Richard worked it out and he was the one who got the pictures taken down. I did the techie side of it."

"Who?"

"Guess?" Josh cocked his head.

"Ashley," Lucy rasped. "At first, I thought it was Brooke. Maybe she was still in contact with Jason or something."

"You were right about that part." Josh pulled a face. "Brooke managed to get the pictures out of Jason years ago, but it was only recently that Ashley came up with a use for them."

"Where are they now?" Lucy's fingers touched the edge of the glass. She rolled it against the pads of her fingers and nudged it a bit closer. One quick, practiced flick of her wrist and it would rush down her throat on a rich burn.

"Richard managed to get the originals. Fortunately, they weren't digital and he could destroy the negatives."

"Great." Lucy curled her hand around the glass. The liquid sloshed lazily against the side of the glass. She watched the way it left a residue against the side of the glass. If it was a wine, they would call that its "legs."

Josh sat silently and waited.

"Can you take me home?" Lucy turned to him.

An expression of instant relief flooded his face. He closed his beautiful, indigo eyes briefly and breathed. It mattered to him and Lucy felt the ice inside her start to shatter bit by bit and melt.

"Fuck, Lucy." Josh shook his head slowly. "I thought for a minute you were going to drink that." He gave a short laugh.

"Nope." Lucy shook her head. "I'm done." She pushed the glass away and swung on her barstool to look at him. "Did you look at the pictures?"

Josh's eyes flickered away and to the left. "Only a little." He gave her a disarming smile. "What?" he demanded when Lucy looked at him. "I had to open the site to get rid of them."

"And that's all you saw?"

Josh went a guilty, dull red. "They were naked pictures of a beautiful woman."

"You're a dog." Lucy glared at him.

"You're right." Josh pulled a rueful face. "But I kept my eyes on your face."

"Sure you did." Lucy gave another short laugh. "God, this is not funny."

"No," Josh agreed, "but it could be worse. You could have taken that drink."

Lucy drew a shaky breath. "You're right." She reached out and squeezed his hand. "That would have been a whole lot worse."

"You going to be all right?"

"Yes." Lucy got to her feet. "Although, I am about to make a scene and I really would like you to get me out of here."

"What kind of scene?" Josh was already on his feet. He dropped a couple of bills on the bar and gathered up her stuff.

"The crying kind." Unshed tears gummed up her vocal chords as Josh slipped her coat around her shoulders.

"I know just the person for those sort of scenes." His arm was warm as he led her out of the bar.

"I found her," she heard him say into his cell phone.

"Belle fille." Donna opened her arms and Lucy walked right into them. "We have been frantic." Donna enfolded her in a Donna-scented hug that shattered the last of Lucy's composure. She started to cry in big, ugly, rasping sobs that shook her body.

Donna held on tight, her hands stroking Lucy's back. She didn't ask questions and she didn't offer platitudes, she held Lucy. She was much shorter and Lucy had to drop her head onto Donna's shoulder, but still she felt completely surrounded by the love of the other woman.

"Your Mads has been calling most of Willow Park trying to find you," Donna murmured against her ear. "Josh will call her and let her know you are all right."

Lucy wanted to ask where Richard was, but she dared not. Richard would have hated those pictures and what they represented. She had left him for that and it was so horribly sordid. Fresh sobs shook her and Donna's arms tightened.

"You cry, *belle fille*," Donna whispered. "And when you are done, we will see what is to happen next."

Chapter Thirty-Two

Donna fed Lucy breakfast. There was no sign of either Richard or Josh this morning. Donna didn't say where they were and Lucy lacked the courage to ask. Lucy wasn't really hungry, but she ate anyway. It promised to be a long day.

She had cried for a good while the night before and when she was done, Donna had put her to bed. Surprisingly, she'd slept well. This morning, she was calm, but resolved. Whatever she had come here to do, it was done. You couldn't go back and rewrite the past, you could only move forward.

"What will you do now?" Donna asked as Lucy shrugged into her coat.

"Go home." Lucy looked away quickly. She had done enough crying for the time being.

"Are you sure?" Donna fastened her scarf around her throat. "You could stay here. If you wanted to stay."

"I can't do that." Lucy shook her head. "Tell Josh, thank you very much. I left a message on his phone this morning, but will you make sure he gets it?"

"I will," Donna responded, nodding, and turned her

blue eyes on Lucy. Lucy struggled to hold their keen stare. "What should I say to Richard?"

Lucy opened her mouth and then shut it again. She had no idea what to say to Richard.

"You promised me, *belle fille*," Donna said softly, "that you would be careful with him this time."

"I know." Lucy swallowed past the lump in her throat. "I didn't know this would happen, though."

"I think you should talk to him before you go," Donna suggested. "He will not like it if you leave without saying anything, like you did before."

"I'll . . ." The idea of lying to Donna did not sit well. "I will try, but if I don't, will you tell him something from me?"

"No, *belle fille*." Donna shook her head sadly. "If you cannot find it in you to say it to him yourself, then it is not worth saying."

Lucy nodded and looked down at her feet. "Thank you," she whispered. "Thank you, for everything."

"*Bonne chance, belle fille.*" Donna gripped her face between her palms and kissed Lucy on the forehead. The touch of her lips was like a guilty brand on her skin as Lucy opened the door and let herself out into the morning.

Willow Park had thrown out its best this morning. It was a clear, crisp winter day. The sun shone out of a sky so blue it made her eyes water. The fresh, clean snow glittered with millions of points of light. Its pristine beauty tugged at her. *See, Lucy,* it seemed to say. *You can go, but there will always be a piece of you here, with us.*

Everywhere she looked, people were out and about enjoying the milder weather and the sunshine. A group of young girls clustered outside Mr. Martin's store and argued about something, happily and loudly. They were like a flock of chattering magpies, all made up and blinged out.

As she passed Mr. Martin looked up from the service counter and waved.

Lucy waved back.

He was totally immune to the chatter of teenage girls. He had seen them all go from buying Twizzlers to squealing and parading on the sidewalk outside his shop.

A small group of boys parted for her to walk through. About six hundred pounds of testosterone and the same again in attitude, they slunk closer to their target. Sooner or later, every teenager in Willow Park found their way to the old bench outside Old Man Martin's. Nothing much changed here.

Except for Lucy Flint. Lucy Flint had changed. The woman she was today was not the girl she had been. She was not even the woman who'd driven in on a blizzard a few short weeks ago.

Past the bank she went. Somewhere in there, Guy Lewis would be working, Guy who she'd used and abused merrily for a short while. He'd cried when she made her amends and hugged her and told her she was still the most beautiful girl in the world.

Lucy smiled and looked through the window of the bookshop. Not such a success. Mr. Baker was not inclined to forgive Lucy's attempt to get sexist literature burned. They had been learning about the sixties at school, feminism and banning the bomb. Lucy had gotten carried away. Mr. Baker still nursed a grudge.

Across the street, the old restaurant had changed hands. Lucy worked there in her final year of school. The former owner had been her kind of boss, never around to check on her, but always there before closing for a drink. She had not managed to track him down. Apparently, he was drinking his way through liver failure. It made her sad and it reminded her of why she was still at this, one day at a time.

Nope, not much changed in Willow Park. She went through her mental travelogue, ticking off the made amends as she walked. For the most part, people had been kind and overwhelming in their generosity of spirit.

In the bakery, she caught sight of Brooke and her son. His little-boy death stare tracked her motion past the shop. Brooke caught sight of her and looked away as quickly. Sometimes, there was no going back.

The house was silent as she strode down the deck toward the front door. The ghosts were still there, hanging around the corners of the house, but they had lost the power to frighten her. The front door jammed. Lucy tugged it slightly toward her, turned the handle, and then shoved. The door opened.

"Lucy?" Her mother appeared at the top of the stairs. "Oh Lucy, where have you been?" Tears glistened in the depths of Lynne's faded eyes.

"I was with Donna." Lucy took off her coat and hung it up. "Didn't she call you and tell you?"

"You should have called." Lynne sniffed, and hunted up the sleeve of her cardigan for the Kleenex always tucked there. "Your father has barely slept all night."

"You're right, Mom. I should have called." Lucy pulled a Kleenex out of her pocket and handed it to her mother. She was done with tears for the moment.

"What are we going to do?" Lynne took the Kleenex and mopped at her eyes.

"Nothing." Lucy reached over and gave her mother

a hug. "We are not going to do anything. As much as can be done, has been done."

"Your father had a very bad night." Lynne tucked her hands up the sleeves of her cardigan. "He is very disappointed in you."

Lucy paused in midstride and then walked past her mother and into the kitchen.

"I'm disappointed in myself. I let myself down when I was drinking." Her mother opened her mouth to say something, but Lucy cut her off. "But I'm not drinking anymore and I don't need to keep crawling for forgiveness. Not from anyone."

"Well, of course, *we* forgive you, Lucy," her mother insisted.

"Really?" Lucy looked at her mother. She almost laughed. "From where I'm standing, your forgiveness feels a lot like judgment. But it doesn't matter," Lucy continued. "Because I forgive myself."

Making amends to Richard had been hard. This one was like swallowing razor blades. Carl sat in his new chair—a brighter, more colorful version of the old one—and gloated at her triumphantly.

"I'm on my way, Dad," Lucy said to him. "I came to say good-bye."

"So, now you've said it." Carl sniffed, and turned the sound up on his remote.

You can be right or you can be free, Lucy reminded herself sternly.

"Um, Dad, could you turn that down?" She motioned to the television. "I wanted to say one more thing before I left."

"I don't have any money for you." Carl didn't look

away from the television. He pointedly put the remote down on the arm of the chair.

So be it. Lucy stepped into the room and raised her voice slightly. "I wanted to say I was sorry, Dad."

He kept his eyes glued to his program, but there was an almost unnatural stillness as if, for once, she had truly surprised him.

"I am sorry for all those times I worried you or embarrassed you. I want you to know how truly sorry I am for any harm I have done you. I was a confused and angry little girl and I didn't always think of what my actions would cost other people. I know better now and so, I'm going to do better."

Carl stared straight ahead of him. His mouth moved as if he were chewing something over silently.

This was for her peace. At the end of the day, it was all about that and now it was done. This was about being able to hold her head up high, free of the guilt and free of the anger. It was time for Lucy Flint to step out of the shadow of her past and into the sunlight.

"I really am sorry, Dad. I'm going to make it up to you, in any way I can." And there it was, lying in the ether between them. The one, true instance of honesty they had ever shared. Father and daughter, locked in an eternal battle, constantly circling each other like a pair of bristling dogs.

"Hmph." Carl pulled down the corners of his mouth as he watched the television. "Is this what they teach you in those meetings of yours?"

"It's what I have to do to be free of the stuff that could make me drink again. I need to be proud of myself again and to do that, I need to break free of the past."

"That easy, huh?"

Lucy had to laugh. "Trust me, Dad, this is not easy."

Carl shook his head sharply and then he smiled, a small quirk to the side of his mouth. "No," he said, and gave a gruff chuckle. "I am sure it's not. You always did have your share of pride, but you came by it honestly. I was never one to apologize easily."

An answering smile tugged at her mouth. The silence stretched between them as Lucy stood there, reluctant to let go of the brief flicker of accord.

In the background, the television blared hockey statistics.

It was as good as it was going to get and it was enough for now. "I'll see you around, Dad."

"See you, Lucy."

She turned to go, but he stopped her before she left. "You got everything you need, Lucy?" She didn't turn. He wouldn't like her to see him unbending. "For your studies and all, you got everything you need?"

"Yes, thanks, Dad. I have."

"Hmph."

"Bye, Dad."

Lucy closed the door quietly behind her.

Lynne waited on the other side wringing her hands anxiously. She blinked slightly when Lucy gave her a calm smile.

"I think he's ready for his lunch," she said. "I'll go and finish packing up."

"Did you upset him?" Lynne wanted to know.

"No." Lucy shook her head. Amazingly, she hadn't upset her dad.

"Where the fuck have you been?" It was the first time Lucy had ever heard Mads yell. "I have been having a purple shit fit over here."

"Hey, Maddie Mads."

"Don't you 'Maddie Mads' me. I am so mad at you. I have been going crazy trying to find you." Lucy heard Mads haul in a ragged breath. "Are you all right?"

"I am, now?"

"What does that mean?" She could hear Mads trying hard to get over her temper and be rational.

"It means, I was shit, but I'm all right, now." Lucy looked around her bedroom, checking to see if she had left anything. "You saw the pictures?"

"Yes." Mads went quiet, briefly. "Do you know how they got on the Internet?"

"I do and now they are off again. For what that's worth."

"Fuck." Mads drew a ragged breath. "Why are you so calm about this?" she demanded suddenly.

"Can you think of a better reaction?" Lucy gave a dry laugh. "I didn't drink, Mads."

"Of course you didn't," Mads huffed indignantly, "because that would be the most fucking stupid thing you could ever do. Even more stupid than disappearing on your sponsor."

"I really am sorry, Mads."

"I'm still sulking, but I'll get over myself in about a year or two."

Lucy smiled. Her face felt stiff with the effort it took.

"So, are you coming home now?" Mads asked softly.

"Yes, Mads." Lucy blinked away a tear. "I am coming home."

Lucy drew the zipper around her suitcase. She reached over and straightened the heart-shaped pillows. She would leave the room as she had found it. Elliot had called it right, it was a shrine to a girl who had been.

That girl still existed, she hadn't disappeared, but she had grown up and grown stronger and she wasn't hiding anymore.

Lucy unpinned a picture of her and Richard. She couldn't even remember where it was taken, but he was looking down at her with his heart in his sky-blue eyes and she was laughing. The pain almost made her double over and she tucked the picture into the side of her suitcase. *Later,* she promised herself.

It took Lucy about twenty minutes to disentangle herself from Lynne. Now that the car was loaded and Lucy all ready to go, Lynne started to fuss. Did Lucy have her ticket? *Yes, Mom, it's all electronic now.* Did she have a passport? *No, Mom, I don't need one, just my driver's license.*

And then, Lucy must call her as soon as she arrived and wasn't it good the weather was so clear. It gave Lucy something to concentrate on other than the growing ache in her chest.

Carl did not appear to say good-bye and Lucy didn't look for him.

The walk had still not been shoveled. Richard had not been by.

Lucy shook off the thought as she left her mother inside the front door. More promises to call as soon as she got in and to come back soon.

She was so intent on getting out the door that she didn't notice Brooke until she almost barreled into the other woman.

Brooke had her little boy with her and he stood by his mother's side, clasping her hand with a huge, red mitten. All Lucy could see over his scarf was a pair of pale-blue eyes that matched his mother's.

"Brooke?" Lucy prompted when it didn't look like the other woman was going to speak.

"Lucy?" Brooke wore her zebras again. Her gaze shifted from Lucy to the boy by her side. "This is my son, Brad-Leigh."

"Hello." Lucy dredged a warm smile up from somewhere.

The boy blinked back at her.

"You're leaving?" It was more of a statement than a question and Lucy merely nodded.

"I needed . . ." Brooke stopped and took a careful breath. "I didn't know what Ashley would do with those pictures," she said, the words tumbling out of her. "They were sent to me a few years ago, because Jason had left me as a forwarding address."

Brooke shook her head in confusion. "I don't know why he did that, but he did. Anyway, he left them behind him with some other things and the owners of that apartment sent his stuff to me. I threw everything else away, but I kept those."

"Well." Lucy took a slow breath.

Brooke's little boy stared up at her warily, as if sensing the tension in the air.

"You got what you wished for, Brooke," she said eventually. "You made me crawl."

"It doesn't feel like I thought it would." Brooke frowned and blinked her eyes rapidly. She shook her head abruptly, as if clearing it, and looked up at Lucy again. "I have two children now with my husband, Christopher." She paused again and her eyes gleamed with moisture. "I wanted you to know that I am happy, now."

"I'm glad, Brooke." Lucy looked down at the child again. It was easier than looking at his mother.

Inside some of the pressure eased. It must have taken all she had for Brooke to come here like this.

She was not Ashley, neither of them was, because both
she and Brooke had within them the capacity for forgiveness. Lucy took Brooke's hand. "I'm truly glad you
are happy."

"Good." Brooke nodded and returned the pressure
on her hand before releasing it. "Take care, Lucy Flint."
The other woman turned to go. "And be happy. I
wanted you to know that I wish that for you, too."

Brooke helped her son down the steps and loaded
him into a shiny SUV. She waved as she drew away
from the curb.

Lucy quickened her steps toward her car.

Chapter Thirty-Three

The rental car started easily and Lucy put it into gear. Behind her, she could see the light in her old bedroom go on.

Lynne would be up there stripping the linens to be washed. Then, Lynne would put the room back to the way it had been before she arrived. Next, Lynne would clean the bathroom. Before Lucy landed in Seattle all the signs that she had been home would be carefully erased from the house.

Lucy let her eyes stray to the house next door. The light in his bedroom was on. Richard would be up there. Maybe he'd be getting ready to go for a run or a bike ride. By the time he came back for his shower, she would be gone.

Would he look over as he walked across his room toward his bathroom and see her light was not on? Would he wonder where she was?

It didn't matter. She wasn't leaving with her tail between her legs or screaming off in the slipstream of anger and rebellion. This time, Lucy Flint was leaving with her head held high. She had come here to repair what damage she could and make peace. And she'd done that.

She pulled away from the curb into the road.

Tomorrow morning, the grapevine would be able to report to Richard that Lucy had left town. Would he understand why she hadn't stopped to say good-bye? He wasn't stupid. Of course Richard would understand. There was nothing more to be said.

Or was there?

Lucy stopped the car. Behind her a horn blared. Mr. Stevens from down the road raised his hands in question. What was she doing?

It was a good question and Lucy pulled to the side-walk again.

Mr. Stevens gave a jaunty wave and accelerated down the street.

She wasn't quite finished here. Because the annoying thing about knowing you were worth more was that it made you kind of want to have more. Before she could talk herself out of the idea, she was out of the car.

Her boots were loud and intrusive on the wooden planking of the porch. With an unsteady hand, she rang the bell. It peeled through the house with rather more enthusiasm than she'd intended and reverberated through the empty foyer. Lucy nearly lost her grip then and turned to run.

The door opened behind her and she was caught.

Lucy blinked at Josh standing in the doorway.

"Hey, Lucy." He gave her his knee-trembling smile.

Lucy grabbed hold of her courage with both hands. "Is Richard here?"

"Yeah." Josh opened the door wider to let her in. "He got back about·ten minutes ago."

"Back?" Lucy peered around the interior of the house cautiously.

"He was with Ashley," Josh explained.

"Lucy?"

And her heart started to leap wildly inside her chest. She looked past Josh's shoulder to see Richard coming down the stairs. He looked like hell, as if he hadn't slept the night before. Her heart didn't care and twisted violently inside her chest.

"I came to say good-bye." She breathed nervously.

"Good-bye?" Richard's brows snapped together over those incredible eyes and his attention turned onto her like the arcs of a laser beam. "Where are you going?"

"Home, I'm going home."

"When?"

"Now."

"NOW?" His brows lowered thunderously. "You're leaving now?"

This was not what she wanted to say at all. This was not the conversation she wanted to be having. Lucy took a shaky breath and held up her hand to stop him. He looked ready to rip into her and if she let the moment go, she would never do this.

"Actually, I had already left and then I turned around again and came back."

"You were running out on me, again." Richard shoved past Josh.

Josh took a step to the side, but stayed where he was.

Lucy threw him a look of discomfort, but Josh gave her the same look as his older brother. He wasn't going anywhere.

"Yup," Lucy said, nodding. "And then I decided to come back and give you the chance to man up and stop me."

Nobody moved for a long while. The pound of Lucy's heartbeat reverberated in her ears.

"The thing is, Richard." Her voice came out in a dry croak and she stopped and swallowed. "I couldn't leave here without saying this. It would be too much like the past. And I'd like to say that I'm doing this for you, but I'm not."

"Lucy . . ." He took a step toward her, but she held her ground.

Inside her coat, sweat slid down the sides of her body.

"Could you let me get this out? I promise this is going to be the end of my big confessions." She sucked in a hasty breath. "So, I was on my way out of town and it occurred to me that there is something I need to tell you."

"I can't believe you were just going to leave."

"Richard," Josh snapped from behind him. "Would you shut the fuck up?"

"Do you mind?" Richard turned and snarled at his brother.

"I've got this." Lucy said, peering around Richard at Josh. And she did. All she had to risk here was pride and that wouldn't sustain her through the years to come. It was time to finish this thing. Closure. She hated that word, but it fit as neatly as a key in a lock.

Josh hesitated and then gave her a brusque nod. "Make it good," he grumbled as he trailed out of sight.

"I love you." Lucy looked back at Richard. "I really, really love you and I don't think I have ever stopped loving you."

Richard's head jerked, as if she'd delivered an upper-cut straight to the jaw.

There was no point in half-assed and Lucy hurried on. "I loved you as a girl and I love you now that I'm all grown up. And it's different now, because I think I could love you right and love you better."

A muscle worked in the side of Richard's jaw.

Finish it, Lucy.

"And I don't want you to remember me as the girl who broke your heart, but I want you to see me as the girl who loved you despite how broken she was and would have done anything to change the past."

Her face felt hot and uncomfortable, but she had already come way too far to back off now. She deserved this chance, both of them did. "And if this is not what you want"—she swallowed hard as her voice shook a bit—"if I am not what you want, then I will leave you with this thought. If you ever change your mind and if you ever decide you might be able to love me and trust me again, I'm probably going to be waiting around for a while, as pathetic as that sounds."

Lucy bit the inside of her cheek to keep back the tears threatening to spill over. "I don't believe people die from unrequited love or because they didn't get their happily-ever-after. I sincerely believe that we get over things and move on." She ran out of breath and had to stop and drag air into her starved lungs.

He hadn't moved and it was better that way because if he as much as twitched she would never finish this.

"But it's been nine years, Richard, and I'm still hung up on you. So I think, in all likelihood, it's going to take me a good long while."

Richard blinked down at her.

Doubt crowded into her mind. Maybe it would have been better if she had left and said nothing. An awful tearing sensation started in her gut and crept over her chest as she watched him look at her.

"Say something." Josh's voice hissed from the other room and Richard started suddenly.

Lucy willed her shaking legs to move. She took a step back toward the door.

"What are you waiting for?" Josh poked his head around the door and glared at his brother. "You've heard everything you need to hear."

"I know." A stupid grin suddenly split Richard's face and Lucy forgot how to breathe.

He reached out and hauled her closer. "You don't honestly think you are going to deliver a mouthful like that and drive away?"

He towered over her, grinning at her like the village idiot.

"Which reminds me," he said, his eyes growing momentarily angry. "What do you think you're doing, arriving on my doorstep and announcing that you're leaving? You only get to walk out on me once and you've had your chance, Lucy Flint."

"Get to the point, dickhead," Josh sang out.

"Thank you," Richard snapped over his shoulder.

"Go away, Josh," Lucy said. She kept her eyes on Richard.

For once, he didn't guard the look in his eyes as he stared down at her.

Her heart started to clamber out of her boots and expand as it rose. She recognized that look and it was one she had never thought to see again.

Richard stepped forward, pinning her against the door. "Tell it to me again." He clasped her face between his hands and tilted her head up. "Look me in the eye and tell it to me again. Start with, 'I love you, Richard.'"

The world tilted all around her and Lucy's mouth went dry.

"Please, Luce." He leaned closer until his forehead rested against hers. "Tell me again. I need to hear it."

"I love you, Richard," she whispered obediently, her heart in her throat, clinging to her vocal chords.

"I always have loved you," he intoned as his hands tightened around her face.

"And I always will," she responded.

His breath stirred through her hair as he released it in a rush. His cheek moved against her head in a slow caress.

"Then where are you running off to?" It came out in a hoarse whisper that brought stinging tears to her eyes. His hands dropped to fasten on her hips and hold her still.

"Seattle," she said, because nothing else came to mind.

"Were you planning on loving me from Seattle?"

"Actually, I didn't have much of a plan." She closed her eyes and took a deep breath. The scent of him surrounded her and she breathed deeply. Against her hips, his fingers flexed convulsively. "I thought it better if I left, but then I thought it would be best if you stopped me."

"Consider yourself grounded." In his neck, his pulse kept rhythm with her pounding heart. "I was coming to see you later," he said.

Lucy's eyes popped open. "You took too long."

"I was up all night talking to Ashley."

Lucy's entire body tensed. "I didn't want to hear that."

She tried to step away, but he crowded her backward. The handle of the door pressed against her side and she could feel the mail slot against her butt.

"I was signing my divorce papers." His lips pressed against her temple in a gentle caress. "I needed to make sure I was free again."

That sounded better and Lucy stilled against him.

"You know this could be classified as Revenge Porn. You might be able to press charges." His voice vibrated through his chest. The comfort of it wrapped around her.

"I don't think I want to." Lucy pressed her face against his shirt and drew in a long, sweet lungful of Richard. "But, I might change my mind." She raised her head to stare at him. "You're ruining the moment."

"You're right," he conceded, grinning down at her. "Forget your flight, Lucy. Forget going back to Seattle and stay here with me."

"You're not afraid anymore?" Lucy closed her eyes again. It was like whispers in the dark and if she kept her eyes shut, then it would never end and reality would not be waiting for her in the light of day. She could feel his breath against her face. He smelled of coffee and Richard and his warmth reached out to surround her. She wanted to believe this was happening, but it didn't seem entirely real yet.

"I'm terrified," he replied, "but I'm more scared of losing you again." His hands cradled her hips, pulling her closer, as if he needed her physical strength against him. "When you left, you took the sun with you and I want it back, Lucy. Bring it back for me. Please, Lucy. Don't let my fear get in the way. I don't want to go back to the way things were since you've been gone."

"That was very poetic, Richie Rich."

"I hate that name."

"I know that."

"Of course you do."

Neither of them moved. Their breathing mingled

and fell into rhythm as he held her pressed lightly against him.

"Will you stay for a while longer?"

"I have a life in Seattle."

"I know that, but if you stay for a while, we can figure it out. I don't really care where we go or what we do. Let's just make sure it's together, Lucy."

"Okay," Lucy Flint gave a happy sigh.

"Richie Rich?"

"Sweetheart?"

"We'll do it right this time."

"No running," he said.

"No hiding," she responded.

They stayed like that for a moment more, before Richard spoke again. "I think we should get married."

Lucy gave a watery little snort of laughter. "I think you should get divorced first and then you can give me a proper proposal, not some half-assed suggestion in a doorway."

"Man, you're tough."

"I'm worth it."

"You have a point."

"Richard?"

"Umm?"

"My butt is getting cold. The wind is coming through the mail slot."

"I can help you with that."

Lucy shrieked as she found herself upended and hanging over his shoulder.

"Trust me, I'm a doctor." He patted her frozen anatomy and carried her up the stairs.

* * *

Josh dragged his cell phone out of his pocket and hit dial. The call was answered almost immediately. "She's staying," he reported. Upstairs a door slammed and he grinned.

"Looks like forever," he responded to the question on the other end. He jerked the phone away from his ear and scowled into it. "Shit, Ma, don't scream like that."

Wondering what happens to Josh next?
Keep reading for an excerpt from

NOBODY'S FOOL,

the next Willow Park Romance
by Sarah Hegger.

Available in
Fall, 2015
from Kensington Books!

The sign above the glass door scrolled out SCANTS in hot-pink neon, blinked twice, and started again.

"Bugger." Holly yanked her clinging sweatshirt away from her body. You should never ask how much worse a thing could get, because Murphy's Law went right ahead and showed you. She squared her shoulders and braced for hell. Good thing she had her bloody passport with her, she was about to enter another galaxy.

The door flew open and the clamor from the bar roared out onto the sidewalk where she stood. A couple of girls brushed past her, giggling as they hurled themselves into the preening frenzy. On the other side of the window, a mass of beautiful bodies circled each other. She was way, way out of her element. There was nothing for it, though. According to his doorman, Josh Hunter was in there.

As Holly stepped over the threshold, the noise crashed into her. It was the manic melody of singles bars everywhere; the clink, the chatter, the bass rumble of male voices juxtaposed against the higher pitches of women. Underscoring the babble, the throb of amplifier and subwoofer ground out an elemental jungle beat and quickened the blood.

Welcome to the mating ground of genus Homo sapiens. What a bunch of posers. Exactly where you would expect to find someone like Josh Hunter. Proof she and Joshua were an entirely different species. She'd suspected as much in high school. The evidence was now incontrovertible.

Her phone buzzed in her hand and Holly checked the screen.

Emma, again. This made it the fifth call in the last hour. What a pity Emma hadn't panicked four days ago when Portia first went missing.

"Yes." She had to stick one finger in her ear to hear what her sister said.

"Did you find her?"

"I just arrived in Chicago."

"What have you been doing?" Emma wailed loud enough to rise above the storm of noise around her.

"Driving." Holly clenched her hand into a fist by her side. Did Emma expect her to hop on her bloody broomstick?

Only this morning, she'd discovered Portia missing. Emma, Portia's twin, had broken down and confessed Portia left four whole days ago for Chicago. Not only was their younger sister gone, she'd left London, Ontario, without her medication. The sheer stupidity of it made Holly want to growl.

"Did you find Joshua Hunter?" Emma persisted. "Portia spoke about him when she called."

"Yes, you told me already." Holly cursed her height as she levered herself onto her toes to see over the heads in front of her. "I'm looking for him now."

She had no idea if she would even recognize Josh Hunter anymore. A lot could have changed in the years since they'd gone to high school together. Maybe he'd grown another head, to admire the one he already had.

"She didn't sound good." Emma's voice quivered. "You have to find her, Holly."

"I know I do." Holly almost snarled.

Four days and Emma hadn't said a word. Holly could barely get her head around it. A phone call from Portia, flying perilously high and prattling about Josh Hunter, had sent Emma scurrying for Holly and help. "I have to go." She hung up while Emma was still talking.

The name of her high school nemesis had knocked Holly off balance for a moment. It was not a name she'd wanted to hear again. She shook it off. It couldn't be helped. The most important thing was finding Portia and she'd make a deal with the devil if she must.

In his school days, Josh had lived in Willow Park and it seemed the most logical place for Holly to start. Their house had been down the street from Holly's and she'd guessed it was where Portia had run into him. She'd been hanging on to the secret hope of Portia standing on the sidewalk, gazing wistfully at the old family home. If you could call a house you'd only lived in for two years an old family home.

Holly dodged a weaving waitress and stopped to avoid a collision.

The two women in front of her spotted each other and squealed like a pair of happy piglets.

Holly waited for the cheek-kissing ritual to end.

Cheek kissing gave way to feverish chatter and Holly finally pushed past. She was on a mission.

Why had Portia gone searching for Josh Hunter? Holly wobbled on her tiptoes and tried to see past the mass of bobbing heads. It was one of the questions she would ask her sister when she caught up with her. And catch up with Portia, she would.

She'd been standing outside the house in Willow Park earlier, wondering where to go next, when the door to the house opened and luck stepped out— trailing spangles and a cloud of perfume. God knows how, but the woman had been thrilled to see her. Holly was still hard put to recall anyone called Brooke from her days in Willow Park. Fortunately, Brooke of the sequins and Christian Dior had remembered Holly and her sisters clearly. And better yet, had been able to tell her the name of the upscale condo on the Gold Coast where Josh now lived.

Brooke went on to say yes, she had seen Holly's sister. Portia had been by a couple of days ago, also looking for Josh. Brooke confirmed Emma's report that Josh and Portia had found each other and were briefly spotted together. Here, Brooke had given a dramatic pause and treated Holly to an abbreviated version of Josh's infamy. Most of it went over her head, but the gist was women and more women and when was he going to settle down.

Holly ran for cover between Brooke's pause and an invocation to God for Josh to stop breaking his mother's heart and get married already. So, same old Josh Hunter.

Holly had located the condo building easily enough and a bit of creative truth-bending with the doorman had her standing on the sidewalk outside Scants, exactly the sort of place she would rather chew her arm off than enter.

The crowd in front of her parted and, oh, sweet Mother of God, there he was.

She would have known him anywhere. Like she

would know if someone had shoved their fist in her gut.

He'd barely changed since high school except to get even hotter and more chiseled and more—whatever. Holly huffed in irritation.

Low blood sugar was her problem. She'd been driving all day, having a shit fit about Portia the entire way and steeling herself to come into contact with Joshua Hunter. So she'd forgotten to eat and the peanuts on the bar were calling her name. That's all it was.

She sidled past a blonde cackling over the top of her designer blue martini. Holly dragged her eyes away from the peanuts and eased closer to Joshua. There was no need to tell him the whole story. She'd tell him only what was strictly necessary and nothing more. Right now, she was leaning toward *"I see you're still a prick. Where's my sister?"* She was willing to concede, however, this might be the blood sugar talking, and probably not the most constructive of beginnings.

Holly managed to wedge herself between two thirtysomething suits who paid no attention to the short woman in the tatty sweatshirt with the whack-job hair, but carried on posturing at each other, simultaneously scanning smartphones that jittered and hummed away at them.

From here she had an even better view of him.

Of all the people who had lived in Willow Park when Holly and her family did, Portia had chosen him. *Why?*

He stood with one hand propped against the bar and spoke to another man whose back was to her. The dim lighting in the bar played peek-a-boo with the finely chiseled lines of his face. His eyes were shadowed, but they were blue. Blue as the inside of an iris, blue as a pansy, blue enough to break a girl's heart and make her want to come back for more.

"Excuse me." One of the suits deigned to look down from his lofty height and notice her jammed between him and his companion. He smoothly sidestepped her and Holly was closer to Josh and the mouth you wanted to suck on.

He wrapped his lips around the neck of his beer bottle. If his face were any less hewn his mouth would make him look girly. As it was, its full, sensuous sweep made an irresistible counterpoint to the aquiline strength of the rest of his features.

This was so screwed up. Why couldn't Portia have chosen someone else to cling-wrap herself to?

Josh laughed at something his companion said. It was a broad slash of white teeth across his tanned face; a heart-stopping affair of crinkling eyes and deep, sexy brackets on either side of his mouth. God, she didn't want to have to make nice with him.

He looked up and Holly was trapped. His glance narrowed in on her like a Scud missile.

There was music and the earth moved.

Maybe it wasn't her blood sugar after all.

More from Bestselling Author
JANET DAILEY